AL

THE LADIES OF BATH

Winning Lady Jane ~ A Christmas Regency Romance

The Duke's Daughter ~ Lady Amelia Atherton

The Baron in Bath ~ Miss Julia Bellevue

The Deceptive Earl ~ Lady Charity Abernathy

THE LADIES OF THE NORTH

The Duke's Winter Promise ~ A Christmas Regency Romance

The Viscount's Wayward Son

THE HAWTHORNE SISTERS

The Forbidden Valentine ~ Lady Eleanor

THE BAGGINGTON SISTERS

The Countess and the Baron ~ Prudence

Almost Promised ~ Temperance

The Healing Heart ~ Mercy

The Lady to Match a Rogue ~ Faith

CONTENTS

THE DUKE'S WINTER PROMISE

The Duke's Winter Promise

A Christmas Regency Romance

The Ladies of the North

Isabella Thorne

Part 1

Home for Christmas

*M*iss Emily Ingram woke to a drizzle on a fine December morning in the English countryside. The pattern of raindrops on the rooftop brought a comfort and solace to her soul that could only be attributed to the depths of her British roots.

The cold rain matched Emily's mood. She was here. In the country, away from London and all of her problems, she told herself. She should be happy. Instead, she felt bothered.

She supposed it was hard to feel beautiful in weather such as this. She paused with brush in hand. The rain had made the fine strands of her hair as limp as a dishcloth.

Emily sighed. She would have to call her maid to do something with the locks. It hung in strings. Surely a grown woman should be able to brush her own hair, she thought as she rang the bell. She was on the cusp of womanhood. Perhaps, that was what bothered her most.

Emily made her way over to the armoire to find her gowns hung in a neat row by the attentive servants. The room smelled of lemon oil and polish, fresh and well maintained. The once-vocal chamber door now glided on smooth hinges, the product of proper oil application and keen observation.

It pleased Emily to know that her aunt and uncle were still capable of running Sandstowe Hill and that the manor had not fallen into disrepair as they aged. Of course, she thought, Cousin William took care of things, since he would one day inherit. Cousin William was a year younger than Emily and had already taken up the yoke of adulthood.

Mother thought she was an adult, Emily reminded herself. Father was determined to marry her off by the spring. Yet, Emily did not feel equal to the task. Had she not already had a London season? Had she not attended the finest of finishing schools? In spite of her mother's thoughtful advice and her instructors' careful teaching, Emily still felt unfinished.

She had never thought of herself as beautiful. She was interesting and unique, but not beautiful. She thought of all the girls who were dull, even in their youth, and thought things could be worse. She was distinctive. Emily was never dull.

Womanhood must come easily to them, she imagined. These imaginary dullards would embrace adulthood and all the rules set by previous generations of gloomy adults. It was the path all young girls must take as they became women. She must do the same. She had very nearly set her mind to it.

"I *have* set my mind to it," she hissed. "I must."

Carrie peeked into the room. "What must you do, miss?" The lady's maid asked.

"I must make some semblance of order of this hair," Emily replied touching the strands although the true problem was not her hair. It was the whole issue of finding a husband and becoming a wife. The entire notion was so very permanent.

"Oh posh," said Carrie with a wave of her hand. "That is my job. Yours is to make pretty conversation, and catch a fine husband."

Carrie's words made Emily's stomach turn.

Carrie took up the brush. "Sit now, miss. I shall make short work of it."

"Thank you, Carrie. Will you miss London?" Emily asked her.

"Oh, no, miss. My sister is here in Northwickshire, my mum as well. I haven't seen my little brothers in an age."

"Oh." Emily had forgotten that Carrie had family in the Northwickshire district. The girl fit in so well in London, and rivaled the very best of lady's maids with her talents. Emily sometimes forgot Carrie's humble beginnings. She had kept the girl away from her family for too long. She had been gone for far too long as well, but her parents were adamant that she marry this season.

Emily's father, the Viscount of Kentleworth, was an active member of the court and a resident of Grosvenor Square. He rarely abandoned his post for fear that some catastrophe or other might strike in his absence. Mother stayed by his side. As a result, the Ingram offspring, Emily and her brother Edmund, had often taken their holidays with their maternal Aunt Agnes and her husband, Uncle Cecil, the Earl of Stratton.

Uncle Cecil's northern home at Sandstowe Hill provided a reprieve from the expectations of high society and a haven for the genteel youth of the area. Uncle Cecil and Aunt Agnes had no children of their own and seemed to welcome everyone else's, but Emily reminded herself, she was no longer a child.

She had other obligations although Aunt Agnes would not push her to it like her mother would. She would allow Emily her holiday, but there were visits to make and people to see.

"Are you going to go skating?" Carrie asked. "I've heard that the pond is nearly frozen over, although I cannot testify to the thickness of the ice."

"Perhaps later in the week," Emily said. "I want to be sure it is thick enough to hold."

"Ah, let some of those towering gents go first," Carrie teased. "If it should hold them, it should hold you. Or perhaps if you were to lose your balance it is the gentleman who would do the holding." Carrie giggled.

Emily smiled, but that was not why she wished to go skating, at least not entirely.

During the years of their childhood, Emily and Edmund had spent their days gallivanting across the sodden fields with Cousin William and the children of all the neighboring country manors within riding distance.

Edmund could most often be found in the company of Alexander Burgess, the son of the Duke of Bramblewood, from the neighboring estate to the north. Emily was friends with Anne and Eliza Albright, the daughters of the Aldbrick Viscountcy to the southwest, as well as Henrietta Milford, daughter of Baron Shudley.

Both Emily and her brother had fostered many life-long friendships, although some of those friendships had been maintained only through correspondence over the last years. Emily dearly missed her Northwickshire friends.

While Emily had been sent to finishing school, Edmund, with all the freedoms that his gender allowed, had continued to make the journey to Northwickshire on an annual basis, usually with Alexander by his side.

Edmund used any and every excuse to slip the confines of the cobbled streets of London, and mostly the harsh authoritarian nature of their father. Emily was lucky that Father considered his daughter in his wife's purview.

Lord Kentleworth felt his job was molding his son into a shadow of himself. Emily could not fault him. He was a good man, but Edmund was not his father. Edmund's best and most successful excursion was the week long opportunity to take provisions from London to his northern relations.

Emily envied him. She knew her mother would never have allowed her such freedoms. There was a bout of influenza in the town of Northwick the year past. Rumors had filtered south to London that several people had died of the illness.

Emily worried greatly for her aunt and uncle who were getting on in years. She had wanted to come and help, but Mother's crippling fear of contagions had put a stop to all thought of visits. Emily's maternal grandmother had passed of such a sudden fever years ago, and Lady Kentleworth was terrified of the infection.

She ordered her children home to London although Edmund had simply stayed on with the other gentlemen outside of the town proper in spite of his mother's displeasure. Gentlemen, as it were, were often allowed, to do as they please, or so her father would say to silence his wife, and then he would chide his son for failing to attend when he spoke of politics.

It was no wonder Edmund escaped to Northwickshire at every opportunity. Especially now, that the danger from the influenza was past.

"Who has come to winter in Northwick?" Emily asked Carrie.

"Well, I'm sure I don't know," Carrie said.

"Come now. I am sure that Mrs. Tanner was bending

your ear with the news," Emily said. She knew the cook was a fount of gossip.

Carrie shrugged. "Your brother, of course, and the young Mr. Singer. And his sisters, the poor dears, losing their mum. Mrs. Tanner was speaking of her this morning. Christmas will be hard for them at their age."

Emily thought losing one's mother at any age was difficult.

She had heard of the bout of influenza that claimed Cousin William's mother, Kate. His father Mr. Singer had died years ago so now the sole responsibility of his sisters rested with him.

"I'm sure it will be good to see Miss Albright," Carrie said.

That made Emily smile. She was forever thankful that one friend from her childhood exploits was sent off to school as well, her dear friend Anne Albright. Through Anne, Emily tried to keep abreast of the news in Northwickshire, but after school was completed, both Anne and Emily had gone on with their lives.

Emily had traveled to London for the Season and Anne returned to the country. In spite of their attempts to stay in touch, they both grew apart until Emily worried there was little left that might be shared.

Besides, Anne was a terrible letter writer. Despite regular correspondence, Emily gleaned more from the pages written by Anne's mother, the Lady Aldbrick who was more like to speak of her own friends and family than the goings on of the younger generation.

"I shall be glad to see her, and the others. Have you word of Alexander?"

"I am sure I do not know of the young lord."

Emily nodded. Of course Carrie would have no way of knowing. Emily would just have to wait and see, but it had been so long since she had seen the duke's son, she thought she might not recognize him at all.

No, she told herself. Alexander, she would recognize no matter how he changed in the journey from childhood to adulthood, but would he recognize her? Would he even care to see her? The thought filled her with nervous anticipation.

She remembered the last winter before she and Anne had gone to finishing school. Everything changed after that. They were children no more, but that last winter they had gone skating and sledding nearly every day, staying out until darkness called them home; Edmund, Anne, Alexander and herself.

Their skin became raw from the wind and the cold, and Aunt Agnes fretted. They had not cared. Edmund would wake Emily first thing in the morning with a pounding upon her door.

They would bundle up, never enough to ease Aunt Agnes' anxious mind, before they would race out the doorway invariably forgetting something that Aunt Agnes had reminded them of at least a dozen times. As long as they had their skates to tie on over their boots, that was all that mattered.

Emily remembered a day when it was particularly

cold. Edmund and Anne were racing back and forth, trying to put each other off balance, but they had not a care, not a worry that they could be hurt. The world was theirs.

Emily had wanted to sit for a moment. She simply collapsed in a snow bank and stared up at the branches of the pines above her. It was a beautiful day, full of sunshine although still cold. Emily remembered watching the friendly quarrels, content in the juxtaposition of the bright sunshine and the icy cushion beneath her. Eventually, Alexander flopped down beside her, winded from his own skating.

Alexander complained that Edmund was no fun when Anne was present. "Anne goads him into these harebrained ideas," he said cheekily. "Silly girls."

"Silly, are we? And none of the schemes are ever Ed's fault or yours? You tease." Emily replied with fire, knowing full well that the boys gave as good as they got.

"Not at all," Alexander laughed. "We are gentlemen, and Mother says a gentleman must never tease a lady."

"And we are ladies," Emily countered, thinking with excitement that the next autumn she would be in finishing school. She would indeed be a lady, but not yet.

Somehow a handful of snow was tossed and there was a grand snowball fight, girls against the boys. They had rushed off in pairs: Anne and Emily. The girls took the high ground for the boys could throw further. It was the only gentlemanly way to proceed, Anne had insisted.

"And you should not give the ladies the side with the sun in their eyes," she added.

Edmund and Alexander graciously agreed and soon the battle of the century began. The girls were making a go of it, especially when Henrietta joined their side; until William joined the boys. William was taller and his longer reach added distance to the boy's snowballs. The girls were pummeled, but when they admitted defeat, the boys helped them brush snow from their cloaks.

"You alright, Em?" Alexander had asked, even then watchful and careful of others, so unlike his brutish father. He had taken off his hat and brushed back his sweat damp curls and jammed the cap back on his unruly locks.

"Are you cold?" he asked.

"Just my hands." Emily tucked her gloved hands into the sleeves of her coat and smiled up at him. Alexander held her hands in his and afterwards he had always remembered to bring an extra pair of mittens.

Emily remembered it as the last innocent touch she and the duke's son had shared. It was an end of childhood. The following winter Emily was home on holiday from school, but the Christmas season was a solemn affair spent in London with her parents.

Emily missed those carefree days in Northwickshire. Days when waking to the fullness of the day brought a fresh surge of excitement for a new adventure, rather than dread at what new suitor Mother had found, along with the reminder that Emily was an adult now, and ought to get on with things.

Emily looked at her visage in the glass. She was dressed in a warm woolen gown of forest green. The color looked exquisite on her and it was properly festive for the season.

A matching ribbon gathered her long tresses up into a neat knot at the nape of her neck and completed the ensemble. Her chestnut strands had darkened over the years, leaving bronze highlights that danced in the light and matched the flecks in her amber eyes.

Gone were the too-long limbs and childish freckles. No longer did her feet get caught up in the hems of her dresses nor did the careful pinning of her locks take a wayward tumble down her back after a mid-day slide on the sledding hill with the duke's son.

Emily looked quite presentable, a proper country lady. Would Alexander have changed as well? The thought excited her. Emily had not seen him in years. She could only picture the shy somewhat awkward boy she once knew.

Emily thanked Carrie for her assistance and the maid bobbed a curtsey. "Is Aunt Agnes awake?" Emily asked.

"I believe so, miss." Carrie replied. "Lainie took tea up to her only a little while ago." Lainie was Aunt Agnes' ancient maid. Emily marveled that the woman could still climb the stairs.

Carrie continued. "But I'm sure Lady Stratton will be in the breakfast room shortly. Your uncle awaits her."

"Very good. You may take the day off and enjoy the countryside or visit with your relatives." Carrie must not have seen them for as long as Emily had been away.

"Thank you, miss." Carrie broke into an excited smile.

Emily knew that there would be little for the maid to do here in the country where no one stood upon ceremony. Carrie shut the door softly behind her and Emily went back to her musings. It felt strange that there was no hurry to be anywhere, no breakfasts or balls called her to rush.

No matter that most of her life had most recently been spent in London, she felt at peace here in the country in her childhood bedroom. The blue curtains that draped her bed were the same that she had slept beneath during her most recent visit several years prior.

Perhaps it was this room that made her long for the days of her childhood. The summers or winter holidays spent living life to the fullest. She was older now and ought to be thinking of marriage, rather than childhood games. Not that her mother would ever allow her to forget.

Emily fully expected daily letters from her mother asking whether or not she had made a decision between Robert Hawthorne, Reginald Beatram, or some other fine London gent. Emily could put aside the letters, but she remembered the conversations with distress.

"Robert Hawthorne will be an earl one day," her mother said firmly.

Emily nodded, but silently she thought, only if his ogre of a grandfather ever shuffles off this mortal coil.

She was quite sure that Robert Hawthorne's father, Lord Hanway, thought he would be an earl one day too, but Lord Hanway was over fifty with no sign of Lord Thornwood giving the reins to him. Instead, the old man kept the entire family under his thumb, and Emily feared that if she married him, she would be under Robert's thumb.

"What of Lord Barton? Reginald is kind, if not strictly handsome, and his sister is a joy."

Her mother was right. Emily did not find Reginald handsome. Oh he was personable enough, but with her chestnut hair and his, just this side of ginger, they would raise a brood of carrot topped, freckled faced children who would be mercilessly teased for their ginger hair just as she had been.

Emily could not willingly be party to torture. Besides, she could not quite wrap her mind around the thought; children with Lord Barton. He was nice, but the thought of kissing him, left her cool.

She liked both gentlemen well enough, and she adored their sisters, but she was not in love with either of the men.

Her mother continued naming others and their attributes, including Cousin William and Emily had finally put her foot down, flatly refusing. Cousin William was Uncle Cecil's nephew.

Mother pointed out that they were not related by

blood, and since it was most unlikely for her aunt and uncle to produce a son at this late date, when Uncle Cecil passed, William would inherit Sandstowe Hill and be made the earl. Still, William felt like a brother to her. Emily could no sooner marry Cousin William than she could Edmund.

She pushed the thought away with a smile.

Lady Kentleworth had continued with her list of names of eligible gentlemen. Emily had gone to wool gathering, but she knew she must eventually come back to reality.

She could not deny Cousin William would be a catch, as would her brother Edmund, but the thought seemed as strange as considering young Alexander as a suitor. Perhaps when they were all older and responsible enough to inherit it would make a difference.

William would have the Stratton Earldom, Edmund would have the Kentleworth Viscountcy and Alexander would be made the Duke of Bramblewood. Emily smiled at the thought. She could not quite imagine Alexander with his shy smile as the formidable duke. Still, William had settled into his responsibilities. Alexander must one day grow up as well.

"Emily," she said to herself. "You are a woman grown. It is time to settle into your own responsibilities. Mother is right." She sighed. "Isn't she always?" Emily traced her fingers over the ribboned edge of the curtains and flicked them away. If only she could push her willful thoughts away as easily as the curtains.

She promised herself, one last Christmas enjoying the country. One last holiday before she would be packaged and parceled away to a husband.

Emily would enjoy her visit to Northwickshire in spite of the current inclement weather. Until such a time as she returned to London, she would collect as many memories as time would permit: memories to last a lifetime.

Afterwards she would return to London. She would do as she ought and take responsibility upon her shoulders. She would make her choice of a husband and submit to society's expectation.

It would not be such a hardship, she told herself. She liked order in her life. It was the way of things. Like her mother, and all ladies before her, Emily must put childish things aside and henceforth be a proper lady. But not yet. She was on holiday.

*E*mily intended to have a leisurely breakfast with her aunt. She smiled and admired the Christmas decorations as she headed toward the breakfast room. The stairs and mantle were hung with boughs of pine and holly and red ribbons festooned the dining room. The scent of pine was heavenly.

Aunt Agnes always did love Christmas. Sandstowe Hill looked and smelled like Christmas for a month before the holiday. She hoped the frivolity would cheer William and his sisters.

Uncle Cecil and Aunt Agnes had insisted that William stay on with them after his mother's passing since Sandstowe would one day be his, and surely he did not want to go home to an empty house for the holidays. Time enough to take up the reins of the household after Christmas, Aunt Agnes had said, and as usual, Uncle Cecil agreed with her. William and his two sisters, Claire who was twelve and Caroline, ten, had moved into Sandstowe Hill.

Emily had brought Christmas gifts for all along with fruit and sweetmeats for the children although they were hardly children any longer. When Emily was eleven, she was already in finishing school.

Still, she knew that all the presents in the world would not give the girls what they truly desired, their mother back with them. Still, she hoped that for a little while on Christmas Day, they might be happy.

Emily gave strict orders that the presents were not to be opened until Christmas Eve, but she shared the candy and fruit cake. She hoped she could be friends with the girls, but they seemed very shy. They did not know her well. She had been away too long.

As Emily descended the stairs, she could hear her aunt and uncle's voices raised in their habitual disagreement, but even their banter could not quell her festive spirit. Emily slipped into a seat beside her brother, well clear of the fearsome glare that her Aunt Agnes was directing across the table toward her Uncle Cecil.

"It is not proper, Cecil, as you well know." Aunt Agnes was determined to have her say, and she did so for the next quarter hour while the servants put breakfast on the table.

The girls, Claire and Caroline were in the dining room, seated with their brother William, their breakfast plates before them. They smiled shyly as Emily greeted them both.

She wanted to bring them some Christmas cheer, but she was utterly clueless as to how to proceed. Emily turned her attention to her aunt.

"What is not proper?" Emily interrupted at long last.

"It is rude for the men to go out on a ride at such short notice, when more company shall be arriving any moment!" Aunt Agnes insisted. "Anyway, it is raining."

"Nearly snow," Edmund added with a solemn nod followed by a covert grin.

Emily in feminine solidarity with her aunt kicked her brother under the table.

Caroline noticed and grinned at her.

"I do not see the problem," Uncle Cecil said. "The women will take ages to change their traveling frocks and make themselves presentable. We shall be returned before they even take notice that we have gone."

"The problem is, you will catch your death," Aunt Agnes said, and with the recent bout of the flu, the words had an ominous meaning. Aunt Agnes flipped an apologetic glance towards William and the girls.

"I'm going into town," William said. "I trust my sisters can stay here. I will be back before the party."

"Of course," Emily said including Claire and Caroline in a bright smile. "I would love to get better acquainted."

"The gentlemen will have many fine mornings to go about their sport later in the week," Aunt Agnes continued. "They do not need to go today."

The sound of horses gathering on the lawn drew the party's attention. "Somcone is coming," Claire said.

"A lot of people are coming," William added. "You can spend the day in your rooms reading or playing games or you can sew or play your music. I'm sure Mrs. Catchpole has schoolwork for you. I shall come up before bedtime."

Claire nodded. "Mrs. Catchpole said we should return right back up to our rooms after breakfast."

"You should practice, Caroline, before too many people arrive," William added.

Caroline wrinkled her nose. "I would rather ride," she said.

Caroline gazed longingly toward the window and Uncle Cecil shook his head. "Not today, Caroline," he said to her unasked question. "It is too wet."

"So you agree with me," Aunt Agnes persisted.

Edmund leaned over and patted his sibling on the crown of her head. "I am certain that my dear sister would rather not be bothered with gentlemen milling about while she reacquaints herself with the ladies of her youth. Is that not true, Em?"

"Do not try to engage me in this argument," Emily laughed. "Why should I help you to escape?"

"I could smuggle you with us," Edmund teased.

Emily sighed for she knew that it was not to be. She was no longer a child and such ways were to be left in the past. Instead, she tried to look to her Aunt Agnes for example. She observed the woman's stern look and disapproving shake of her head, as Uncle Cecil pulled her into the doorway.

"Mistletoe," he said glancing up, but Aunt Agnes just turned her cheek to him.

Uncle Cecil waited until she turned back to him, no doubt to scold him, and then kissed her full on the mouth.

Laughing, Aunt Agnes pressed a hand to her husband's cheek. "Go on with you, then," she said. "But wear your woolen socks, and do not stay out too long." She shook a finger under his nose.

Emily had to smile. Aunt Agnes sounded much the same as if she were speaking to the children. While Lady Stratton chided her husband Edmund turned to Emily.

"Surely you see, Em. You know that it makes sense for the women to meet with you first," Edmund urged. "They will all want to change clothes. Once the ladies are in the drawing room, the gentlemen can greet them all at once. That way, the gentlemen will not find themselves in the way of the ladies' conversations."

"*You* would, no doubt, find yourself in the way, brother," Emily smiled in reply.

She knew when Edmund was trying his best to wheedle out of a task. Even as a child, Emily had found little joy in the intricacies of female companionship, except Anne, of course, but her words usually had purpose. Emily preferred to steer clear of the drama that seemed to follow the female sex.

Years earlier she and Anne would have been outside on horseback among the gentlemen, rain or no. Today, she would remain in the drawing room to fulfill her duties and receive the other ladies. She was after all, a lady herself.

"Get on with you then." She said at last waving her brother out of the room.

"That is why you are my favorite sister," Edmund called over his shoulder as the two men raced for the door, the elder moving with surprising speed for a man who had, only the night before, claimed an ache in his back.

"I am your only sister," Emily called after him.

"Either way," her brother's laughter rang from the hall, "you are first-rate, Em."

"You are welcome," Emily muttered to herself. A glance at her Aunt Agnes revealed the woman shaking her head in apparent displeasure. Then, a slow smile crept across the elder woman's face and she sighed.

"That man will be the death of me," Aunt Agnes laughed. "Only The Lord knows why, but I love him."

"We might pray in advance for whichever lady finds herself the focus of Edmund's fancy," Emily replied with the phrase her own mother had oft repeated over the years. "She must have the patience of a saint."

"That, indeed," Aunt Agnes agreed with a pointed glance at Emily. "At least we can be grateful that one of you found the right path. The other," she shook her head at the sound of hooves beating past the window. "You should not coddle him so."

"He is my little brother," Emily said affectionately. She could not help it. She wanted Edmund to enjoy what time he had left in his bachelorhood. Soon enough Emily would be married and their mother would have little else to focus on than her free spirited son. Edmund would have the undivided attention of both Mother and Father.

When such a time would come, she shuddered to think of the battle of such stubborn wills. Edmund was already stifled enough in London. It was no wonder he spent so much time away. For now, Emily would bear the brunt of her mother's attentions and Edmund might breathe freely for a while when Father was engaged in politics.

Emily turned to her aunt. "Who will be here tonight?" She asked with interest.

Aunt Agnes began naming families. By Lady Stratton's estimation nearly all of the nearby families would be represented in one form or another. Some, of course, had sent regrets, but most were happy to be invited to the celebration. It was, after all the opening of the holiday festivities.

Aunt Agnes said that the Earl of Pelburton had promised to come with his new wife and his son from a previous marriage. It had been rumored that the countess had fallen deep into her widowhood, vowing never to love again, but the earl had, by some miracle, managed to change her mind.

"Or perhaps they just wanted to join their properties," Emily said with her utmost practicality. She knew their abutting estates had now been joined into one of the largest properties in Northwickshire, save Bramblewood Park.

"Perhaps they fell in love," Aunt Agnes added. "In any case, I am eager to speak with her."

Emily was not eager to become acquainted with the earl's son again. The young man was already full of himself and now with his father's marriage, and the extended property, Emily expected the gentleman to be insufferable.

"And the Duke and Duchess of Roswell?" Emily asked.

Aunt Agnes shook her head. "They have sent their regrets."

"Oh, I do hope your friend feels well," Emily said with a bit of worry.

3

*A*s it drew nigh on towards mid-afternoon, Emily and her aunt went to dress for company, and still the gentlemen were not back from their ride.

Emily knew they had decided to "take the round" as they called it. Her brother and uncle would ride the full circle of the lower property. The trek took several hours, and eschewing a canter in the icy mud, it would take longer.

As promised, the gentlemen stayed away as the company began to arrive.

The Lady Harcourt entered with a flourish and kissed Aunt Agnes on both cheeks. Lady Harcourt was one of the most upstanding citizens in Northwickshire and several years older than her aunt. She commented on the lovely greenery that Aunt Agnes had used for Christmas decoration.

Emily greeted Mrs. Ladley who arrived shortly

thereafter and they talked for a bit about what new books might interest her while her aunt entertained the Lady Harcourt.

Mrs. Ladley ran the ladies book club in town. She was also a friend of her aunt's from their season in London. Emily knew Mrs. Ladley was called so for respect, but she had actually never married, being a confirmed old spinster.

Many of her aunt's acquaintances exclaimed their pleasure at Emily's return and she was pleased to note that she recalled the names of all except one, whom she had not known well. Still, all were nearer Aunt Agnes age than her own and she hoped some of the younger ladies would arrive soon.

The visiting gentlemen retired to the drawing room while Aunt Agnes fluttered about belying the absence of their host. Emily was sure her brother and uncle would be back soon and told her aunt so.

It was about that time that William returned and after handing off his packages to the footman, he took charge of the gentlemen to Aunt Agnes' great relief.

Although Emily noticed that with each offer of condolences on his mother's passing. William's face contorted in a mask of pain. "Thank you for your kindness," he muttered softly.

Emily moved to welcome the guests and offer him some reprieve. She realized that there were many residents who were advanced in years that she was only just meeting for the first time beyond name, now that she was among the adults rather than the children.

After a dozen people had passed by, turning to greet one another, Emily found that she could no longer put names to faces. There was, however, one individual who did stand out above the rest and always would: her long-time friend, Miss Anne Albright.

Anne spotted Emily before she even removed her cloak and bubbled to her side with a squeal. "Oh, Em," she cried. "It has been too long."

The ladies hugged one another, ever mindful of dresses easily wrinkled and coifs easily mussed, but it was an exciting homecoming.

Anne had found occasion to visit the Ingrams in London several times in recent years. The rural lady had taken every opportunity to join Emily in Town and debut her beauty about the *Ton* in search of a husband, but as yet Anne had not settled.

A part of Emily was glad that Anne also remained unmarried for they could cling to each other during this time of transition. Emily pulled Anne aside to chat while Aunt Agnes was busy with the older women.

"So you have no prospects?" Emily queried.

Anne shook her head, but the dreamy look in her eye said otherwise.

Emily frowned and prodded her friend.

"I have someone in mind," Anne admitted.

"Who is it?" Emily demanded.

"All in good time," Anne said enigmatically.

Emily was amused that Anne seemed particularly choosy for a woman with little dowry, but nonetheless, Emily loved her as one loves a sister.

"Wretch," Emily teased. "I have told you about all of my suitors. Why will you not tell? Do I know him?"

Anne thought about the question for a moment. "Passingly well." She said her eyes sparkling, but she was close lipped with the name, and so Emily let her keep the secret.

She and Anne were best of friends regardless of the fact that they had been separated. Emily's worry was alleviated as the pair of women fell back into an easy camaraderie as if no time at all had passed since their last meeting.

Their friendship rekindled and Emily could say with complete assurance that Anne was the individual she most longed to find herself in company. She was excited to spend the Christmas holiday together.

"I am so glad that your mother allowed you to visit," Anne said as they made their way to a settee on the edge of the now crowded room. "Whatever did you say to convince her?"

"I didn't do it alone," Emily replied "Edmund said I must come."

"Where is Edmund?" Anne said. She glanced around the room. "I have not seen him."

"He is riding with Uncle Cecil, much to Aunt Agnes' consternation. They should be back soon. I expect they are making the circle and found some compatriot along the way. In any case, it took all of our powers of persuasion to convince Mother that the threat of influenza was past."

"Yes," Anne agreed with a solemn nod. "I was so sorry to hear of the death of William's mother. Kate was a dear woman. I am most glad you did not come this autumn," Anne continued. "It was dreadful."

"You did not catch the influenza, did you?"

"I did not," Anne said. "But Mother and Father were both ill. It was a nightmare. I was so worried for them. Neither are in the best of health and then, when I learned that Kate had passed, I worried even more. Those poor motherless lambs," Anne added with a sad smile.

"Yes. I must admit, I am at a bit of a loss," Emily said. "Edmund and I are so close in age I never had a significantly younger sibling. I hope I can be some comfort to the girls."

"I am sure you will," Anne said. "Just remember how your Aunt Agnes was with us."

"Those are large shoes to fill," Emily protested.

"When shall you need to return to Town?" Anne asked as they clasped hands. "Not soon, I hope. You will stay all the way through the holiday, shan't you?"

"Mother would prefer I return after the New Year, but Edmund is determined to make it all the way through the Epiphany, or further." Emily revealed. "Of course, Aunt Agnes said she wrote and invited my parents to join us for Christmas."

"You don't think Lord and Lady Kentleworth will come, do you?"

"They haven't in the past. They have no love of the country. They will expect me to arrive for the Season with bells in my hair, so to speak. Spring will be soon enough for me."

"Then it is decided?" Anne whispered. "You will wed this spring? I know your father is determined, but certainly your mother can be reasonable."

"Such was the agreement," Emily shrugged. "I will have the Christmas holiday to consider and then I must put aside my dilly-dallying and make my choice."

"And have you? Made your choice?" Anne was well aware of the two leading prospects although Emily had never sensed any interest at all from the position of her dear friend. If Anne were given the choice, since the Albrights had maintained a lasting friendship and loose family relationship to the Firthleys, Emily knew that Robert Hawthorne would not be her preference.

"I have been considering Robert Hawthorne," Emily admitted.

Anne confirmed her opinion. "Oh, but Emily, if you marry a Hawthorne, your husband will never consent to you visiting a Firthley."

"*You* are no Firthley," Emily said shaking her head.

"But visits will be curtailed, rest assured," Anne said.

"Mother reminds me daily that he shall be an earl one day."

"When pigs fly," Anne retorted.

"Do you not mean when pigs die?" Emily whispered, and Anne burst out laughing.

"Oh Em you are awful. You see, you cannot marry that man feeling as you do about his grandfather."

"There is something to be said for hardy stock," Emily argued.

Anne shook her head. "It will not do. Have you forgotten, I am related by marriage to the Firthleys."

"Oh, bother that old feud. Who cares about that ancient thing?"

"Ancient men, I imagine, one of which is Robert Hawthorne's grandfather, Earl of Thornwood. The odds of visits between us would be increased with your marriage to Reginald Beatram, and his sister Lady Patience is a button."

Emily could not help but sigh dramatically.

Anne smacked her with her fan. "Lord Barton is nice," Anne said. "If not exactly handsome."

Emily still wrinkled her nose, and Anne shook her head. "Now, who is being particular? Reginald has much more chance of becoming an earl in our lifetime," Anne added dryly.

"His family is from the south." Emily argued. "There is no feud to think of, but it would put even more distance between us. Besides, I just do not think Reginald Beatram will do for me. I cannot even imagine. I mean... the thought of children with Reginald..." Her face must have blossomed into a blush, because Anne poked her shoulder.

"Oh that," Anne teased.

Both girls dissolved into giggles.

"So who else?" Anne insisted.

"I do not know."

"Very well, then. We must find you someone suitable nearby. You do want to visit Northwickshire, do you not?"

Emily nodded.

"What about Sir Joshua Clements?" Anne said. "I hear tell he is looking for a wife."

Emily shook her head. She did not think her Mother and Father would accept a simple knight. They had high expectations for their only daughter. Nonetheless, she spoke. "I do not know him. You will have to introduce me."

"I think he shall do very well." Anne sniggered.

"Truly?" Emily sensed her friend was up to some mischief.

"Truly. And you shan't have to live with him long. He is nearly as old as Robert Hawthorne's grandfather and not half so hardy."

"Anne!" Emily chided, while Anne burst into a fit of laughter. She nearly bent in half with merriment.

"It is a pity Ned Compton's character is questionable," Anne said once she had recovered. "Rumor is he has more money than the Duke of Bramblewood, but I would not wish him on my worst enemy."

Emily shivered suddenly.

"In spite of his wealth," Emily said, "and you know I care nothing for it, I feel that Mr. Compton's new fortune could be as easily lost as it has been found. That sort of pendulum swings both ways."

Besides, she thought, Ned Compton was a man too much like the Duke of Bramblewood; only Ned did not have a title to recommend him. He was the sort of man who might wed a lady and lock her away from society, only so that he might gallivant about beyond her notice.

This brought home the fact that Emily had to be careful. A husband was in control not only of his wife's purse, but also her person. Best to find one who was kind above all else and from good family. It always came back to the Hawthornes or the Bertrams.

The Bertrams were wealthier than the Hawthornes, but Emily felt nothing when she looked at Reginald. Still, he was kind. Robert Hawthorne was tall and good looking.

"Robert is steady," Emily said. "I cannot see him carousing, or drinking and gambling away the estate."

"His grandfather would make you an early widow if Robert tried," Anne said as she sipped her wine, and then she grew serious. "There is something to be said for steadfastness," she added. "Drunkenness is the bane of marriage." She raised her own wine glass with a giggle, and Emily shook her head.

"It sounds to me as if you have made up your mind," Anne questioned with a lift of her brow.

"I don't know," Emily said, but she thought, yes. Robert Hawthorne was her preference if she had to choose. He was everything that she had been taught to desire in a man.

He was calm and reasonable, staunch to be exact. He was independently wealthy and stood in line to inherit his grandfather's earldom. He had outgrown his childish ways, if he had ever had them at all. Honestly, Emily could not imagine him being playful or surprising in the least.

He must have been a very steady child, she thought, and then she remembered her earlier thought about dull women. Well, there were dull men too. Robert was quite possibly one of them.

"I do enjoy Robert's sisters," Emily admitted after a time, thinking of Eleanor, Lily, and Grace. She did not know the youngest sister well. Although it was no profession of love for the man himself, it was the closest thing to approval that Emily could muster. He did, after all, check all of the necessary boxes.

"You cannot marry a man for his sisters," Anne laughed. "Although they are fine ladies and would make willing companions. Do you love him?"

"Not as yet. *Could* I love him?" Emily corrected. "Therein lies the question..." She considered her own words for a moment. "I think I could, in a way. He is all that is proper. How can there be unhappiness in that?"

Anne hummed in response, neither in agreement or refusal of her friend's estimation. Both ladies were on the brink of considering such things and the logic must be weighed no matter how coldly the weighing might seem.

"Let us find a more pleasant subject." Emily released a breath and with it all the tension of the previous discourse. "I have missed our conversations. It seems an age since we last spoke face to face."

"It has only been since the end of the Season when I stayed with you, but I agree," Anne replied. "It seems an age. I did see Edmund upon his visit for the end of summer hunt, before this business with the influenza. He promised to pass my love to you." She laughed and shook her head. "Did he not?"

"Of course he did, but it is not the same as visiting."

"You know, every time he arrives I know it within an hour because the town bursts into an uproar." Anne took another glass of wine from a footman's tray and sipped it, looking over the glass at her friend.

"Have the troublemakers not stopped their antics?" Emily pretended to be cross with her brother and his dear friend, Alexander. Neither were boys any longer, but Emily could not think of them as men. "Edmund doesn't tell me anything because he is sure I will scold."

"Not at all," Anne giggled. "They are out until the early hours at the tavern and stumble home shouting and singing loud enough to wake the dead."

"Gentlemen will have their fun," Emily said. "Edmund and Alexander have always been nearly inseparable."

Anne grew quiet. "Well, there's a thought," she murmured.

"What is that?"

"Another suitor for you."

"Alexander?"

Anne nodded. "He has grown quite handsome."

The image of a smiling boy with tousled hair came to Emily's mind. She tried to imagine what Alexander would look like now as a man. What sort of man might he be? The thought gave her pause, but she pushed it away.

"He would never do," Emily said firmly.

She would not have the duke for her father-in-law. Robert Hawthorne's grandfather was bad enough. The Duke of Bramblewood was as unyielding as the Earl of Thornwood and as scandalous as Ned Compton in one. As children they had all feared Bramblewood Park. It was little wonder Alexander spent his time at Sandstowe with Edmund.

"If your parents are looking for a title they cannot reach much higher." Anne went on, but Emily shook her head.

"I could not consider Alexander," Emily said. "Have you forgotten what he was like when he and my brother got together? They were insufferable."

"That's true," Anne said at last. "I suppose you are right. At least I have not heard of any recent horse races. Mama said last year they took several spills until it became widely known for drivers to take the long route around the forest rather than the shortcut down Bramblewood's lane."

"Foolishness is the folly of masculine youth," Emily commented.

"And those two have it in spades," Anne continued. "Although, we have also been caught up with such foolishness on occasion." Anne admitted.

"Not any longer," Emily objected. "We are finished now. It seems that it is only boys who are allowed to go on unchanged."

"The boys and perhaps Henrietta Milford." Anne teased.

Memories of the past surfaced in Emily's mind. Miss Henrietta Milford, daughter of the notorious Baron Shudley, had been in Emily and Anne's circle since they were very young and they could not make the choice to exclude her.

As they had grown, Henrietta's tomboyish ways, her cutting comments and flirtations had not endeared her to the other girls of their age group. Her neglectful father had let her run wild with the boys long after it was proper. Emily and Anne had gone to finishing school, and when Anne returned on holiday, she found Henrietta displayed an obsessive pursuance of the town's young gentlemen.

"I have had letters from her," Emily confided. "As if we were the best of friends."

"She has written me also," Anne said. "Her father was one of those stricken by the influenza. He passed almost at the onset." The two grew quiet, Anne sipping her mulled wine and Emily drinking cider.

Emily had not crossed paths with Henrietta since before she had been sent away to finishing school, but their encounters in childhood had been many. Although Henrietta was not well received, Emily saw how her young cousins suffered from the loss of their parent and she could not wish that pain on anyone.

4

A feminine voice chimed from the doorway. "Emily? I never expected that you might be in residence! Oh, and Anne, it has been years, has it not?"

"Speak of the lady and she shall appear," Anne muttered before turning to smile at their guest. "Henrietta, how are you?" She asked.

It had indeed been years. Emily recognized Miss Henrietta Milford at once, but she was hesitant to engage Miss Milford in deeper conversation.

Emily was old enough to choose her own circle of friends now. She could give Henrietta the cut. Indeed, she should. The girl's reputation bordered on scandalous, and Emily wished her circle to be exclusive. But it was the Christmas season: a season of love and harmony. Emily would, at the very least, make an effort to be friendly.

She took a breath and put a smile on her face. "That

it has," Emily agreed. "What a fortunate occasion."

"Might I join you?" Henrietta asked with a tentative smile. "I would hate to be an intrusion."

"Not at all," Anne shifted to make room for the third upon the cushion. Emily nodded her approval as well.

She was surprised to find that Miss Milford had insinuated herself into the conversation with aplomb. It appeared that much changed since their last encounter. Henrietta seemed amicable and willing to please. She asked after their families and spoke with knowledge of the harvests, expressing concern for those most affected by the flood and the flu.

For once, her golden angelic appearance matched her behavior. Not only did she greet the other girls with warmth, but she seemed genuinely interested in developing an acquaintance of substance. Emily felt silly for being so standoffish.

Henrietta sat beside Emily on the settee and grasped her hand.

"I am just glad of some female company. I cannot deny that I have longed to renew your acquaintances," Henrietta admitted. "The whole neighborhood is filled with young men and I am in desperate need of some feminine companionship. An afternoon tea or picking ribbons would be such a relief. I cannot tell you how drab it became when you all went away to be finished."

She cleared her throat and her expression turned serious. "I am afraid that I might have been... coarse in the past but I doubt any here would claim to be unchanged over the years. I might only hope that you will not hold me to past indiscretion and that we might begin anew."

Emily raised an eyebrow at Anne behind Henrietta's view. She could almost be convinced that she had never met the lady. So dramatic was the change, and so welcoming was the expression upon the lady's face, that Emily could not help but be inclined to agree.

Anne shrugged delicately and Emily took the lead.

"Of course," Emily said. "Tell us how you have been. I was so sorry to hear of your father's passing."

Henrietta hesitated before offering her reply. "I am well enough," she admitted with a vague smile. "Father has done the best he could raising me on his own, and I am determined to make him proud."

Emily recalled Henrietta's father and his inability to care for his children in any sort of structured way. He had always been too wrapped up in his own activities to take notice of the young girl roaming about without proper chaperonage or instruction.

For all her position, Henrietta had been raised mostly wild. It might not have been an excuse for her uncouth behavior, Emily thought, but it was certainly contributing factor. For that at least, Emily decided, Henrietta could not be held to blame and as the lady said that was past now.

"You certainly have done. So it seems," Emily offered in compliment. Henrietta beamed at the praise and opened her mouth to speak when she was abruptly called away by her aunt who wished her to make an introduction of some sort.

"Excuse me," Henrietta said with a glance towards her waiting relative. "I do hope to renew our acquaintance." She gave a small nod and turned away.

"She seems quite changed since her return," Anne commented.

"Return?" Emily asked. "I had not heard that she had left."

"Neither had I," Anne admitted. "If I am to be honest I had only thought that on my trips home I had just missed seeing her. It was only recently that I learned she had gone away shortly after your last visit."

"Away?" Emily wondered aloud. "Was she sent to school?" Henrietta had made it seem as if all of the other young ladies had gone away to be finished except herself.

Anne's voice dropped to a whisper. "Had you asked me prior to speaking with the lady I would have assumed some scandal, but she seems quite refined. Still, you know her father held hunts?"

Emily frowned. She did not know what her friend meant.

Anne leaned in and whispered. "Hunts! Revels, such as the Duke of Bramblewood once hosted."

Emily's eyes opened wide at the scandal.

"There is little enough in terms of specifics, but obviously Henrietta was in the manor house." Anne continued.

"When her father held such a party?" Emily asked

askance.

Anne nodded. It was well known what sort of event the duke held. If the Baron Shudley hosted the same no wonder there was talk. Such parties were sordid things that no lady of quality would attend. Such a flagrant disregard of decorum was unusual and the height of impropriety, and although the duke was above social censure, the baron was not.

Anne leaned in conspiratorially. "It seems the baron tried to out-do the duke in terms of debauchery, and did quite well in the attempt. At least that is the word. The baron hosted grand hunting parties that last a month at a time and Shudley Hall has been the recipient of frequent visits from many notables."

"My goodness!" Emily exclaimed. "That must be terribly expensive. Should he have not been thinking of his daughter's future instead?"

"Perhaps he was." Anne said with a pointed raise of her brow. It was true that many gentlemen hoped to pawn their daughters onto the upper echelon, and a drunken encounter with a peer would necessitate a marriage.

Emily blanched with the thought. "So there *was* a scandal?" She urged.

"Apparently, it was averted somehow," Anne confided. "Then the baron sent Henrietta off to some aunt in Scotland. Scotland! Can you imagine, heaven forbid." Anne shivered at the thought.

"Oh, but Henrietta must have been devastated to be

sent away." Emily said thinking of her own longing for Northwickshire.

Anne shook her head sadly. "Henrietta returned a month past, just after the harvest, of course, her father was ill by then. He passed the following week."

"That is awful." Emily commented. She said a silent prayer for the baron, that on his deathbed he may have repented. He was not well-liked, but he was still Henrietta's father and Emily thought perhaps the man was more in need of prayer than most.

Anne admitted that she had not crossed paths with Henrietta until this day, but that she had only heard of improvements to the lady's position. "Although, it couldn't have gotten much worse," She added regretfully.

"What of the entail?" Emily asked.

Anne lifted a delicate shoulder in a shrug. "Perhaps, you should ask Henrietta. We are sure to see her again. In only a few days' time, Bramblewood is hosting a gathering for St. Nicholas Day. I am certain that your brother has already received an invitation."

Emily turned up her nose. She was not a fan of the Duke of Bramblewood. His parties were just the sort they had been discussing; renowned for copious drink and raucous behavior. In the past, Emily had been too young to attend. Now it would be a slight to decline such an offer. One did not offend a duke.

Emily hoped that she might be able to avoid the invitation entirely although if Edmund wished to go, that would be difficult. Still, Emily certainly did not think

Bramblewood was any place for a lady of quality. Or a gentleman for that matter

For years, when Alexander appeared repeatedly on Uncle Cecil's doorstep, she had wondered if the duke realized that he even had a son. Like Henrietta's father, the duke had often left Alexander to neglect and disarray. If the duke had noticed his heir, he certainly had no qualms about leaving him to poor influence, or rather, any influence at all.

Once Emily had asked Aunt Agnes if William and Alexander were brothers because they were both at Sandstowe so often they seemed not to have another home. A vision flashed through Emily's mind of a tall, skinny boy who had once been inseparable from her brother. The duke's son had been a constant presence in her uncle's home and was still the fellow that Edmund descended upon during his visits.

Alexander's mother, the duchess, was well-known to Aunt Agnes. Emily recalled what she could of the Duchess of Bramblewood, a sweet unassuming woman who was in direct contrast to her philandering husband. In spite of the onslaught of rumors, the duchess had always carried herself with poise and an inclination toward kindness for all.

Emily remembered sitting in the drawing room late in the evening hours as the elder ladies had laughed and shared tales of their season together. The mishaps and near-romances were recanted until the ladies had clutched their sides aching from the laughter.

Emily would often tell Anne that they would be the same when they were old. Their friendship would remain just as easy and important. Emily hoped she could rekindle all her past relationships, even with Henrietta. She hoped that they could see past the serious nature of their futures and just be friends.

Aunt Agnes held the duchess in the highest esteem, and Alexander had been devoted to her. Emily was sorry to hear that the lady had passed on several years ago. Emily was probably eleven or twelve when it happened. She remembered she had been away at school.

Aunt Agnes had been distraught over the death of her friend, as had everyone who knew her. The wasting illness had taken the duchess in a slow and painful way. If anything, from what Emily had heard from Edmund back then, it had hardened her husband even more fully. Emily wondered if the tragedy had hardened Alexander as well.

Emily had been away, and Edmund had been tight-lipped about his friend's hurt. She had heard, however, that the duke reveled in his debauchery. If possible, he drank even more heavily after the passing of his wife.

Perhaps it was grief, but Emily secretly thought that with his duchess gone, he had no further inhibition. Emily's own father, who was rigid in his duty and never missed a parliamentary session, had complained that the duke was a drunken lay-about and had not been to Lords in an age.

Emily did not know much of the duke, but she did

recall when they were younger; the boys had raised the
tempestuous wrath of the man at every turn. It was not
that Alexander and Edmund were overly rowdy, but the
duke was constantly annoyed when anything took him
from his own pursuits. He had had no time for children.
Not even his own son.

Perhaps that was part of the reason that Alexander
and his mother had spent so much time at Aunt Agnes'
home. Their own manor lacked the love and happiness
that was found at Sandstowe.

Many times Emily had walked with her friends along
the river path, skipping stones or sharing stories. Once
the group of them, Anne, Edmund, Alexander and
herself had been determined to catch a frog, but she had
slipped on a moss covered rock. Only Alexander's quick
reflexes had saved her from a dunk in the water. She sat
down hard on the rock with her wet boots while Anne
ran on to catch the frog with Edmund.

Alexander had sat with her then. They chatted about
meaningless things that surely had meaning in their
child's minds: why the baker in town never made custard
poufs in the winter and how much cocoa was too much
in a cup of chocolate. They both agreed that as long as
one could still stir the cup, there was room for more
chocolate. Laughing, they fell back in the grass

They did not always speak of trivial things.
Sometimes, they spoke of things close to their hearts,
things Alexander might not have even spoken to
Edmund about, things of which children were not

supposed to be aware, but always were, such as his mother's sadness at his father's philandering and the rumor of another bastard that his father may or may not have sired.

"I might have a brother or possibly sister that I have never met," Alexander said. "Can never meet. Do you think he wonders about me?"

He turned questioning eyes on Emily and she did not answer. How could she? But she listened.

Emily wondered how the young Alexander had fared after the loss of his beloved mother. Had he, too long exposed to his father's debauchery, forgotten the lessons of his kind mother? Alexander would have been only just barely a man when she had passed on from this world.

Emily recalled Edmund coming home disgruntled, saying that the duke wished Alexander to join him in the hunts. What about afterwards? She wondered. Would his father allow him to stay and drink with the men? Would he in fact, encourage it? What had happened after she left for finishing school?

Perhaps the duke did not care one way or the other. Emily guessed that for much of the time, the duke would forget entirely that he had a son. How much had Alexander changed from the boy she had known?

It was not something that she had been brave enough to ask of her brother. Even family had to maintain propriety.

In spite of her distaste for the thought of one of the duke's notorious parties, she found herself looking forward to attending if only to speak to Alexander once again. She even wondered if he was at this moment off with her brother at some sport.

"Emily?" Anne's voice broke through her musings and drew her back to the present.

"I am sorry," she said. "I was spinning webs in my mind."

"Pray, tell," Anne grinned.

"Just silly things from when we were young," she replied. "Do you recall the winter holidays when we all used to go skating on the pond?"

"Of course!" Anne grinned. "The whole village still turns out every year when the ice is thick enough. Last year, I was sure that the surface would crack under so many skaters." She grinned at Emily. "Edmund still can't keep up."

"Surely not," Emily said laughing. "He always was a clumsy child," she added.

"He was not," Anne argued a spark of fun in her eye.

"Oh, I remember Mother trying to teach us to dance. It is a wonder Edmund did not cripple me."

"I thought you had a dancing master," Anne added.

"Oh yes, the dancing master! Please, do not remind me." Emily allowed herself to smile and lean into the earlier memories of childhood. Together the young ladies reminisced well into the evening.

5

Darkness began to fall on Sandstowe when at last, no less than a dozen gentlemen and their sons poured into the drawing room in search of a warm hearth and warm company. Emily wondered when the others had joined Uncle Cecil and Edmund. Still, a day's sport had left them exhausted and cheerful.

Warm liquors were brought to hasten their comfort while the ladies abandoned their window seats to gather round for hearty conversation. Sandstowe was large, but the room not so much so that the assemblage could not be called cozy.

Several of the gentlemen were unknown to Emily, who watched the group with contented pleasure. She never felt so relaxed in London.

Edmund, in particular, was made for country life, she thought. He looked happier than she had seen him since they were children. Well, no wonder, she thought. He did not have Father breathing down his neck.

Emily's parents flourished on the bustle and chaos of Town. Both Lord and Lady Kentleworth loved the elite society, theater, and powerful companions. How they had ended up with two children who did not thrive in the environment was beyond comprehension. Emily, unlike her brother, did enjoy the parties that boasted hundreds of guests in the London ballrooms, but she quickly grew tired of the bustle and needed time to recuperate.

She liked the country. She liked the quiet company of close friends. She had dearly missed Northwickshire, but a love for life in Town was something that she was attempting to cultivate. She expected to live in London. The man she was likely to marry would certainly be of her father's choosing and of her parents' temperament.

Edmund, a deep lover of nature, had little outlet for his energies in the narrow streets of London, but here, he looked positively joyous. Emily observed his wide grin and the frequency with which he threw his head back in laughter. She wondered if he had imbibed a bit too freely, but she did not chide. They were on holiday.

Instead, she smiled. He deserved a little fun; at least for a short while longer. He was younger than she, and gentlemen did not marry so young as ladies. He still had time to enjoy his youth. She raised her cup to her lips and allowed the hot cider to soothe her tongue.

A sip was more than enough for a lady, particularly when she knew not who might be watching. A lady must be above rumor. The tenets of her finishing school ran through her mind, and she smoothed her dress, thinking that she should not drink another cup and keep her wits about her.

Soon enough, Anne was pulled away by her sisters, Eliza and Susanna. Emily would have been dragged away too, but her aunt had called to her, and she must answer.

"Emily," Aunt Agnes placed a petulant hand on her hip but still giggled when her husband tucked her neatly beneath his arm. Emily smiled at their antics. It was the season for merriment.

"How shall I ever hear the end of it when he is always such a success?" Aunt Agnes said.

"Success at what? Were you shooting, Uncle?" Emily asked. "Surely you were not on foot all this time. I thought you were riding. Your feet shall freeze."

"Riding. Hunting," Uncle Cecil said with a shrug. "No fox can out fox us."

"So it was an impromptu fox hunt? Was it a success then?"

Uncle Cecil nodded. "With my horses and the duke's hounds how can it be anything but a success?" He went on to boast about how within only a few miles they possessed the finest animals in all of England.

"You see!" Aunt Agnes laughed. "He shall never grow up, and besides, he is returned empty handed."

"Better that then empty headed," Emily replied.

"There's my girl," Uncle Cecil said patting Emily's hand and then pulling Aunt Agnes into an embrace. He held her close. "Now, I am not empty handed," he teased.

Aunt Agnes sighed and gave in allowing herself to be maneuvered under the mistletoe where Uncle Cecil kissed her. Emily allowed herself to laugh at the strange couple. Sometimes she thought her Aunt would wring her husband's neck. Other times, it was clear that they mooned over one another. Emily could make no sense of it. They were so very different from her own parents, who hardly spoke to one another unless it was of the utmost necessity.

Even then, Mother became annoyed when Father showed up unannounced in her dressing room. They seemed to make appointments to discuss her season. Emily knew they sometimes went months at different estates with nothing more than the occasional letter between them.

The Ingrams were not harsh and unloving, only perhaps more tepid in their willingness to show affection, she guessed. Unlike Uncle Cecil and Aunt Agnes, Emily thought they would wither and die if they could not lay eyes and perhaps hands upon one another each day. It was quite unseemly and would not be tolerated in London. Perhaps that was why they spent so much time in the country.

Emily was lost in her thoughts again when Edmund called out to her.

"Dear sister," Edmund's impressive voice sounded

from the far side of the hearth which was not in the best of manners.

Emily cringed, but Edmund was sure to be heard over the frivolity in the room. He could probably be heard in London. "Do not be cold. Come and greet our old friend!"

Which old friend? She wondered. She furrowed her eyebrows and scanned the trio of men beside Edmund. Not a one of them looked familiar. Still, she made her way over to her brother's side.

Edmund's introductions were sloppy and haphazard. Emily could gather no distinct name from any of the three who stood before her. The gentlemen bowed over her hand one after the other, while Edmund mixed up their titles and called them all by nicknames that meant nothing to her ears. It was not until the third guest took her hand and she met his deep blue gaze that she realized that she did in fact know him. It was none other than Alexander himself.

A spark of warmth rose from their joined fingertips and straight to her midsection. For a moment Emily forgot to breathe. She felt giddy and strange at his touch so she pulled her hand away. It was only that the shock of the recognition had caught her off guard, she thought, but she still could not quite draw a full breath.

The gentleman looked nothing like she would have expected although Anne said he had grown handsome. The last time they had met they were of a height. Now, he stood a head taller than most of the men in the room.

Emily's own head landed well below his shoulder, in spite of her own improved stature, and she found herself taking a step backward to have a more comfortable view of his smiling face.

His teeth were incredibly even and white. She could not help but be surprised at the power and confidence that he exuded. Although still lean, he had filled out from the scrawny child she remembered into a more muscular and balanced physique. Was this the skinny boy that her brother used to entertain? He had grown handsome, devastatingly so. Dark lashes covered expressive eyes, and a hint of a curl at the end of his hair was the single flaw to be found. Even that was endearing for it seemed all that remained of his childhood visage.

Emily could not help but wonder at his character. Having spent his most recent years under the wing of his notorious father, she expected that some of the elder's ways must have rubbed off. From her brother's too-wide smile, the same which seemed present upon many of the faces that had partaken in the impromptu hunting party, Emily had no doubt that a lively atmosphere and deep cups were still well-kept traditions.

She could not help but think it a shame that men were still allowed to be boys for so much of their lives, and yet, girls must become ladies.

Alexander, however, seemed to have his wits about him, moreso than her brother, truth be told. Either, he had restrained more than the others or, perhaps, had a stronger stomach for the drink. She observed him for another moment, but he seemed steady. Well-practiced, she decided.

"Goodness," Alexander said without apparent notice of her shrewd appraisal. "This is a pleasant surprise. It has been, what? Eight years since you last visited Northwick?"

"About that," Emily nodded. "An age, to be sure. Finishing school and then London."

"Then you are quite finished?" he teased, and Emily smiled.

She made a show of evaluating herself. She glanced at one shoulder, and then the next, picked at the elegant fabric of her skirt, and nodded. "It seems that all of the loose ends have been tied," she said in conclusion.

"What a shame," Edmund piped in and tweaked his sister upon the nose. "I much prefer the loose ends."

Emily swatted his hand away and did her best to maintain her bearing. She would not fall prey to their picking as she had used to. She was above such silliness now.

"Emily is not allowed to be amusing anymore," Edmund said in a feigned whisper. "Mother says."

"Ah, I see," Alexander nodded with a look that one might think meant he agreed, but Emily recalled that that particular, slight raise of his brow meant he thought the information ridiculous.

"We do not all have the luxury of reveling in childish ways," Emily gave her brother a serious look. "We are adults now."

She tweaked his nose in return just to make her point, as well as show that she could be amusing when she wished. So long as mother did not see, Emily amended. She would not get a lecture on deportment from her aunt since Aunt Agnes had much less restrictions than Lady Kentleworth.

"You too will soon learn the way of it, brother, or else you shall get yourself a silly wife with no money, no sense, and no sympathy from me."

"I shan't have a silly wife," Edmund grumbled.

"Oh, you probably will," Alexander muttered and Edmund gave him a look.

"That's what happens when you are simple-minded," Alexander teased.

This comment precipitated Edmund switching his glass to his left hand and giving Alexander a swift punch in the arm. "That is exactly the inappropriate behavior to which the lady was referring," Alexander scolded while he attempted to control his laughter.

"Em doesn't count," Edmund said with a dramatic roll of his eyes. "Buried somewhere beneath all the polish that finishing school heaped on her, Em is still my sister, and I know her best."

"I suppose you would," Alexander said with a wry smile at his friend and a glance towards Emily.

Edmund raised a finger in admonishment. "Em would rather ride than sew and she still prefers blueberries off the vine and plum pudding to mincemeat."

"Somewhere in your coat is a gentleman," Emily laughed in reply. "Besides, I can ride and sew and be a lady. Although I do prefer blueberries, I no longer eat them from the field."

"Ah, but how many blueberries is it proper for a lady to eat?" Edmund teased. "I'm sure that school gave you an exact count, not to be exceeded."

"And how much cocoa is appropriate for a cup of chocolate?" Alexander added and Emily felt her face color. As much as can be stirred into the cup, she thought, but she did not voice her opinion. She suddenly felt out of sorts.

If she teased him as before then she wondered if it might be mistaken by onlookers as flirtation. She could certainly never flirt with Alexander; it would be unnatural to their friendship. Even more, as an eligible lady, she could not afford to give others in the room the wrong impression.

She glanced around as if to find them watching or perhaps it was just that she could no longer bear the intensity of Alexander's gaze and must look away. She sensed Alexander's eyes still upon her.

Her skin felt tight and tingly as if her London suitors were at her shoulder saying you cannot choose here. You must choose in London. How could she choose another with Alexander right in front of her? How could she think of another gentleman when he was within her sight?

She looked up at him through her lashes. Lud, he was

handsome. What had happened to the skinny boy who was once her friend? He grew up, she reminded herself, as we all must.

Emily got control of her galloping emotions and the small group talked on for a while longer. Emily enjoyed the banter between the men, proof that their friendship had remained the same throughout the years. She looked for William, who was always their third.

She found her cousin speaking with another gentleman she did not know, and surprisingly, Henrietta. She tried to turn back to the conversation, but found herself standing awkwardly to the side as the gentlemen conversed, aside in Edmund and Alexander's friendship. She had never been on the outside before.

She did not know how to speak to this new Alexander. She decided to keep her interactions formal, safe. That felt wrong too, especially as old stories were told and she found herself mentioned in many of them. Still, it was the best option if she were to keep Alexander at a distance.

It was not as if they had remained close. For all that she knew he might be an entirely different person. She might very well disapprove of him now, especially if he had his father's habits, which seemed likely. No one could be so handsome and be uncorrupted.

Edmund suddenly called across the room with his hand in the air. "Oh, look! It's Anne. Em, you didn't say that the Albrights were here," He castigated his sister.

He spoke again to catch the lady's attention and

stepped forward. Never a particularly graceful man, even when he was not drinking, Edmund lurched forward giving the fire a wide birth and bumped into Emily instead.

Edmund's apology from over her shoulder could not save Emily as she stepped forward tripping on the front hem of her dress as she had as a child. She would have fallen most embarrassingly in front of the whole crowd if a firm hand had not grabbed her by the elbow and held her upright. Alexander. Her breath caught in her throat.

Emily felt her face grow hot with the thought of her averted embarrassment and realized she was sporting her colors. She was acting like a girl right out of the schoolroom. She was a woman grown. She stared at the ground for a moment as she collected herself, aware of the hand that remained warm on her arm. It was quite a large hand; firm and warm. It shifted to her mid-back as Alexander drew her close.

"Careful," his unfamiliarly deep voice coaxed. His hand upon her back guided her to the empty spot at his side, safely away from further disaster. But what disaster would his touch lead her to, she wondered and her face flushed even hotter.

Alexander released her and adjusted his position so as to give her the space that she thought she desired. Emily instantly felt the lack of his touch and almost leaned back into him before she caught herself. She drew a shaky breath and tried to convince herself it was only from the near-fall.

Sudden whispers must have reminded the young Edmund of his blunder and he immediately took a more subtle note in calling Miss Albright to join them. Anne shook her head at Edmund's antics and she offered him her best scolding look, then she giggled which entirely countermanded the chiding expression.

"Edmund, you are a beast," Anne snipped as she finally joined the group. Like Emily, Anne could hardly stay mad at the lovable lout that was Edmund, in spite of the fact that he had been trying their nerves for as long as they all could remember.

"Not to worry," Edmund replied. "I take full ownership for the fault, but Emily fared well enough."

"She might have landed in the fire," Anne scolded.

"I thank my friend for the save," he nodded at Alexander. "However, my sister is not so graceless as she once was, if you recall. Quite the opposite, in fact. She has taken the *Ton* by storm, but still refuses to choose amongst her many, many..." Edmund raised his glass and took a drink before continuing. "Many suitors."

Emily felt the heat rise in her cheeks once more, and she could only hope that her constant state of flush could be explained by the proximity to the fire, and the warmth of the room. She wanted to press her hands to her cheeks to cool them, but she did not. "Not so many," she whispered.

"It only takes one," Alexander's deep voice whispered in her ear. His breath was so very warm it seemed to melt her insides.

"I didn't. I don't," she said stumbling over her words with as much aplomb as she had just stumbled over her skirts. Her face burning with embarrassment.

"A lady has a right to take her time," Anne came to Emily's aid once more. "Besides, she has nearly made her decision. Only, it is not for you to know."

Emily stifled an inward groan. She hoped that information did not get back to her mother. She understood Anne's saying it to silence her brother though. It was not as if he or anyone else near had a real care of whom Emily chose for her husband. Still, she wished for a few more months without the threat of impending marriage hanging over her head. There would be no more avoiding it once she returned to London.

"By that, you mean *Mother* has made the decision," Edmund said. "Or, at the very least given her strong recommendation to the one or two which Em can pick. It's a farce. My sister does not care for London any more than I do. She certainly shan't choose a man who lives there exclusively."

"Why not?" Emily asked, curious as to her brother's sudden strong opinion on the topic. "I do not mind London so much. As Father says, it has access to everything one could possibly need."

"So you will let Father choose?" Edmund counted off on his fingers. "Not a Frenchman, not a Whig, not a commoner, not in debt, but a peer that will vote accountably in Lords, which means with Father. Who is marrying the man then? You or Father?"

"Come now. That is not so."

"Yes it is." Edmund scrunched his nose as if he could not agree with her statement less. "Pfft. Hawthorne or Beatram? Slim pickings if you ask me."

"Well, no one asked you," Emily snapped.

"You deserve better that's all, Sis."

"Shall we speak of a more pleasant topic?" Alexander broke in to ease the growing tension between the siblings.

Emily offered him a look of gratitude and was struck again by how handsome he had grown. His eyes danced with merriment. His cheekbones were high and rosy and his lips were so full. Why was she even thinking of his lips? Would they be soft she wondered or would they hold just the bit of firmness she had felt in his hands? A liquid heat filled her and she looked down, gaining control of her thoughts.

Alexander had saved her pride twice this day it seemed. She told herself that the bubbling tension inside of her was embarrassment at the personal nature of the conversation, but a secret voice inside of her head whispered that her sudden and unaccustomed awkwardness stemmed from the gentleman himself. It was, after all, a strange conversation to have with someone who was only a distant memory of a friend.

She reminded herself this handsome stranger was Alexander, the boy with whom she had once shared secrets, as had he done with her. Only he was no longer a boy and she was no longer a graceless freckle-faced little girl.

It had been years since they'd had a serious conversation. She wanted to flirt and to prove with wit that she was no child, but there was no going back to casual acquaintance. Alexander was not some stranger whom she could tease in fun and then brush aside. What could she say? Nothing at all, she supposed.

Instead, she forced herself to smile and stuck to simple topics, making polite conversation for the appropriate amount of time before she and Anne made some excuse to return to the other Albright sisters. The conversation was wholly unappealing. Emily could not remember a single interaction with Alexander ever being so forced.

Before she turned away, Alexander asked, "You will accept my invitation for dinner on St. Nicholas Day, will you not?"

Emily nodded, but she felt a niggling of unease. She remembered again the duke's parties from days past. There was always a big to-do at Bramblewood for Christmas, or any other time there was an excuse to celebrate.

She knew that her brother would want to go, if only to be near his friend, and found that she did not abhor the idea, not if Alexander would be there. Surely, the duke would keep his proclivities in check if he was inviting ladies.

"Yes," Emily replied. "Of course. If the Duke of Bramblewood is hosting a dinner, please inform His Grace that I would be honored to attend."

"You just have!" Edmund chuckled lightly, the sound turned into a full-fledged snicker and she realized that her brother's garbled introductions at the beginning of the evening were a-purpose.

"Oh!" Emily gasped. She did not know that Alexander's father had passed away. She did not imagine many missed the old goat, but nonetheless, propriety must be kept. Condolences must be spoken.

"I am truly sorry. I did not know." She tossed an annoyed glance at her brother and then looked back at the new duke with kindness. "May I express my deepest sympathies?"

Alexander shook his head and revealed a sad smile. "It has been difficult since my father passed," he explained. "But, the wound is not so fresh. We were never close."

Emily's heart broke for the hardship that this man had endured. It broke for the boy that she remembered, who was now entirely without family. She thought of her own parents. She differed so much from them, but if they were gone, she would still miss them. She did not feel a strong kinship with them. Even so, she would be devastated to have them pass.

She was grateful for their care and all that they have done to ensure her future. That, at least, was a form of love. What love did this man have since his mother died?

She hoped at least that her Aunt Agnes and Uncle Cecil had stood in for what was lacking.

Alexander seemed to bear the burden of responsibility well on his broad shoulders. Her thoughts stuck as she considered those broad shoulders and she was once again suffused with heat. Emily realized she very much wished to attend the dinner and observe him in his home. Truthfully, observing him in any way was a delight.

She lowered her lashes and peered at him. He was a treat to the eyes, but she did not know his character any longer. She hoped that he had not continued in his father's ways, although with such an example to follow she could not be sure. Still, she could not think unkindly of her old friend. This was Alexander, in spite of the unfamiliar feeling he raised within her.

"Well, then, Al—your Grace," Emily corrected herself before she fully spoke his given name aloud and dipped into a curtsey. "I would be most honored to attend." She looked at Edmund with narrowed eyes. "You, I will speak to later."

Edmund smiled his eyes bright with merriment.

Oh, he was cruel to have tricked her so.

Alexander scoffed at Emily's new level of formality, but he said nothing, seeming to know that Emily would cling to the title over their childhood familiarities. She could only hope that he suspected her motivations to be led by decorum, rather than by the truth, that his title now held him at a distance. Use of his Christian name even in her own thoughts felt too familiar after all of these years passed.

Whatever was wrong with her? She chastised herself for the discomfort that should not exist between them, but the feeling rankled. The young Duke of Bramblewood was nothing more than a boy with whom she had once raced across the countryside along with her brother, Anne, and numerous other local children.

Emily had to force herself to think of him with dirt upon his nose, spindly limbs, and skinned knees. Why was it that this new meeting, after such time, should hold any sway over her composure? What difference should it make that he was now a duke of great standing? None. That was not the problem, she told herself. It was not because he was a now a duke. It was because he was a man.

The boy that she thought she knew as a friend was gone, and now, there in his stead was a man grown: A most attractive man that she found deeply intriguing. Emily glanced over her shoulder to find him still watching her, and she quickly turned away.

6

For the remainder of the evening, Emily kept herself at a distance while using great stealth to find out more about how the duke had faired in the years she had been away. Keeping her ears turned toward any hint of information about her old friend. She found that he was well liked and seemed to be respected for the choices that he was making in progress of his land although they were, understandably, slow in coming.

She found her way back to her aunt and uncle, and they were speaking of Alexander. No, they were speaking of the young duke, which was not really the same thing at all. Curious, Emily joined them. She was not outright collecting information on Alexander. She was only interested in the news.

Sir Eldorf, an elderly gentleman whose sons were off at war, greeted Emily and then turned back to his conversation with Uncle Cecil.

ISABELLA THORNE

"He is off on the right foot," she heard Sir Eldorf say to her uncle. "It is well that he has taken your advice, Stratton"

"He and William have always been friends." Uncle Cecil admitted with a solemn nod. "And not unlike sons to me."

Of course, Emily had known that and was not surprised to hear that Alexander, the duke, she amended in her mind, took her uncle's council. After all, Uncle Cecil had experience in managing a large estate and in the teaching of such things. He had already done so for Cousin William, but William would inherit Uncle Cecil's title and property.

Uncle Cecil considered while he sipped his drink. "Although he still has much to learn," he added.

Aunt Agnes spoke up with a comment that echoed what Emily hoped. "He is no different than young William."

Well, Emily thought he was quite different than William in form and appearance. She smiled as she thought of the figure Alexander cut across the room, but said nothing. She only wanted to listen and learn about him. There was no purpose to her wonderings.

It was not as if he was the object of her desire. Was that what he was? Was she enamored of Alexander? She startled at the thought. Surely, it was not so. She turned her attention back to her aunt who was speaking.

"Once he takes a wife and has children of his own, he

will settle more. You shall see." Aunt Agnes smiled with fondness for her neighbor.

Emily blushed heatedly at her aunt's comment, but kept her own council.

"Alexander is about more things at the moment than the quest for a wife," Cecil replied, his eyes rested searchingly upon Emily. She looked down into her cup.

"Nonsense, the harvest has passed, and he has the full winter to explore the possibility," Aunt Agnes argued.

"What he has is the full winter to reevaluate and plan for the coming spring. It will be here before we know it and he had two full fields that lost crop to flooding. The lands must support the entail, and there is Lords."

"But you said that he was well received by the other members of the Peerage," Aunt Agnes pressed.

"Yes, even those with more years to their name," Uncle Cecil agreed. "That does not mean he can neglect London society, not at his age."

"Not like an old codger like you," Aunt Agnes teased.

"No. I have told him, he cannot neglect Parliament, although I doubt he will love the trip to London." Uncle Cecil considered. "The young duke has a long road ahead in more ways than one."

"Will he and William travel together?" Sir Eldorf asked.

"More likely, he will travel back with Edmund and myself," Emily added, the thought sending a little thrill through her. She felt her face heat, but she could blame it on the closeness of the crowded room.

Uncle Cecil's eyes stayed upon her, studying her queerly. The old man saw entirely too much, Emily thought.

"In any case, he cannot repair his father's blight in a day, my love," Aunt Agnes placed her hand along her husband's arm and he turned to her. She offered him a soft look that Emily could not understand as they were supposed to be arguing. "And a wife will take time as well."

"Fiddlesticks," Uncle Cecil said. "I saw you. I wanted you. I married you."

"Is that how it was?" Aunt Agnes said with fire in her eyes. "I beg to differ. It took me decades to sort you out, and I have only just now got you right where I want you."

"Is that so?" Uncle Cecil whispered something to his wife and she blushed like a schoolgirl. He raised his glass then in salute. "If that is how it is, I pray that the duke sorts out Bramblewood before a woman comes to sort him!"

"She would have to be quite a woman to be equal to the task," Eldorf said.

"Indeed," Uncle Cecil replied.

Emily laughed and the conversation turned to the winter's grain storage, the spring floods and the devastation left behind by the influenza.

She was glad to hear that the young duke had taken the role of his title to heart and attempted to make improvements to his estate. Emily knew he had learned little enough of such things from his father, who had cared nothing for progress and only kept up Bramblewood Park for his own amusement.

Alexander would have much to test on his own. Emily was happy for his successes, but there was a small part of her that wished the man had been covered in flaws. Perhaps then she could more easily dismiss him from her mind.

She heard of the new duke's adventures and exploits, mostly those tales included her own brother. Emily felt that as most men do, Alexander was still in need of maturation. Although, that was not so much a flaw; it comforted her somewhat to know that the boy she once knew may still exist to some small degree within the new duke.

Robert Hawthorne did not need maturing, her interfering conscience interjected. You can always marry him, but compared to Alexander, Robert was made of stone. Alexander was flesh and blood, deliciously so, and Emily was not the only one who noticed his virility.

Whispers and ladies eager eyes followed him about the room. Emily could determine one thing; the young duke was a distinct cause of interest. Whether that was the result of feminine fancy or his own flirtatious ways, she could not say, but it left her most unsettled.

LATER THAT EVENING, Emily cornered Edmund in the hall.

"What can you mean by not telling me that Alexander's father died? How much time has passed?" she exclaimed. "I might have sent my regrets rather than looking like a selfish and uncaring fool. He was my friend once."

"Is he not still your friend?"

"He must think I am a horrible person," Emily said.

"Nonsense," Edmund replied with a wave of his hand. "It's Alexander's fault really."

"How so?"

"He asked me not to tell at first, and perhaps that was a wrong choice. He said you would never think of him the same, unless you learned of it in person and could see that he was unchanged by the title. Of course, I do not think he expected you to be away for so long."

"But it was years ago," Emily said weakly.

"Truthfully, it has been so long, I forgot that you did not know until just this night. And he was right. You do look at him differently, don't you." Edmund asked raising a questioning brow.

Emily let her eyes find the young duke in the crowd. He was surrounded by beautiful ladies, and she felt her eyes narrow. "Of course not," she snapped.

"Truly?"

"Well, yes. Of course, I look at him differently. That is true!" she agreed. "But not for his title. We are both different people now."

"Not really," Edmund laughed. "Your dresses are fancier and you are a bit taller; that is all. You are still Em in here." He tapped her most inappropriately on the chest. "Where it counts you are the same," Edmund said, "and so is he."

"Edmund, when will you see that things have changed? That they must change," Emily sighed. "I am a grown woman now, soon to be married. How I interact and with whom must reflect accordingly upon my character. The same goes for you. You cannot go about plucking at braids and hopping in puddles any longer."

Edmund raised a shoulder in a haphazard shrug. "I shall hop in puddles as I wish," He said. "And as for braids, well a lady's hair is much more fun to pull these days."

"Oh Edmund, you know what I mean. People shall talk."

"You make it all sound so dismal," he complained. "As if our lives are over before they have even really begun. Is that really how you see things?"

"I don't know," she said miserably.

"Is that the marriage you want for yourself?" Edmund pressed.

"Of course not." She snapped heatedly.

"Then don't let it happen, Em. Simple as that." He drained his glass and rejoined the party, leaving his sister deeply confused.

7

*A*lexander Burgess, the Duke of Bramblewood, let his eyes follow Emily Ingram as she walked across the room. Seeing her again was nothing like he had imagined. He was not sure he knew what he had expected. It was awkward. He had not expected it to be awkward.

Alexander was glad when Edmund found him. He never felt out of place at Sandstowe or in the presence of his friend, but the number of people at the party, people his father had castigated, was daunting indeed.

After Mr. Grimes, the butler, took his coat and hat, the young duke scanned the room. He saw Emily immediately, talking to her friend Anne Albright. For just a moment, the years melted away. She glanced at him and looked away as if she did not know him. The thought stung, and then Edmund was there with a hand on his shoulder.

"Come. I will introduce you to some of my friends from school. You know Harry Westlake of course, and Edgar Wickham." Harry was most jovial, and in someway related to the Albrights. Edgar's smile did not reach his eyes.

Alexander knew why. Not all of the people of Northwickshire were as accepting as Edmund's aunt and uncle. In fact, most were not so. He would not think of that just now. He was at a party. It was Christmastide. He should be festive. He spoke, commenting on the weather and various families. His conversation degenerated to single word answers and then he stopped altogether. They assumed he was listening. No one noticed he was not.

He looked out over the crowd. He smiled but he could see the break: those who spoke and those who avoided him. The town seemed to solidify on both sides of the issue as if his parent's marriage was a spectator sport. He supposed that was because his father never made any attempt to keep his degeneracy secret or even low key.

On one side, there were the people who either were invited to his father's parties, or those who wished they were. On the other side was everyone else. These were the sincerely good people like Lord and Lady Stratton and the self-righteous who thought his mother was vastly maligned. Those who gave sage advice from the comfort of their own homes, but would not speak to him directly.

Truthfully, Alexander himself thought his mother was maligned. No, he corrected himself. He knew she was. His problem now was, for the most part, people put him in the box with his father, not unjustly so. After all, he was invited to the parties, in fact, quite often was commanded to attend. Except when he had not done, which bought him to a whole new kettle of stinking fish. Perhaps he should have just listened to his father. If he had, things would be vastly different.

More than once in his lifetime he had cursed the chance that had taken his mother from him in such an untimely way. His father had said he was grown, and should not cling to his mother's apron strings any longer. She was dead anyway, his father said callously.

It was the first time Alexander hit the man. It felt good. He should have done so sooner, but Mother would not have approved. Mother would not have approved of much of his life lately, he thought. Accept for Emily. His mother would have approved of Emily. That he knew.

The young duke let his eyes follow Emily Ingram as she walked across the room her head held high as a queen. She was as he remembered her and not.

At first, he just watched her from a distance. She glanced in his direction, but obviously she did not recognize him. The thought unsettled him. He would know her anywhere.

The amber depths of her eyes were unlike any other. In the dark he would know her voice, and the scent of her. Across a room, he would pick out her silky hair, the color of sunshine and autumn leaves. He would enjoy the tiny wisps that fell along her freckled neck. She did not have so many of the tiny spots now. The duke was disappointed. In the years while she was gone, he had fantasized about kissing each and every one. Just the thought made his blood heat. He shook the image away.

This was Emily. She did not deserve such thoughts. Still, he enjoyed drinking in the view of her as she spoke with Anne. She was so animated. He remembered that about her: how she just exuded life. As she gestured, he watched her hands, gloved now, and he thought of how many times he had clasped her hands in his, warming them. The thought made him smile.

He had imagined Emily growing up more angular. He supposed, that notion was because he remembered her as an eleven year old, lithe and strong. She had a softness to her form now. He could see that even from a distance.

He was content to watch her, but Edmund saw the direction of his gaze and was impatient.

Edmund called to his sister and she came. She was beautiful and poised, and perfect. Still, Emily did not recognize him, not until her hand was in his. Yes, he thought, she knew him at a touch. It made sense.

Then, Edmund, thinking to give them a moment alone had bumped her. Alexander wasn't quite sure if that was a-purpose or not, but he had caught her nonetheless, reflexes born of ducking blows at Bramblewood.

He was instantly transported to one of the dozen or so times they had tripped as children, sometimes laughing at each other; sometimes catching each other from hurt, but never awkward. How had their interaction become awkward?

He half expected her to turn and laugh, but her eyes were glued to the floor filled with mortification to find herself in his arms.

In that moment everything changed. They should have laughed at the silliness. That is what they would have done once, but he caught her and was instantly aware of how very soft she was, how very feminine. His body stirred at her nearness and somehow she knew. She knew the improper turn of his thoughts.

Silly him. She always knew. Emily was always half step ahead. How could she not know what he had done; what he had become?

She froze beneath his touch, but he could feel her trembling.

The duke expected some comment filled with innuendo, or scorn, but she only blushed, ignoring the sudden heat between them as he could not.

They stood so for what seemed like years and yet it was only a fleeting second too soon lost. She gave him an inane smile the likes of which he had never seen on her face. He released her, and stepped back.

What followed was bland conversation about the weather and the troubles in the land. He didn't want to talk about troubles. She was here at last. He wanted to revel in her presence, but he felt as if she had turned to glass, or perhaps he had. If they touched; if they were real, they would both shatter.

When she walked away, he didn't know how to call her back or how to fix the gulf that had sprung up between them, so he said nothing.

Later, in his usual room at Sandstowe, the young duke realized the truth of it. She had become tongue tied; Emily who always knew exactly the right thing to say. Suddenly she could no longer talk to him, and he didn't want to talk either.

He had thought it had been so long since they had seen each other that they would want to talk and become reacquainted. He thought that they would be eager to share where their lives had gone in each other's absence, but none of that happened.

In the moment, all he wanted to do was pull her close and kiss her. Would she have let him? He wondered. Or would she have run? Some of the self-assurance that he had so loved in her seemed lost. No. not lost, buried, he thought, buried under what the finishing school had taught her. At least that was what Edmund believed.

Emily was full of spirit. He did not think it could be gone. It was too much a part of her.

8

----

*T*he winter morning dawned over Sandstowe Hill. The duke's mind was still on Emily, but he did not see her again before he was forced to take his leave. He had a meeting in town to distribute the dwindling grain. He was sure if he were not there to keep order the Northwick townsfolk might come to blows.

He was still unaccustomed to the chaos of the regular meetings held each month in the Northwick town hall, but he held firm on the notion. Lord Stratton was right. The people needed to see him, and truthfully he had learned a lot from them. He wanted to be sure everyone had all that they needed. These people were his responsibility, but there seemed no end to their complaints in spite of his best efforts.

People who lived in want for most of their lives were quick to take from their neighbors. It was not something he could rectify in a single season. On the other side of the spectrum, many of the people of the area were proud. Those like Mr. Marksham, and would not take charity easily. They would rather starve than ask for help.

The truth was, Bramblewood Park and all of its outlying Northwickshire properties had fallen into disarray under his father's haphazard guidance and the trust of the people was lost. When he took over the duchy the tenants thought of Alexander as irresponsible. They knew him too well as a child and not enough as a duke.

It would still be many more years before he proved himself to the locals. Although he had their best interests at heart, there was little understanding between them. In truth, there was little trust among the townspeople themselves, never mind the nobility. He hoped his presence at the town meetings would ease their minds and let them see that he cared about them and their worries.

As Lord Stratton said, he must convince them that together they would solve whatever problems befell them. The most open-minded were beginning to see that Alexander was not his father. Some were willing to work with him, but the influenza had taken a toll. Now with winter in full swing and the tally of foodstuffs scarce after last year's flooding, the people were worried. Frankly, so was the young duke.

He wanted his people happy and well fed with meaningful employment. Only then would he count himself a success as a member of the peerage. If his tenants could feed their families this winter, then Alexander would be one step closer to being a man worth the pride of his position.

Now, what to do with Mr. Marksham? The man had moved back to the area from London, but his acreage was all but useless with the flooding, and he had lost most of his harvest. Alexander had gone to school with Marksham. He hated to see the man in such dire straits, but he was too proud to accept help or charity. Just stubbornness, the duke thought.

With a sigh, Alexander turned to his land steward, Mr. James Barnes. The man had been packing up papers while the duke's spoke to the men. He sent a boy to call for the carriage. Alexander thought he would have to hurry if he wanted to be home before dark.

Thoughts of completing the repairs on the manor made him smile. Alexander had, admittedly, already done much to improve the appearance of Bramblewood in the main rooms, but most of the repairs were only cosmetic. All of the rooms where his guests might wander at a party had been given some updates. Everything beyond that still needed work.

The servant's quarters were barely livable; a matter which he intended to address as soon as possible. The guest rooms were horribly out of date. So much so that he rarely invited anyone to stay. Except Edmund, of course, who did not care where he slept so long as he was free of London and his own father for reasons much different than those Alexander once harbored.

The duke thought if he could manage to make one or two presentable rooms, then he might feel more comfortable having a group of guests descend upon him without cause for worry. Still, he must remedy the problems which were draining money from the coffers and work to make the land profitable before he did anything else. That was more important than cosmetic fixes and his own comfort or that of his servants.

He had once thought of inviting all of the Ingrams to Bramblewood after the passing of his father, but was glad that he had not done so as he thought of Miss Emily Ingram. She was far too refined now to be put up in outdated rooms with broken cabinets and musty curtains.

As a young girl, she would have thought it an adventure. Now, he was not so sure. Her mother and father, the Lord and Lady Kentleworth, who had never approved of Alexander's father, would have taken one look at their accommodations and hopped straight back into their carriage for London proper.

His mind turned to Emily and his surprise at seeing her once more. In their childhood, he had been enthralled by her. Not necessarily in a romantic sense, but rather, he had been drawn to her vigor and surety. She always knew just what to do and how to get on, while he and Edmund seemed most often to flounder and only hit upon a correct notion by chance.

He remembered when he and Edmund had crashed the wagon and he had injured his arm. Unconsciously, he let his fingers trace the scar. He and Edmund had both sat there dumbfounded, a little silly and punch drunk from the ride and the collision.

"You're bleeding," Edmund had said, and it was only then Alexander noticed. There was a piece of wood stuck in his arm. Stupidly, he pulled it out. He was so amazed to be in one piece that a little blood did not seem a concern, but the blood did not stop.

Truthfully, he had fully expected to bleed to death on the spot, but Emily had taken charge, yelling at Edmund to give her his shirt. When Edmund didn't move fast enough, she pulled it from him, buttons flying. She had shoved Edmund towards the house with the sharp command: "Get Uncle Cecil."

Then she turned on him, wrapping the limb with Edmund's white shirt. It was blood soaked in moments, but the bleeding did eventually stop, probably from her ministrations. The whole memory was a bit hazy, but he remembered her voice chiding him: "Stupid, idiot boys!" and then repeating in a frantic demand: "Don't die, Alexander. Don't you dare die." Of course, when Emily commanded it, he could not.

She was always like that. She kept him out of trouble, or if she could not, she bailed him out of the consequences of his own stupidity. He understood now she had quite literally saved his life.

Emily always knew what was right, what to do and when to stop. He had no one who could tell him those things now. He had missed Emily and now she had returned, and yet she had not. He hoped Edmund was right and the Emily he had known still existed within the poised young woman he had met last evening.

Other than Edmund, and on certain sensitive topics certainly more so, Emily had been his sole confidant. She had listened and consoled without judgement. She had soothed him when his embarrassment over his father's philandering had been made known. She had not allowed the gossip to mar their friendship.

She had given comfort and kindness when his mother first fell ill with the disease that would take years to sap her strength and her life. He had missed Emily dreadfully when his mother passed, and she was not nearby to offer the comfort of her presence. The Ingram siblings and their Aunt Agnes and Uncle Cecil had been more like family to him than his own father. For that, he had always been grateful.

Alexander recalled once, saying to his mother that if he married Emily then Aunt Agnes and Uncle Cecil would really be his aunt and uncle. His mother had agreed with that half smile she had and then said that a gentleman should not marry for the lady's family, but for the lady herself.

"Oh, Emily is first rate," he had told his mother. She still was, he thought with a smile.

"Yes, she is," his mother replied. "One day she will be a fine lady, and she would make a marvelous duchess."

He did not take it to heart at the time. At his young age he had scoffed and said. "No Mother. You are the duchess." He snorted with laughter. "And why would I want a fine lady, anyway. I want to marry Emily."

The duchess had chuckled and told him that one day Emily would grow into a lady with more life in her than the ninnies that his father would push upon him.

"But I don't want a lady," he had insisted.

"You will. Mark my words," she had said, and he did mark her; only Emily had moved to the city.

His mother had not been wrong. Emily had grown into a fine lady. Perhaps too fine for simple country life, he thought. She was born and bred for the finery of Town. Lady Kentleworth had made sure of it.

The duke wondered if that meant that all of the things that he had enjoyed about Emily had been wrung from her in finishing school. Edmund said it was not so. Of course, the school had made her appear proper. He had seen as much the other night. Alexander worried that it had taken away the spark that had always made her stand out above the other ladies of his acquaintance.

In recent years, he had thought of Emily often, especially when Edmund came to visit. Of course, that was because she was Edmund's sister. Still, they had not spoken or written. Both had been far too busy with their own lives to keep in touch. Edmund could visit, but it would have been inappropriate to bring his unmarried sister to a house filled only with gentlemen. It seemed a shame that their friendship should be curtailed for the simple reason of the expectations of their sexes.

His father had had no qualm exposing the boys to his

wild evenings of drinking, smoking, and gambling. Perhaps he should not have done so, Alexander thought. His friend Edmund knew of the rabble rousing, but not all. Alexander wondered if he would ever dare to tell him, or if that would mar their friendship. Even if it did not, Edmund would be wary of Emily, and Alexander did not want either of them to be wary. He decided there was no need to tell tales of events past.

Alexander knew that even if he had a sister in residence his father would not have done things differently. Certainly, Henrietta's father had not. No, if he had a sister, Alexander was sure she would have been ruined, in reputation if not in fact. Emily had been protected from his father, and therefore from him.

The duke knew now how very inappropriate such actions were. He supposed he had known that even when he was younger. Where his own father had not cared a whit about society or what rumors flew, Edmund and Emily's father ruled them both with attention to sensibility.

Alexander only hoped that Lord Kentleworth's uprightness had not squashed all the bite out of Emily. There had been a few moments of witty retort that had made him think that the old Emily was still there somewhere; buried beneath the fine silks and rigid backbone. He hoped he could find her again.

At that very moment, one of the objects of his musings happened to waltz through the door of the meeting house. Edmund sauntered over with a devilish grin. Ed was always up to some sort of trouble although never anything too terrible.

"Your Grace," he said with a flamboyant bow.

Alexander sighed and pretended to ignore his friend. Edmund flopped down at a seat at the table, his one leg, draped over the other. "Are you finished holding court?"

"I have work to do," Alexander replied as he set about placing his seal upon several documents that had been drawn up that afternoon. "You will see it too soon when your own father passes."

"No," Edmund said flippantly. "My father shall never die. Heaven doesn't want him, and the devil is afraid he will take over his position."

Alexander gave a hearty laugh. It felt good to let go. "Just let me finish this. I am not too busy for my friend," he said.

"Good," Edmund said. "I hoped we could stop by the Arms. You must be hungry."

Alexander finished his work and spread the pages out so that the wax might dry and turned to face his companion. "I am a bit."

"Good," Edmund leaned forward with a conspiratorial grin. "You'll never guess who just took a room at the inn." Edmund went on to explain that several of their old friends from school were passing through on the North Road and had decided to stay for a night.

Alexander raised an eyebrow. "On the way to Gretna Green?" he questioned.

"No," Edmund said with a laugh.

Alexander could not help but grimace. "I dare not put them up at Bramblewood," he said to his friend.

"I do not think they expected it."

Still, Alexander felt shame that he could not. Those guest chambers needed to be finished, he thought with a muttered curse.

"Do not let it bother you," Edmund said.

"Well, ho!" Alexander grinned. "Then we shall have an evening on the town, I assume?"

"Of course," Edmund replied. "Just like old times. You've become far too stiff in my opinion."

The duke sighed. He certainly had not. Although there were many responsibilities that now fell on his shoulders, he would always make time for old friends. Edmund just did not wish for either of them to become so caught up in the work of running of an estate that they did not remember what was most important: things like family and friends.

Alexander could not blame Edmund. His friend often complained that responsibility had ruined many of their old companions who now had little to talk about, but wealth and the securing of more of it for their heirs.

"Allow me to finish up here." Alexander nodded. "Tell the others that I will join you shortly. We shall make a night of it."

Edmund clapped his hands together and sprang from his chair. In an instant, he was off. The duke glanced about the room to see if there were any other business matters that must be addressed. Barnes returned with the news that his carriage was ready for the ride home.

Alexander grimaced. "Change of plans," he said. "I am staying at the inn tonight." He felt a twinge of guilt that his man, who had waited patiently for the duke's business to be finished, would now have the ride back with only the carriage boy.

"Very good, Your Grace. As you wish. I shall take the carriage back to Bramblewood and send it for your pleasure on the morrow."

Alexander shook his head. "I will acquire a horse from the livery and ride home," he said. He stopped the man as he was about to leave. "A moment," he said.

There was no time to change his attire or refresh his person as Bramblewood sat no less than one half an hour outside the village by horse, a bit more by carriage.

He would be as he was. Tonight, he would not be the duke. He would only be a gent out with his friends, he thought as he ran a hand through his thick dark hair. He shrugged off his jacket, loosened the knot at his neck, removed his cuff links and rolled the crisp white sleeves back.

As he replaced his jacket, Alexander dropped the expensive cuff links into Barnes' palm. They had belonged to his maternal grandfather and although appropriate for the duke, he did not want to wear them carousing with friends. As he put them into Barnes' care he thought of the many times he had caused his mother grief for losing cufflinks.

"Give those to Jervis, and return these papers to my desk. Then take the night off." Even if he decided not to remain at the inn, the duke would end up at Sandstowe rather than to his own home. "Do not expect me before mid-afternoon," he said. "Take the morning off, too," he added with a grin. The year had been difficult. Everyone needed a bit of time to recoup.

"Thank you, Your Grace."

Then, without another word, Alexander went to join his friends for some much needed ale and laughter.

Part 2

All is Bright

9

*T*he following afternoon, after some shopping in Northwick's town proper, Emily was seated at a table in the tea room of the Northwick Arms. The room was decorated with bright ribbons and pine boughs. The delicious smell of tea mixed with the scent of pine.

The owners of the Arms brought the tea from Twinings on The Strand and served it at the inn. Consequently, anyone who had to stay in town past teatime stopped in for a cup, and the tea room itself did a thriving business aside from the inn. The main pub served guests more hardy food and stronger drink.

In conversation, Anne told Emily that the occasional tea shop had sprung up in France, separate from inns. She took a sip of the excellent brew and closed her eyes in bliss.

Emily said, "No doubt giving the widows of the war some occupation to keep body and soul together."

The other girl nodded. "Other than the pubs," Anne added. Both knew what sort of girls would work in a pub.

"Some tea shops sold loose tea as well as by the cup. It is done in the East too," Emily said. "Why, Mr. Carrington spoke of drinking some wonderful tea in the East."

"Mr. Carrington?" Anne asked. "I do not believe I know him."

Emily shook her head. "He has done a great deal of traveling. I do not believe he was in London during your last visit. He is an odd fellow."

Anne's sisters Eliza and Susanna, along with Henrietta, joined them. Emily had extended the invitation to meet her and Anne at the tea shop.

"Your Aunt Agnes will be so envious when she hears we stopped at the tea shop," Susanna said. "She loves the Earl Grey tea, but generally she just buys tea in a block to last the year."

"Truly?" Emily said thinking this was a good Christmas gift idea. "Then, the Earl Grey would be a treat for Aunt Agnes?"

"Oh, yes," Anne said.

Emily moved aside to allow the girls to join them at the table.

She smiled politely at Henrietta who hugged her and gushed. "What a pleasure I had upon receiving the invitation to meet you," Henrietta said with a nervous smile. "I cannot tell you how dull this town is without female conversation."

"I thought that you might like to join us," Emily said as the other ladies settled themselves. Although Henrietta may have been uncouth in her childhood, here she was, smiling and overflowing with Christmas spirit.

"I was indeed glad of the invitation, and I thank you," Henrietta said with a sincere smile.

"We are glad to share tidings of the season with you," Emily said.

"Yes," Anne added without further comment.

The conversation stalled a bit with the newcomers. Emily sought to rescue it.

"So, I heard you visited your aunt in Scotland," Emily said. "That must have been an adventure." Emily wondered at the thought of the cold wild land.

"It wasn't exactly a pleasure visit," Henrietta said while the tea was poured. "Father wanted me...out from under foot." She was picking at her handkerchief.

Anne and Emily exchanged glances. So there was some scandal there. Emily did not want to pry. She wanted to put Henrietta at ease, but the conversation seemed to be dredging up unhappy thoughts.

"Will your aunt's visit here be an extended one?" Emily asked but Henrietta shook her head.

"No, not for long," she said, "only until we get some things settled for my young cousin." Henrietta seemed a little hesitant at first to talk about Scotland, but soon warmed to the topic when she saw that Emily had a genuine curiosity rather than just an interest in gossip.

"It's very cold," she said. "One is nearly guaranteed snow for Christmas."

"Oh, how wonderful," Susanna said. "I hope we have snow for Christmas."

"At least it was cold before we took to Peckridge Isle," Henrietta continued. "It is nearer the sea, and so gets the sea breezes, but it is still colder than here."

"Is that your aunt's property too, or rather your uncle's?" Anne asked.

Henrietta shook her head as she stirred sugar into her tea. "It belongs to a friend. I was visiting."

"Is it really an island?" Susanna mooned. "I would love to live on an island. It would be so romantic."

"Not at all, although it does border Lake Mchearen," Henrietta laughed. "Why it is called an isle I have no idea. Perhaps long ago it might have been, I suppose, but a land bridge has been made, so that you can walk to it from the North Road, straight east towards the sea, although it is quite the trek. It is rather a pleasant day's ride in the summer."

"I would like to hear more of it," Emily said with sincerity. Perhaps if she got to know Henrietta better she would have a stronger sense of the lady's character.

"What I would like to hear more of," Susanna said with a conspiratorial lean into the table and a wink toward Emily, "is Robert Hawthorne!"

"Do tell!" Henrietta perked up with interest.

"He is Emily's intended," Susanna said.

"Not exactly," Emily said with a blush. "Mother is certain he will offer, but he has not." She gave Susanna a look. "Even if he had done, I have not decided that I will accept. I suppose that is why I have run off to the country."

That was exactly why she had run off to the country. Northwickshire gave Emily a chance to clear her head. Perhaps it was not entirely the district, but more specifically the people here. Thoughts of Alexander bombarded her.

Emily gave a strained laugh.

"Hawthorne, you say? As in, that feud that started some dozen generations ago?" Henrietta asked glancing from Emily to Anne.

"I do not think it was that long ago," Anne added.

"But you are related to the Firthleys are you not?" Henrietta asked.

Anne nodded.

"On our mother's side," Eliza supplied. "They are our cousins."

"Second cousins," Anne added between bites of teacakes.

Emily grimaced. She did not want to talk about that. It was such old news that no one ever spoke of it anymore. The elders of the families avoided one another as if their opposites carried the plague, but no one of note paid it any mind. Still, she imagined that Robert's grandfather would be resolute in his hatred. He was entirely the type to hold old grudges.

"So, this Robert is one of those Hawthornes?" Henrietta pressed.

"Yes," Emily replied. "He is of that family, but I can't see that it would matter. The argument between the families was long ago."

"You cannot honestly entertain his interest," Henrietta gasped. "Why, you would never be permitted to visit Sandstowe or Bramblewood again. Likely not even the neighborhood unless you came alone, and that would be a push. Your aunt and uncle would certainly be most distressed, let alone those of us that call you friend."

Emily smiled. She had some reservations about calling Henrietta friend when the tea began, but it was clear that the lady needed a friend or two. "Thank you, Henrietta, for your kind thoughts of me," she said.

"Of course," Henrietta said.

The two of them smiled at each other over their teacups.

"I like Robert's sister, Eleanor." Emily said. "She is always up for a lark."

Anne took a sip of tea and nodded. "Father's family has been able to maintain a friendship on both sides without conflict, so perhaps it would do."

"Only, you must be careful of invitations. You must not include both families on invitation to the same event," Eliza added with a nod. "You could still see us,

Emily," she said with a kind squeeze to Emily's hand. "I am sure of it."

"That is good to know," Emily replied. "I admit that I had not given much thought to the feud. Still, I have made no official decision and so we shall cross that bridge when the carriage draws close."

She was glad when the subject drifted away from her romantic endeavors. They were an uncomfortable topic for an afternoon spent with friends. She would much rather think of happy things over necessities. Marriage was a tedious business: one to be dealt with in the spring, she decided. "I do not have to think about marriage just now," she said.

"We all must think of marriage," Henrietta replied.

"But," Eliza added, "spring is a much better time for weddings, or perhaps summer when all of the flowers are blooming." Her eyes were alight with the thought. They all knew that Eliza was quite the gardener.

"Right now, let us talk of the Christmas presents we purchased." Susanna said digging in her satchel to show the girls several items.

For a while they did just that.

"I do want to find something special for your young cousins," Henrietta said.

Emily nodded.

"I know that the vicar would say that Christmas is a solemn holiday," Emily said, "and not all about presents and merrymaking, but I am sure that Claire and Caroline need some Christmas cheer in their lives right now."

All thought of the poor girls and the loss of their mother. They knew that presents would not really take away the sting of that loss. It would be their first Christmas without their mother, and although the ladies were uncertain what to do to help, they all wanted to bring joy to the young girls.

"I've brought a few tokens from Town which I hope they enjoy," Emily said.

Anne said, "I have made them both scarves which they can wear skating once the lake freezes."

"Oh, do you think it will be soon?" Susanna asked excitedly.

"Without a doubt," Eliza answered.

"I am not even sure I remember how to skate," Emily lamented. "It has been so long."

"I am sure it will come back to you," Anne consoled her.

Susanna shivered with delight. "It shall be so much fun!"

"I am more excited for the party at Bramblewood," Henrietta said.

"Yes," Anne admitted. "That will be sooner."

Emily admitted that she too was looking forward to it, although she had mixed feelings. "I suppose it will be a very different party than has been held there in the past." At least she hoped so.

"Oh yes," Henrietta agreed. "Alexander hated those parties," she said in an off-handed way that revealed she and the duke had discussed it.

Emily raised an eyebrow and exchanged a glance with Anne as Henrietta began a story from several years ago about the Dowager Mayberry's fur hat. "She said it was a gift from a Russian prince, but Alexander and I thought it looked like a fox perched unhappily on her head. I must say, we laughed until our sides ached."

"You are so familiar as to use His Grace's Christian name?" Susanna asked with curiosity. Her young face was alight with romantic notions of familiarity. She had yet only one or two gentlemen who were close enough to refer without title; and those for family reasons.

The truth was, she was young and naïve enough to ask what they all were thinking, even though they were too well bred to pry. Emily thought it was not only the familiarity of calling Alexander by his given name, but the very awareness of knowing his feelings about his father's parties. It made Emily uncomfortable although she supposed she could have guessed the same.

"We have long been close," Henrietta explained with a wave of her hand, "since childhood really. You know, Anne. We all played together." She seemed to want validation for her familiarity, or perhaps she was trying to draw Anne into the conversation.

"Nonetheless," began Anne shaking her head. "He is the duke now, and we are not children."

The truth was, Emily thought herself and Anne were much closer to the duke in childhood than Henrietta. Emily's mind conjured several fun childhood excursions. She remembered Henrietta tagging along rather than being completely included, and yet it was Henrietta who called the duke by his first name.

"I do not recall your spending much time with Ale... His Grace in our youth," Emily added. She had almost slipped up herself because she always thought of him as Alexander in her mind.

She had called him Alexander since childhood and it felt somewhat strange to refer to his as the duke, but that was his proper title. It was extremely forward to refer to him with familiarity now that they were no longer children. Emily much preferred the honorific for its formality. It reminded her that he was no longer the boy who was her friend. He was a man and a peer of the realm.

"No," Henrietta admitted explaining, "not in the years that you might recall. It was afterward, when you were away and we were a little older, that we became close."

How old? Emily wondered. She shot a glance at Anne who was frowning mightily.

"Oftentimes we were the only two of an age in the neighborhood with any real position," Henrietta continued, but Emily knew that was not the complete truth. There were the Albright sisters and several other girls their age, but Anne had said previously that they were discouraged from visiting with Henrietta.

"Everyone was always coming and going, Alexander and I were quite left behind," Henrietta said with a pique.

Left behind together, Emily thought miserably. She

chided herself for her uncharitable thoughts, but she knew it was true. Her mouth felt dry at the implication. At the same time, Emily realized that they *were* left behind.

Henrietta said the words as if it were no great hardship, but Emily heard the pain behind them. Emily felt terrible as she realized that this must be true. It was clear Henrietta felt abandoned by the friends who had gone off to finishing school.

She wondered if the duke had felt abandoned as well. Lady Aldbrick did not even want her daughters to visit Sandstowe when the rowdy Edmund, Alexander were there, most certainly not Bramblewood. It was a good thing that Edmund had continued to visit, Emily thought, and of course William, but where did that leave Henrietta.

"Your fathers were close," Anne observed with caution. "Were they not?"

Henrietta clicked her tongue. "Somewhat," she said. It was clear she did not want to continue on this topic. Her eyes began darting around to other tables as if looking for another topic upon which to latch her interest.

Emily knew it was common knowledge that the two nobles had been cronies of sorts. The baron and the duke were of differing status, and yet, in character, they matched each other perfectly. Both enjoyed a deep glass and a party that went well into the morning hours, with women of the questionable variety.

"They shared company often back then," Henrietta agreed hesitantly as if trying to retreat from her earlier admissions.

"But they had a falling out," Anne urged. Emily knew that when Anne got her teeth in a bit of gossip she really could not let go. Emily wanted to stop her, but she also wanted to know.

"Yes. I suppose. They were always trying to out do one another, and eventually Father could not keep up. The duke had very deep pockets you know." Her voice contained a bit of coldness as if she were stepping around a delicate subject. "Although, Father did not keep me apprised of the goings on or the financial situation." The chilly retort and the topic itself advanced the fact that Henrietta did not want to elaborate.

Rumors of Henrietta's hoyden ways assaulted Emily's sensibilities and Emily wondered if she really should have invited the woman to tea, lest she be labeled so by association. More than that, the thoughts that Emily was entertaining filled her with a strange combination of anger and hurt. Emily had the sinking feeling that Henrietta and the duke were much more familiar with one another than the laughing about hats or the use of Christian names.

10

A buoyant laughter rang from the far side of the teashop and drew the attention of the gathered ladies.

"What could be so humorous?" Henrietta wondered.

It must be the funniest thing as the two ladies across the shop bent over with peals of laughter.

Emily did not feel like joining in the spirit of laughter at all. In fact, she had a strange desire to be home.

"We should ask," Henrietta said with determination. "Melinda Mize has never been one to hold her tongue and is bound to share the tale. It is sure to give us an entertainment."

"No," Emily said, and with a shake of her head, she caught Henrietta's arm as she meant to stand. "It is not for us to pry."

Henrietta raised an eyebrow.

Emily felt guilty. She wished she had not pried about

Henrietta and Alexander. Now she felt disheartened. "Let them get on with it," she said.

It was clear that Henrietta was desperate to escape the conversation into which they had maneuvered her.

Emily's thoughts were whirling. She had to believe that Alexander would have acted the gentleman. Hadn't they spoke of such things, even as children? She exchanged a glance with Anne as Henrietta spoke, waving her hand at the other ladies.

"Mrs. Mize," Henrietta called over one of the participants when it seemed their conversation was complete. Henrietta had to make several tries because Mrs. Mize was nearly deaf, but Henrietta was determined.

"How are your daughters?" Henrietta called loudly.

"Who?" the lady asked and Henrietta repeated herself quite loudly. "Last I heard Nell was going to marry a solicitor or something of the sort."

"You heard correctly," Mrs. Mize said in the same overly loud voice. She beamed with pride. "Not just any solicitor, Mr. Mills. My Nell did well for herself, I should say although he is quite a bit older than she would have liked he treats her well and is as doting as any husband ought to be. I cannot complain that she stayed right here in Northwick."

The ladies offered their congratulations and listened for what seemed an hour on the details of the marriage and her daughter's small but respectable dowry.

"I've just heard the most amusing thing," Mrs. Mize

said when she had run out of other things to say. She brought her voice down to what she must have thought was a whisper, but it was still possible to hear her across the room.

"Do tell." Henrietta gave a pointed smile to the ladies at her table. Her purpose had been accomplished.

"Well, those of the Bramblewood party were out carousing last night," Mrs. Mize said with the sort of stern, yet loving, look only a mother can give.

"Is that so?" Anne said. "What have they done this time?"

Emily felt a bit of worry, but she was not surprised to hear this. Her brother must have been in the fray considering that he had not arrived home until she was waking for the day. He had put himself straight to bed and was still asleep when she had left for her tea. She hoped that the night did not get too out of hand.

"It is the most ridiculous thing," Mrs. Mize clucked. "Honestly, I do not know what made them think of it."

"Well," Emily said, "what have they done?" She had the feeling that she was about to be embarrassed by the actions of her brother and his friends, but it would not be the first time, nor the last.

She remembered that Edmund and Alexander usually made her smile, and she needed a bit of levity at the moment. Her mind was still reeling with the information that had been revealed by Henrietta. She wanted to push it away, but her sensibilities would not allow it.

"Do you know Mr. Marksham?" Mrs. Mize asked.

All four ladies shook their heads. They had not heard the name.

"He is the new magistrate. His family is related to some lord or other. I can't remember which." Mrs. Mize went on for a while trying to remember but could not. "Hosh-posh," she continued. "Anyway, as I said, he is new to the neighborhood and has taken up at Chatterling Cottage. Which, mind you, is more than cottage, but that is beside the point. He is a proud man, you know."

Emily did not know, but apparently Mrs. Mize was going to tell them.

"What of him?" Henrietta pushed the woman to get back to the point with an encouraging nod.

"Well, the party of no less than six gentlemen was at the inn all evening, His Grace included," Mrs. Mize began again. "I know this because my maid's daughter is a serving maid there and she said they had her in stitches all evening with their antics. Her daughter, not my maid, of course."

"Of course," Henrietta said.

"She brought home a silver shilling for her trouble, too," the lady said knowingly.

"A shilling?" Susanna encouraged.

"More than she made in the whole day, no doubt several days," Mrs. Mize said. "The daughter, not the maid," she corrected again.

"Of course," Henrietta said.

"Sounds like your maid is itching for a raise in salary," Anne muttered, but Mrs. Mize ignored her.

"Even the chambermaids came out when they finished their work, and they all had a grand old time."

Emily was taut with anticipation. She was not sure if she was eager to know or afraid to know, but the tale must be revealed. "What happened?" she urged.

She hoped Edmund wasn't trifling with bar wenches. That was a slippery slope. Pulling braids indeed! Surely Mrs. Mize would not find that funny. The thought brought her back to Alexander and Henrietta, unchaperoned in their youth. The thought would simply not go away.

"What is the humor in that?" Anne inquired sharply, voicing Emily's feelings

"Well, when talk came to the new Mr. Marksham's arrival the gentlemen soon realized that he was an old schoolmate of theirs, and they decided to welcome him into the neighborhood properly." Mrs. Mize giggled and held her girth as it shook with laughter.

"How did they achieve their welcome?" Emily pressed when the woman seemed unable to continue. She was now interested in the story in spite of herself.

"Why they crept out in the dead of night, while Mr. Marksham was asleep in his bed," Mrs. Mize let loose several more peals of laughter, "captured a dozen fowl and released them inside Chatterling Cottage!"

"They did not!" Emily cried. Emily could imagine the confused birds squawking and flapping inside the house.

It was too funny. She had to laugh. "Inside the cottage?" She said just to confirm the picture of chickens flapping about the house that she had in her mind.

Around her the ladies broke out in giggles.

"Loose about to their own devices until Mr. Marksham woke to the sound of clucking beneath his bed!"

Emily laughed until tears rolled down her cheeks. The prank was truly harmless. If there ever was any doubt that the boy Alexander was somehow in the duke, this story confirmed it. This was exactly the sort of prank the boys would have pulled when they were ten.

Perhaps his kind nature would not have changed, she thought. Certainly, Edmund's still had the same quirky sense of humor. She had to remember that she has always trusted Alexander as a youth. She would trust him now. He did not have an unkind bone in his body; careless, yes, but not unkind, and Henrietta was their childhood friend. He would not be so crass.

"Boys," Mrs. Mize said, shaking her head, and Emily could not agree more though she wondered at the eventual outcome.

"Was Mr. Marksham cross?" she asked. Very few people liked having pranks played upon them, but apparently Mr. Marksham was forgiving.

"Not at all!" Mrs. Mize chuckled. "He vowed to get his revenge when they least expect it and sent a note to the duke saying that he would be keeping the chickens!"

"Were they his chickens?" Emily asked. "The duke's, I

mean?" She would not put it past her brother to steal them, but she hoped they had grown past such antics.

"Oh, I assumed they were from the duke's own enclosures. If not, I am sure he could have bought them. I did not think about it," she said with a shrug.

"But now that you mention it, the chickens were probably worth a pretty sum," Mrs. Mize said. "And with all the flooding this year well, Mr. Marksham made out the best in the deal." She laughed again. This time the joke was on the duke.

Emily could not keep the smile from her face. No harm done then. Serves the duke right, she thought, to lose his fowl for a prank although he was certain to have plenty more. Emily thought that this Mr. Marksham had gotten the best of them and with good humor as well.

Anne had a bemused smile on her face.

"Remember when we were a part of such antics," Emily mused.

"But we are ladies now," Eliza said.

"Indeed, we are," Anne said. Emily thought she heard a wistful note in her friend's voice.

11

*A*lexander thought it had been a good evening. At least, it had been an eventful one. He slipped off his tailcoat and handed it to his valet, Jervis, while Lucky wagged his tail and coaxed for a rub.

"Lie down," he told the ancient greyhound. Lucky obeyed but continued to wag his tail. It made a continual thump-thump sound on the floor as he watched his master with silent adoration.

A book and a glass of brandy waited on the duke's nightstand, along with fresh wax candles in the silver candelabrum. He told Barnes that he hated struggling to see the letters in his book in poor light although, he knew; his servants thought he spent an extravagant amount on candles for unused hallways.

Perhaps he just hated all the dark corners of his boyhood home. He wanted to dispel all of the shadows.

Candles would not quite do that, but perhaps there was another way. Alexander swirled the brandy in his glass and took a sip not tasting it. His mind was on Emily.

Lucky whined and he gave a low whistle. The dog bounded to him and Alexander put down the brandy to give him a good scratch. He had the animal since childhood and the hound showed signs of his age. He was the only greyhound allowed in the house. Lucky was a runt puppy that his father wanted to put down, but Alexander had intervened. Since the dog had lived to a ripe old age, Alexander thought the dog was definitely lucky.

"Bring me some luck, hey boy?" The duke said patting the dog.

Around him the servants moved silently, about their tasks. Jervis hung up his tailcoat and fussed with his clothes, tsking over the occasional dog hair, no matter that Lucky was well brushed. Alfie filled the bedwarmer with coals while Joe banked the fire.

Alexander remembered when it had been Polly who lit the fires in his room: Polly, with the red hair and freckles. She had looked a bit like Emily then. He remembered the day quite clearly. It was the day everything had changed.

He and Polly were of an age. It had not been long after his mother died. Polly had been kneeling by the fire chattering brightly in the way she had; filling the room with a pleasant sound. He had been by her side talking.

She stood and turned to him, a smudge of soot on her cheek, and he reached out to wipe it away.

She froze, so very still and he had kissed her. It was an impulsive thing, and yet, perhaps he had planned it. In some part of his mind, he supposed he had. He knew he didn't want his father to choose his first kiss; his first anything, and yet he would. He had.

Alexander took another sip of brandy and sat the glass on the dresser. He let Jervis take his cufflinks. He unbuttoned his waistcoat and pulled it off handing it to the man to hang.

He watched Joe now poking the fire and he remembered.

He had kissed Polly and when he stepped away, Polly had stopped speaking. She had stopped moving. There was stark terror in her eyes. He had not meant to scare the poor girl. It was only a kiss, and yet it was not.

"Go," he had said softly and she fled as if the hounds of hell were on her heels.

The next day, there was a new servant to bank the fires, a tall boy, who he thought must have drawn the short straw. Either that or he was the bravest of those offered the job. Jackson was his name.

The entire attitude of the household shifted that day. He knew that Polly had told of the kiss. It was such a simple thing. It meant nothing, and yet it meant everything.

To the servants he was no longer the young master

who snuck biscuits and chatted in the kitchen. He was the duke's son. They did not speak unless spoken to, and he never had another female servant alone in his room.

Alexander realized that the gossip flooded through the house, and by morning everyone knew he had kissed the chambermaid. They watched him then with the same wary eyes they watched his father.

"Be wary of the master. Be wary of the master's son" was whispered from one female servant to the next. They started going about the rooms in twos, never alone. Alexander had not wanted it that way, but he was powerless to alter the situation.

They watched him still despite changes he had made after his father's death. He had not hired many woman in the household since his father's passing even though male servants were more expensive than females due to the tax. He could not stand to see another servant look at him the way Polly had done. He could not stand to see anyone look at him the way Polly had done.

His thoughts went to Emily, and for a moment he paused with the brandy at his lips. Concern filled him. He took a slow sip of his drink and reminded himself, Emily was afraid of nothing. She would certainly have no call to be afraid of him. He would see to it. He would do things right this time.

He went over plans in his mind.

Bramblewood was ready as it would ever be for guests. It was clean. The stairways were hung with pine boughs and holly. Tiny candles glittered among the branches on mantels. He would have to thank the staff for their extra efforts. He was quite impressed. The manor looked beautiful.

The boy finished with the duke's fire, and Alexander nodded to Jervis. "That will be all," he said.

The man bowed and took his leave.

Lucky curled up at the foot of the bed, as close to the fire as he could get.

Alexander crawled into his warmed and yet cold bed and thought of Emily. No, he corrected himself. Miss Ingram.

He must address her as Miss Ingram. He must not make another mistake. Not like he had with Polly. He had blundered through and things had turned out, although not for the best. The result was at least not disastrous, not for him.

Nonetheless, there would be no mistakes this time. Not with Emily. Not with anyone. Emily was a lady. He must treat her as such.

The candles were making flickering patterns on the wall. He must remember to tell Barnes that he wanted every sconce lit. He wanted no dark corners for nefarious actions at the dinner party even though he only invited upstanding persons.

Lots of candles make no dark corners. Wicked deeds happened in darkness, not in the light. He had ordered an extravagant amount of candles for the party.

He wanted the unfinished rooms locked. He knew his kitchen clerk had the meal well in hand, but he ran over the items in his mind anyway. It must be perfect, just like Emily was perfect. Once again he went over all that should be done, and what should be done differently. Not all of the servants had been involved in the hosting of his father's parties, and none of them had been involved in a party like this one.

Previously, the only order was to keep the alcohol flowing. It was much more difficult to host a party like this, and without a hostess to take care of the ladies it was doubly difficult, but the lady was the whole point of the party.

The staff would manage, he thought. They were good people. After his father died, he cleared out any of the staff that had agreed with his father's proclivities. He had retired his father's old steward and promoted Barnes. Several others gave their notice, perhaps anticipating that he was going to sack them which left odd gaps in the staff. He did not care. He would replace them.

He despised the man his father had assigned to be his valet. The man was a veritable spy, passing information to his father as the late duke wished. Distasteful though Alexander may have thought it, the man could not disobey the duke. Alexander took pity on him, gave him a curt reference and the man left his service.

He promoted the most senior footman to the position of his valet the next day, and Jervis had been with him ever since. He promoted Jackson to take Jervis' place as senior footman.

After he was done with his mental tally of things to do, the young duke decided it was too late to read. He leaned over and blew out the candles. He wanted to be up early. He wanted to go over everything again for the dinner party. Everything had to be perfect.

12

St. Nicholas Day came more quickly than anticipated. Emily found herself anxious for the duke's dinner party. She would never admit it out loud, but she felt as if this gathering was a test of the gentleman's ability to behave like civilized company.

In spite of telling herself not to, Emily took special care with her appearance that evening. Pearls glanced out from between her locks; which had been most carefully arranged. The stark contrast between the pale orbs and her dark auburn locks had always been noted by her admirers in London.

The pale golden gown gave her the distinct feeling of femininity. The sleek silhouette showed off her figure to perfection and Emily could not help but feel satisfied with the overall effect.

The carriage ride that took them to Bramblewood Park gave Emily her first feeling that the Christmas season was truly upon them. The gentle flutter of snow swirled around the carriage, enough to catch the light of the lanterns, but not enough to cover the ground.

Bramblewood's sprawling grounds had taken on new life under the change in ownership. The lawns were manicured and the fields and gardens, although tempered for the winter, still held hints of the lush growth that had flourished in the preceding months. Although much still needed repair, the main buildings were revitalized with fresh paint and repaired stonework.

She thought of the late duke's revelries that had often left the properties in disarray. Emily recalled one autumn in which Alexander had spent countless evenings in one of the many guest rooms of his parent's once august home as they waited for the glass to arrive to replace the broken window which had been shattered during a late-night game of cricket.

It had taken place during a drunken revelry in the light of the front garden rather than further out on the lawn. No doubt the guests did not want to travel too far from the spirits.

One glance at the Bramblewood façade now showed pristine glass in every pane and a light in each window. The building glowed with the promise of hope, as if the chaos that had once hung thick within it walls had been chased away by the brightness of the Christmas candles. Perhaps, Emily thought by the care that seemed to have been taken; this party would be a far muted version of past extravaganzas and all the better for it.

The carriage pulled around the circle drive and Emily, Edmund, and their relations were handed down with care and shuffled inside. Their coats were taken by a footman before they were briefly greeted by the duke, who expressed his regrets that he must attend to the next couple and those that followed as they walked through the door of the ballroom.

"You have done well, my boy," Uncle Cecil said to Alexander.

The duke smiled shyly at the praise and returned to greeting his guests. His gaze caught Emily's for only for a brief moment, but that moment was alike a spark to a candle.

She looked away quickly. "Yes, Your Grace," she agreed. "The decorations are beautiful."

The alterations of the interior were, Emily thought, if possible, even more dramatic. The furniture shone with polished curves and the carpets had been replaced, burn holes and stains no longer littered the flooring from the late duke's carousing.

The hounds were apparently in their kennels, because there was no sign of the animals now. They had used to be underfoot and left to do as they may, which left an unmistakable odor in the house. Now, the air was filled with the sweet aroma of pine boughs.

Emily knew that Alexander loved those dogs. One had even slept upon his bed at night. She supposed that he needed the company with the lack of siblings. Yes, she remembered her uncle saying the hounds were with them at the impromptu hunt last week, so Alexander still had his dogs; he just took better care of them than his father.

The new décor was elegant, striking, and most welcoming to the guests as they arrived. In fact, Emily would say that the edifice was nearly unrecognizable. As far as she could see, every inch of the manor was trimmed with Christmas cheer. Boughs of evergreen and festive bows were placed here and there. The mantels and the stairways were done with care and mistletoe hung in the doorway between the parlor and the hall, and no doubt several other places within.

Emily studiously sidestepped it as she entered the room with her brother as her escort. A moment later, Anne and her sisters joined the party. Edmund teased that he did not have enough arms for them all, and Susanna and Eliza joined hands, allowing Edmund to escort Anne, the eldest of the sisters.

Anne looked stunning. Her tawny hair was woven with velvet ribbon that matched her gown and slippers. The regal colors were fitting for the season and made a vibrant statement against the sleeting showers that had persisted during the days leading up to the event. The few bits of soft snow that still clung to her skirt made it appear as if she, by some unknown power, had brought the snow with her.

Both ladies had just finished their greetings and several moments of pleasant conversation, before expressing a wish for thick blanket of snow to celebrate the season. However, it seemed that the English weather would prove otherwise as Henrietta arrived with her aunt. Both were soaked through. Even though it was quite cold, the rain had begun anew.

The golden haired lady shed her sodden wrap and passed it to a servant. Emily admired the pale blue gown that Henrietta wore. It was clearly a style that would not be fashionable in London but it was still lovely: silk velvet and had hand laced edging. Such a garment would be costly due to both the silk and the intricacy of the labor even though the style was several years past. Still, it was the country.

Henrietta greeted Anne and Emily like an old companions, embracing them with vigor and affection.

"What an appealing sight," she commented, gesturing at the elegance around them.

"Yes. It is, isn't it?" Emily agreed. The festive decorations made her wonder even more at the man who had facilitated such a transformation.

"I must say that we set it off to perfection. The jewels of the room, are we not?" Henrietta added with a flutter of her eyelashes.

Edmund excused himself to go speak with another gentleman across the way, and Henrietta tucked her arms into those of her companions and began to tow them toward the drawing room. "What fine work Alexander has done. I do recall that the manor was quite uninhabitable years ago. Do you remember when the side window was broken?"

Emily frowned. "As I recall, it was the front," she said.

"Oh, yes," Henrietta laughed. "It was both of them. The front was broken earlier," she said with a laugh. "To hear my Father tell it, one of the late duke's guests or perhaps it was the duke himself, got into a match of fisticuffs and threw another guest through the side window."

"Lud!" Emily exclaimed. "Was the gentleman hurt?"

"Not a scratch. Do you not know that drunks seem never to suffer for their folly?"

Emily supposed that Henrietta was right, but she would not want test the notion.

"His Grace has made many improvements," Emily agreed. "Although I would not have considered it quite as bad as you say."

Even so, Henrietta's words reminded Emily of things that her own mother used to say. Lady Kentleworth, had no qualms about voicing her disapproval that the late duke was always tap-hackled. Emily recalled one time that her father had even referred to the place as 'Shamblewood' for all the ruckus that went on.

If Emily wrote to her mother this very night about the improvements that she had personally witnessed, she doubted that they would be believed. It seemed to be a miracle that the duke had been able to make this much progress. Although, she thought, Alexander always had been clever.

Henrietta reached out and took Emily's hand in her own. "Now, Emily," Henrietta patted her hand in consolation. "I only wish to give a complement to our dear host on his progress. I meant no offense."

"Of course not," Emily affected a smile, pleased when Henrietta's expression mirrored her own. She could not say why she felt so defensive over anything said about Bramblewood. It was not as if Henrietta had truly meant anything harsh. They had all been friends in those days.

Several minutes later Henrietta rushed off to gain the attention of the subject of their conversation.

The ladies joined Uncle Cecil and several others with before dinner drinks.

Aunt Agnes was not with him, and Uncle Cecil said that she was playing unofficial hostess. "Just to help the poor boy," she confessed as she joined them again. "He was uncertain of the seating arrangements."

Emily was thankful when the group was called to the dining hall. The couples paired up to enter, Uncle Cecil and Aunt Agnes joining several of the older guests and moving towards the lower end of the table.

Emily looked for her brother, but he was already escorting Anne. They were deep in conversation and took no notice of Emily. Rather, she found herself beside the duke, who gave her his arm to escort her.

"Your Grace," she said with a deep curtsey.

"May I escort you to dinner, Miss Ingram?" he asked and she acquiesced. He smiled and tucked her hand into the crook of his arm.

Emily could not help but be flustered for reasons that she refused to evaluate as he led her to the front of the line. She decided her excitability was due to all of the eyes that turned their way and followed their lead, rather than anything to do with her handsome companion.

Try as she might, all she could think of was the warmth of his hand on hers and the comparable warmth in her cheeks. Her heart fluttered wildly in her chest. Alexander seemed to have noted it as well.

The lengthy table had been set for twenty guests. Emily found the room suitably full without being crowded and thought that this was turning out to be quite the exemplary dinner party. The duke seated her at his right and then stood at the head of the table, waiting for the other ladies to be seated. The invited guests gathered round. Henrietta watched them with sharp eyes. Emily could make no sense of the expression and hoped that it was not anger or jealousy that she saw in the lady's features.

In preparation for dinner, Emily pulled off her gloves and put them in her lap. She laid her napkin atop them as Edmund took the place on her other side, with Anne beside her brother. Mr. Martin Eldridge, a county gentleman renowned for his experimental agricultural methods escorted and then sat next to Henrietta.

The lady made a show of choosing the seat to the left of the host. Emily noted that Aunt Agnes and Uncle Cecil took seats further down the table with some of the elder guests. The rest of the assembled company found their chairs and the servants began to usher out the first course a rich creamy mushroom soup, the likes of which Emily had not had since she was a child.

Emily found herself enjoying the meal. There was meat aplenty: beef, mutton and venison as well as several savory sauces. Each course was more sublime than the last and the conversation was engaging.

That is, except for when Mr. Eldridge spoke. Henrietta and the duke were the only ones who seemed to have been able to maintain focus throughout his speech about rerouting the stream that bordered his north pasture so that the plants received the water they needed without being drowned with the spring floods. Of course, Mr. Eldridge had already consulted at Bramblewood so the duke was rightly fascinated with his methods and approving of his success.

Henrietta had said. "It was certainly useful to have your wealth of knowledge in Scotland, Mr. Eldridge."

Mr. Eldridge beamed under the praise of the only lady who seemed to have followed his speech.

"Further north, one must be more cognizant of the weather and water if you plan to have abundant crops," Eldridge said.

Soon enough, Emily found herself laughing at the wit of her companions. Edmund was regaling those nearest to him with tales of the duke's childish follies. Emily shuffled nervously worried about what her brother might say.

"There was that time, do you recall Anne?" Edmund

began. "When your father had given you that small rowboat to take about the lake."

"Yes," Anne replied with a shake of her head. "It had been meant for one person alone. He had thought I would enjoy the solitude. My sisters were expressly forbidden to follow me."

"And yet," Edmund laughed, "we were able to fit the four of us inside for a row."

"For a time," Emily added, "before it sank!"

"I remember this," Henrietta chimed in from across the table, excited to add her part. "I saw you carrying the tiny craft down the lane sopping wet and Emily marching behind with a scowl throwing pinecones at the back of Alexander's head!"

Embarrassed, Emily applied herself to the candied carrots which was one of her favorites.

Everyone laughed at the picture Henrietta's story made and Emily blushed with the thought.

"He deserved it!" She blurted, surprised that she still felt as strongly about the issue as she had years prior. He had deserved her censure once, but now Alexander was the duke. "I'm sorry, Your Grace," she said almost immediately upon realizing what she had said.

"Oh, do not," the duke laughed. "I was completely at fault. I freely admit it. I apologize, Miss Ingram." He bowed his head slightly to Emily. Although, his laughter revealed that he still found her plight humorous.

"Nearly a decade later and you finally take ownership," Emily shook her head.

"I have taken ownership of much of late," Alexander said.

"And about time too," Emily added.

"Whatever happened that made you so cross?" Mr. Eldridge asked. He was the only one present that had not witnessed the friends in their youth and was curious to know more.

Emily scowled and crossed her arms below her breasts unsure how to answer. His question was gauche, but she supposed she was short with the duke, and Mr. Eldridge did not know the complete tale.

Anne answered his query. "Emily's skirt got stuck on a submerged log after we took our spill and she could not break it free," Anne explained.

"My goodness!" Henrietta gasped with a hand over her mouth. "Poor child. Did you nearly drown?"

"Not even close," Edmund chuckled. "Once we helped her gain her footing, she was only a bit more than waist deep."

"You had nothing to do with it, brother dear," Emily said.

"As I recall it was the duke who helped you to stand," Anne said.

"Then why was she so angry with Alexander?" Henrietta asked.

Emily could not help but bristle every time Henrietta called the duke by his given name, but Alexander seemed not to mind. He was chuckling softly, a light in his eyes.

"As I recall, Alexander suggested she remove her skirt," Edmund said chuckling.

"Oh," Henrietta said, and Emily blushed crimson.

She could just kill Edmund. "As *I recall* we were ten!" She defended.

"Perhaps eleven," Anne said.

"But Emily always was a bit of a killjoy," Edmund said.

"I'm not," Emily said glaring at her brother.

Alexander came to her rescue as he had so long ago.

"She wasn't really angry," Alexander replied. "She was just pretending to be. Emily never got angry with us. Not really."

"Then why would she pretend?" Henrietta asked more specifically.

"Because he told me that since I was stuck I must live in the lake forever, but not to worry. He would visit daily to toss me bread as he did the carp."

"Oh," Henrietta said.

"Not like the carp," Alexander corrected.

"You called me a mer-creature." Emily explained with a childish huff.

"Mermaid," Alexander said.

Emily was doing her best to remain indignant, but the laughter kept slipping through. It was a simpler time when it was easy to laugh.

"You did look most enchanting," the duke whispered for her ears only, and she froze with the thought. She set her fork on the side of the plate. Her stomach was suddenly too full of butterflies to take another bite.

Edmund and Anne were still shaking with laughter at the memory.

Emily pulled herself from the reverie and gained her wit. "It was your fault we spilled," she added. "The duke kept leaning over to pick the lilies and the boat would rock ever so violently." She explained.

"As I recall, you still held the fistful of lilies that I had gathered as you stood in the water scolding me," he replied.

Emily grew still as she remembered that part. She looked at Alexander. His blue eyes were sparkled with the mirth of youth and something else, something that did not speak of childhood.

"If anything it made you look all the more a mer-creature," Anne giggled. "You had weeds in your hair and you were dripping. I never remember you being more out of sorts."

Edmund nodded. "Emily who was always so careful about her appearance," he remembered.

"Simply enchanting," Alexander said again, his eyes dark as a night sky. "Like the Lady of the Lake," he said.

"Oh, I remember how we played those stories," Anne broke into the conversation. "Although usually Edmund was the damsel in distress, not Emily."

"Now just a minute," Edmund protested above their laughter.

Emily gave in to the moment and permitted herself to

have fun. It was alright to remember her childish ways, she thought, although she was very aware that the man beside her was not a child.

In any case, she supposed, the conversation was much more interesting than speaking about next years' plowshare.

She glanced at Mr. Eldridge who was listening intently to their tale.

"How did you escape?" Henrietta asked with interest.

"Ale... His Grace," Emily corrected. "He rescued me at last."

"Ah, you remember," Alexander teased. "I have ever been your gallant knight."

"If I would have had a sword, I should have cut my own skirt loose," Emily said smartly.

"My sword is ever at your service, my lady," the duke teased and for a moment there was something more serious in Alexander's eyes, and then he was just the same. Emily thought she must have imagined the overtones, but the heat in his gaze was unmistakable.

Emily met his eyes as she spoke. "He dove under and broke the branch that had ensnared my hem. It was all quite straightforward when it came down to it."

"I would have left you there," Edmund said taking a sip of his wine. "You were being quite the shrew."

"I was not." Emily wished to give him a sharp jab in the ribs as she might have back then, but refrained. It would be inappropriate at such a gathering.

"I never remember Emily being shrewish," Alexander

said. "Opinionated, perhaps, but it is hard to argue when she is so often right."

"Be sure to recall that," Emily teased with a smile.

She had forgotten about the boat incident and several others like it that were shared that evening. Emily and Anne often found themselves an accomplice in the stories. Emily was amused to find that both gentlemen recalled their participation with fondness and did not think less of them for the wild ways of their youth.

"I had always thought myself more of a nuisance," Emily admitted at last when Henrietta and Mr. Eldridge had turned toward one another for a private conversation on their side of the table.

"Not at all," the duke said. "We are forever indebted to you for your ingenious escape tactics, Miss Ingram, without which we certainly would have found ourselves in a great deal more trouble." He lifted a wine glass to toast her as another moment, another adventure, was recounted.

This time Anne recalled that the boys had broken the hay wagon by trying to ride it down a hill. "I remember, it made a terrible noise when it moved," she said.

"We were lucky we were not killed," Edmund said. "There was no way to steer."

"I recall," the duke said. "You crashed us into the side of the barn. I still have the scar."

"You do not," Edmund protested, but Alexander noted the pale white line on his hand which he swore extended all the way to his upper arm where a piece of wood from the wagon had splintered off and pierced his skin.

Emily eyes followed the scar noting where it disappeared within the sleeve of his shirt. Her throat felt tight. She remembered that day. His blue eyes were laughing now, but she remembered those same eyes fluttering closed with blood loss. The thought gave her a chill.

She had run down the hill after Alexander and her brother to find them both dazed and silly. She had begun to scold and then realized that Alexander was bleeding, holding a bloody spike of wood that had come loose from somewhere. She had been torn between running for Uncle Cecil or trying to help Alexander.

In the end she screamed at Edmund to get help and for just a moment he had balked at telling Uncle Cecil of their folly until she had commandeered his shirt and pushed him away.

She had thought Alexander might bleed to death before her very eyes. She couldn't lose him. Not then. Not now. The reality made her feel a bit queasy, although she had not felt so at the time. At the time, she had just acted.

The gentlemen were still laughing at the tale.

"If I hadn't put up my hand I might have put out an eye or worse. We were so foolish." Alexander said shaking his head.

Emily looked at him a moment before speaking. "I remember," she said softly.

Emily could not bear the thought of it. Looking back,

she realized that a part of her used to care deeply for Alexander. Perhaps more than she ever wished to admit. What did she feel now? The thought of losing him still made her mouth go dry and put a cold feeling of terror in the pit of her stomach.

"Uncle Cecil was so cross that he threatened to send me back to London as punishment." Edmund said.

"Of course, he was more scared than angry," Emily said, "as was I."

"Oh, Em, you never get ruffled," Edmund said, but that really was not true. She just did not show it. Certainly, falling apart at the first sign of trouble would not have been helpful.

"As I recall," the duke said, taking up the story, "Edmund and Miss Ingram had only just arrived for the summer the day before. Edmund would have been miserable in London and I would have been left to a summer alone with William, who was always more studious than the rest of us, but Miss Ingram saved us again."

Emily blushed looking down at her plate. She couldn't bear to see Alexander hurt or unhappy. Her eyes drifted again to his scar. He was the same boy she had known. He was different yes, but still marked by past. Was she not the same?

"I still cannot believe you convinced your uncle that it was the fault of the wagon," Anne said to Emily with no little amazement. "That was brilliant." She toasted Emily with her glass.

Emily sipped her drink and nodded. She took a breath and rejoined the conversation. She explained that with calm inducement she had persuaded Uncle Cecil to see that the hay wagon was quite old and already had a cracked axle.

"Broken at that point," Edmund added.

"In any case, it could no longer be pulled by the horses and needed replacement," Emily said.

"This gives you an excuse to convince Aunt Agnes that you ought to have a new hay wagon." She had said. Although her uncle had still been very cross, he had taken to the idea of a new wagon. The following week, it had been delivered and the matter, forgotten. Although Alexander's arm had been bandaged half the summer.

"That was Emily," Edmund smiled at his sister with affection, "never caused the trouble but always found a way to trench us out."

"Yes," the duke said his fingers on his own scar but his eyes on Emily. There was weight in his deep blue gaze. She wondered if they both remembered the event in the same way, but there was no way to go back to that shared moment, even if she wanted to do so.

Emily sighed with dramatic effect and mock distain. "What a pittance I received for the effort. Neither of you were ever able to learn from the experience."

"What would you know of my experience?" The duke chided in good fun, but Emily blushed with the sudden unintended innuendo, or perhaps it was intended. She glanced up to see the duke smiling at her, his dark eyes smoldering.

"Nothing," she breathed.

The moment between them held. She realized she did want to know. There were so many details about this new version of him that she wanted to know. She wanted to curl up by the window and share secrets with him as she had as a child. She wanted to know everything that had occurred while she had been away.

Alexander reached across the table and took her bare hand. The heat of his hand on hers made her deeply aware of him. "Your Grace," she breathed as his fingers moved over hers, bare flesh to bare flesh.

She felt the raised scar under her fingertips. She wanted to trace the line up over the corded muscles of his forearm. She wanted to map out his new form so that he might be known to her as he once was, but in a far different way.

He said nothing, but a hint of a smirk came to his lips and she knew he was thinking much the same. It was no boy's look. His eyes held the full weight of a man's gaze. Emily felt the heat of it against her skin. Her heart pounded in her chest, and for a moment she felt they were the only two people in the room. Perhaps the only two people in the world.

Edmund was still speaking, but his words seemed far away. "Emily has grown-up, sensible and proper. I, on the other hand am without hope of fitting in with London society even if my sister speaks well of me."

"Nonsense," Anne protested. "I am sure you are the perfect gentleman."

"Oh no. According to my Father, I am far from perfect."

"I would not credit it, Edmund. Your sister's opinion is without flaw." Alexander said at last. He released Emily from his gaze and she felt a sudden heaviness drop in the room, as if all of the air had gone out. "I hope she would speak well of me, though I too am far from perfect."

Emily felt as though she had missed something important in the duke's words. Some secret weighted upon him. She wanted to chase away the darkness that had dimmed his smile, but did not understand what he wanted her to say. Once, she would have known. Now, she felt unsettled.

Emily looked about the beautiful room trying to regain her bearings. She was a lady in a beautiful dining room, and her host was at her side. A complement would bring the conversation back to a safe subject. "Perhaps not perfect, but you cannot say that you have not done well. You have restored Bramblewood."

"Oh no," he said. "Only upon the surface. The upstairs bedrooms are quite the mess. I should show you and then you would see ..." he broke off as if suddenly aware of how improper it was to speak of the bedrooms with an unmarried lady. Her heart was aflutter again with his eyes upon her. It seemed as if she could still feel his fingers gliding over hers.

"You have done splendidly," she said bringing the

conversation back to a safe subject. "I do not think that I have ever seen such beauty."

"Nor I," he said so softly, raising a glass and toasting her. The duke's voice was soft, for her ears only and she knew that they were no longer talking about the house. She blushed and lost her train of thought again.

"Do not be silly," Emily said. He could not think her beautiful. She was not. It was only a nice dress.

"Oh, I am quite serious."

She had never been so tongue-tied. What was wrong with her? She hoped the duke did not see how unsettled she was. It was embarrassing. Was it possible that he felt the same as she? Was it possible that he cared for her with more than friendship? No, she was his childhood friend, her brother's companion, that was all. Why did thinking such thoughts fill her with melancholy?

"I still have a lot of work to do." The duke added for the interest of the table. "I would not say that I am completely satisfied yet. Parts of the manor are completely unlivable, so I will warn you do not wander."

"But you are a man of means, Your Grace," Mr. Eldridge said. "I am sure you will have everything tip-top in no time."

Alexander grimaced. "It is my charge, but it is not yet complete."

"Everything takes time," Emily defended softly.

13

*D*essert arrived and Emily turned her focus to the far end of the table, in order to avoid the smoldering eyes that followed her movements. He knew. Of that she was certain. The duke knew that she felt unsettled in his presence. He could still read her as well as ever, even after all of these years.

Like the time that one of the village girls had poked fun at Emily's freckles and she had lied and told him that it had not hurt her feelings. She had been determined to return to her chamber and paint them over. She had already taken the powder, about which her aunt would have had a fit if she had learned was in Emily's possession.

Instead, Alexander had complemented the feature and told her that they made her unique.

"I like every single one of them," he had said, "and if you erase them then you won't be the same."

Together, they had dumped the powder in the river and filled the elegant glass jar with wilderness treasures instead. Her freckles had mostly faded in time, and she was not so conscious of them now. She wondered if he really did like them. No one else ever had.

As a child, the ability to see past her barriers had meant that he could sense her worries and fears; calm her tears when she had been hurt, or bolster her confidence when she needed it most. As an adult, it meant that she was unable to hide the flush of her cheeks, the quickening of her breath, or the wide doe eyes when she realized he was teasing her. Only, they were no longer children, and she no longer knew what to say to his flirtatious taunts.

"Almond cake," he said, taking one of the white pastries from the server and putting it on her plate himself. "Is it not still your favorite?"

Emily nodded. She realized suddenly that the creamy mushroom soup, the candied carrots and beef with rosemary were all her favorites as well. She did not trust herself to speak. How did he remember these things? Moreover, how was he capable of knowing what exactly she felt, when even she could not say?

She had no doubt that he was noting each fluctuation in her exterior manner, although she thought she had hidden her feelings so perfectly. In London, she had never struggled to present exactly whatever image she desired. There were too many people and too many distractions for any one person to be the sole focus of another's attention. Here everyone knew too much about one another.

"You remembered, Your Grace?" she asked in a mere whisper.

The duke laid a hand on top of hers and she felt a sudden rush of heat suffuse her. "I am the same Alexander that I have always been," he said. "Have I not always remembered what you would prefer?"

"Of course, Your Grace," she said, but nothing felt the same at all. He seemed to remember every little nuance about her, and she was at a loss. She could barely speak in his presence. She felt like a giddy schoolgirl.

In a short time, dessert was completed and the dishes were cleared. Emily expected the men to retire to another room with their drinks, allowing the women to refresh themselves, but instead of an extended feminine interest, Emily found herself too soon ushered back into the sitting room with card tables and drinks. Aunt Agnes and Uncle Cecil were directing some of the older guests to card tables. Footmen came to offer after dinner drinks to them.

"I did not wish to neglect half of my guests," the duke explained. It made sense, for he had no wife to entertain the feminine side of the party. Emily felt his eyes burning into her as he spoke, but when she looked up, she found that Henrietta had placed herself at the duke's side and was attempting to engage him in conversation.

Emily wondered, not for the first time, if the lady had designs for the duke. So what if she did? It shouldn't matter, Emily reminded herself. Alexander was certainly not the sort of husband that she expected to find.

She had Robert Hawthorne and several other suitors, if she wished, waiting for her back in London. The thought filled her with melancholy. None of them made her heart race like Alexander did. Still, she should not care what Henrietta might have to say to the duke.

The lady leaned into him and found occasion to settle her fingertips upon the duke's forearm. Emily's eyes were drawn to the scar on his hand and the thought of wrapping that same arm with Edmund's shirt while his blood stained her fingers. She could still imagine the warmth of it. It seemed to have marked her.

Whatever was said could not be heard by Emily, but she did witness the duke nod in reply as Henrietta looked up at him with watery eyes.

Emily felt a sudden spate of anger, and realized that it was a stab of jealousy. She clenched her hands into fists and turned away. All her doubts of earlier in the tea shop came rushing back.

She should not feel so for the duke. It was unexpected. Years of friendship and memory were colored with a new aura of desire. Emily saw that she and Alexander always had an attachment for one another. If they had not been separated for so many years, such feeling might have grown into something more, but now, he had grown in a different direction. He was all sorts of wrong for her, she reminded herself.

He was far too adventurous. She wanted someone

settled she told her galloping heart. Compared to Robert
Hawthorne, Alexander fell short by leaps and bounds.
Life with Alexander would never be steady. She would
forever be out of sorts. It would be messy and upending.
And absolutely wonderful.

No. Robert Hawthorne was the logical choice. She
wanted stability and a rational man with a clear head
who did what was expected. Alexander almost never did
what was expected of him. The thought did not stop her
from wanting him.

Emily need to get control of herself. She could not fly
off in a fit of hysterics. She forced herself to breath
normally.

At that point, Emily would have excused herself to
the ladies retiring room, where a number of the ladies
had gone, but she realized that Mr. Martin Eldridge had
joined her, and was attempting to engage her in
conversation. She found she could not extricate herself
in a polite way.

She found herself an unwilling listener to Mr.
Eldridge's farming projections for the upcoming season.
Although not a lord, he was a wealthy landowner. Her
effort to remain engaged in the conversation led Emily to
discover more about the local farming techniques than
she had ever cared to know.

The conversation could have been most boring, but
the man was so excited that it was hard to speak with
him and not feel at least some of the fervor he extolled. It
seemed that the man was quite accomplished.

He had increased the yield of his land quite spectacularly which had led to a windfall of sorts. The duke had employed Mr. Eldridge to manage some of his properties as well. Eldridge was happy to give the duke the help he needed. Where was the duke? Emily wondered suddenly. He had disappeared.

In fact, when she looked up again, both the duke and Henrietta were nowhere to be seen. An uncharitable thought flashed in her head, a recollection of his father's shameless philandering. She felt a sinking feeling in the pit of her stomach, but she ignored it. Instead, she attempted to turn her attention back to Mr. Eldridge.

At last, he motioned to one of the card tables where a couple of players were needed. Edmund and Anne were already seated at the table and needed a second team for whist.

"Shall we play?" Mr. Eldridge asked gesturing, and Emily agreed. She enjoyed cards and games. Although she did not consider herself an accomplished card player, she enjoyed a round of healthy competition, and the game would take her mind off of the duke. Edmund shifted over.

"Shall I be your partner?" Mr. Eldridge asked Emily or shall we play ladies against gentlemen?

"Oh do," said Anne as she started to stand, but Edmund moved to take the seat across from Mr. Eldridge.

"Emily and I shall beat you soundly," Anne promised.

The gentlemen seated the ladies and then play

began. Several rounds passed without any serious care for the winner. Conversation was light and took no effort to maintain. After a time, Emily glanced around and still did not see the duke. It was his party. Where had he gone? With a start, she realized she did not see Henrietta either. In London, such a disappearance would be cause for instant gossip and censure.

"I do not see Miss Milford," she commented.

"Is Miss Milford another friend of yours?" Mr. Eldridge asked Emily, and she lifted a shoulder.

"We were all friends as children, but have grown apart. I suppose we still do count as friends."

"Of course we do," Anne said throwing out a low trump card in the hopes that Emily would have the trick. Emily grinned and took the hand.

"Miss Henrietta Milford is even more beautiful than I remember her," Mr. Eldridge commented throwing his last card into the center of the table in defeat.

"I say, man," Edmund complained, "you must do better than that, or I shall take back my sister as partner."

"You shall not," Anne said.

"I'm sorry," Mr. Eldridge said. "I suppose my mind is not much on the game."

"Shuffle," Emily ordered her brother, pushing the pile of cards to him.

"How did you meet Miss Milford?" Emily asked Mr. Eldridge knowing he was not originally from the area.

"Oh, in Scotland" he said. "I have an aunt there and so does Miss Milford. When she moved back here, well, I decided to visit my southern cousins. I am considering the purchase of Hancock House and its surrounding properties."

Emily blinked. Such action seemed to speak of an attachment. Was Mr. Eldridge enamored of Miss Milford?

He took a sip of wine. "It will depend upon a certain lady. Her manner seems much changed, though still beautiful."

"A change in manner does not alter one's features," Edmund commented. "Miss Milford has always been beautiful." He passed the cards to Anne to cut, who in turn passed them to Mr. Eldridge to deal.

"Of course it does," Anne said.

"I have never done this pass around of the cards," Mr. Eldridge said as he picked up the deck.

"Edmund cheats," Anne said matter-of-factly and Mr. Eldridge paused in shook.

"I do not cheat," Edmund said automatically, and then frowned.

Anne just stared at him.

"I was a child." He amended finally.

"As I said, Edmund cheats." Anne stuck by her words and Emily had to laugh.

"Also, a gentle manner does make a person more handsome," Anne added. "It alters one's opinion, if not appearance."

"Yes," Emily agreed. "A genteel manner can make one more pleasant to be around certainly."

She glanced back at the table to her left where she had thought the blonde played previously, but Henrietta had not returned. A quick glance around the room confirmed that the duke had also not returned. She tried to focus on the cards for the next few rounds, but found she could not concentrate on her hand. Eventually she said in a teasing voice, "I seem to remember that Henrietta fancied you not so many years ago, Edmund."

"Oh, no. I am afraid that was many, *many* years ago," Edmund laughed. "She did always chase a title. Pray, I should not be the one to draw her eye, although I do think she aspires a bit higher."

Mr. Eldridge dealt the cards. He gathered his hand and studied it much as the others did, but Emily watched the light go out of Mr. Eldridge's eyes as he spoke. "Then, I am certain that I would not be capable of drawing her affection."

"We should not make speculations," Anne said, "when the lady is not here to disavow them."

"Which lady?" Aunt Agnes asked as she and Uncle Cecil made a round about the room. Emily supposed the duke may have asked her to hostess for him.

"Henrietta," Anne answered Aunt Agnes.

"Is Henrietta entertaining a beau?" Aunt Agnes questioned from behind Edmund's chair.

"She has said nothing of it to me," Emily replied with a shrug as she began the play. "We were shopping just the other day."

"She mentioned something of the like. I believe that she wishes to keep it a secret," Anne said following suit.

"What?" Emily said sending Anne a look. How had she kept this secret from her? It certainly seemed that Anne had indeed heard a rumor.

"Certainly something is secret," Edmund said as he took the trick and played the next card.

Anne shrugged delicately. "Nobody seems to know for certain, but there have been whispers that Henrietta is to be wed by spring. The lucky groom, we have yet to discover."

Emily held her cards suspended, shocked that Anne had not revealed this news to her.

Mr. Eldridge seems to sink into his chair as he took a generous swig of his drink. Emily thought that the gentleman may have feelings for the beautiful Henrietta, but if her desire for a title was true, as Emily thought it was, then the poor man did not stand a chance.

"It's your play," Edmund urged his partner, but Mr. Eldridge threw off and Anne took the trick.

"An intrigue!" Aunt Agnes cried. "I do love a good mystery at Christmastide."

"Agnes," Uncle Cecil said lightly. "Do leave the young people to their play." They moved off toward the other guests.

"Perhaps you ladies might discover the truth of the matter," Edmund prodded. "Miss Milford seems to have devoted herself to you Emily. In good confidence, she might tell."

"That it would not be in good confidence," Anne chided as she took another trick.

"No indeed," Emily agreed. "Nor will I pressure her for reserved information. It is no business of ours."

"Are you sharing secrets, Miss Ingram?" The duke appeared at the card tables so suddenly that Emily leapt in her seat with surprise.

"Not at all," she replied with her chin held high as she followed the play of the cards.

14

*E*mily glanced around to see if they were being watched, but only Edmund and Anne were paying any attention at all. Two other card games were in session and the card group at the next table was laughing at Uncle Cecil's tales of a dog that refused to hunt. The wine was flowing freely at all of the tables, and yet, Emily noticed that Alexander seemed not to have drunk to excess. He did, however, seem uncommonly close to her.

The table started to shift so that the duke could seat himself. "What a pity, for I was certain that you were full of secrets," he teased Emily and then when realizing that he had disrupted the game, he held up a hand. "Oh no," he said. "I do not wish to interrupt."

"Shall we deal you in?" Edmund asked. "We can play something else." Whist was a game for partners.

Alexander shook his head. "Finish the play."

"Take my place," Mr. Eldridge said. "I find I have lost my interest."

He stood and the duke took his place. "If you are sure," he said.

When Mr. Eldridge left, Anne said, "I wonder what that was all about."

"I think he was quite done with secrets, as am I," Emily said.

"Truly?" the duke said. "I seemed to remember that you liked an intrigue, most especially shared secrets."

"Perhaps," Emily replied in a low murmur only loud enough for the duke to hear, "you have made a poor practice of imagining things, Your Grace. Much time has passed since we shared secrets. Even then, they were childish things. We are beyond that now."

"Well, more's the pity then," he said. "I remember some secrets quite fondly."

Emily blushed. She remembered too.

Emily tried to return her attention to the card game but found that her mind would not stay on the hand.

"You could not get a secret from Emily for one thousand pounds," Edmund commented as he dealt. "She never was one to share what goes on inside the head of hers. She is unflappable."

That was certainly not how she felt at this moment.

Alexander narrowed his eyes as if considering her brother's evaluation. "That is strange," he finally added. "I have always found her rather expressive." He paused and leaned close, his voice a low rumble in her ear. "If you wished, we could share secrets again. They no longer need to be limited to childish things."

Emily blushed to the roots of her hair. Her face was aflame. How dare he tease her so! Why was he teasing her? It was fortunate that at that moment Edmund exclaimed as he claimed victory of the round.

With their table mates distracted, Emily gathered her wits and plastered a calm and cool expression on her face. Play came around to her again, and she looked at the mixed pile of cards in the center of the table. "What is trump?" she asked.

"Hearts," Edmund said and Emily threw a heart without really looking.

Edmund cheered as he again took the trick.

"I want another partner," Anne complained. "Emily is distracted."

"I am not," Emily protested.

"I shall gladly partner Miss Ingram," the duke said. "With your permission?" He looked at Emily as he stood beside her

"As you wish, Your Grace," she replied as stiffly as she could manage but the duke did not move.

"I wish you would not be so formal," he muttered.

"It is your proper title," she said.

"It is," he agreed, "but you are using it to put distance between us."

"There *is* distance between us," she argued.

"I wish it were not so," he replied.

The duke watched her for a long moment. Too long.

Emily resisted the urge to shift under the uncomfortable weight of his gaze. She raised her chin higher and stared back with assurance. Alexander shifted his chair closer. She gave him a pointed look. He smiled at her. When had his eyes grown so very blue, or his teeth so even? Emily realized that the entire card game was suspended.

"I'm sorry," Emily said, but Anne just looked at her with compassion and Edmund had a rather rueful look on his face.

"I make you nervous, why?" the duke said.

"You don't," Emily said.

"If I have made you uncomfortable that was not my intent." He had not resumed the card play. He sat looking contrite, and Emily felt that she had somehow been unkind.

"Of course not, Your Grace," she answered. She could not call him Alexander in company and yet she wanted to do so. The moment felt too intimate. His eyes were alight. She felt they would have a very different conversation if they were alone.

Was she imagining it, or could Alexander also be recalling their childhood in a different light? Emily bit her lip. He was a child no longer. The thought made her heart beat fast. She was so muddled, she could not speak. Instead, she looked down at her cards once more.

"You have hardly said a dozen words to me since your arrival, Miss Ingram. Yet, Edmund and I are not so different and you adore him."

"Oh, she doesn't," Edmund chipped in.

"He is my brother and I am obligated to adore him," she gave one sharp laugh. "If it were not so, and he still teased, I would keep my distance."

"Then you no longer have the heart to be teased?" The duke said as if he could not believe it.

"You are now a gentlemen and I am a lady. As you have said, we are not children any longer. A gentleman does not tease."

The words brought back a flood of memories shared from that last summer before she and Anne left for finishing school.

"I think we are done with cards," Anne said disgustedly throwing in the hand and sitting back allowing the duke to shift closer to Emily.

Edmund laughed. "Oh Anne, this has always been in the cards," he said.

Emily and the duke sat in silent accord while the duke pondered her answer. Then, so softly that Emily could not be certain whether she had heard it or imagined, he said, "Then we are in agreement." His breath was hot on her ear. "We are no longer children."

She turned. His lips left her ear and instead she found herself staring into his eyes. They were the deepest darkest blue she had ever seen. Her own eyes found his lips as he asked, "Would you allow me to call upon you, Miss Ingram?"

She glanced up at him from beneath her lashes and their gazes locked. He was uncommonly close to her. She could smell the scent of him. It was quite pleasant, like the outdoors after fresh snowfall, and underneath something deeply masculine that tugged at her insides.

She felt as if she couldn't breathe. The request was formal, but somehow more intimate than all their former discourse. She nodded helplessly, her insides roiling like a tempestuous sea. He smiled at her acceptance although it did nothing to lessen the intensity of his deep blue gaze.

THAT EVENING, when she turned in for the night, Emily could not remember ever having felt more confused or frustrated. In barely two encounters the duke had transformed from a childhood playfellow into some paradox of emotion that had defied Emily's best attempts to decipher. Edmund remained oblivious and Emily could not bring herself to confide in him. He may be her brother, but first he was a man.

Well, at least he was male, she decided and the duke's friend. Her aunt and uncle were preoccupied with Henrietta's mystery groom. Even worse, Emily could not bring herself to share her predicament with Anne for fear that her friend would attempt to encourage a deeper evaluation of something that Emily was unprepared to confront. Alexander could always be counted upon for fun and the glib comment, but she did not need such flippancy. She was a lady now.

She had agreed to his calling upon her. Why had she

done such a thing? It seemed as if something had changed between them over cards or over dinner and Emily had entirely lost her footing.

Emily needed someone to remind her to stay the course. Stand firm. She needed someone to tell her that she had a plan, and a good one. There was no point in jeopardizing her future based on some unidentifiable emotion that would most likely lead to heartbreak. She needed someone to sit her down and remind her that Robert Hawthorne possessed all of the necessary characteristics in spades. Yet, there was no doubt that Alexander, the duke, was in her thoughts.

Sometimes she felt she could almost see her Alexander's clear blue eyes staring back from underneath the smoldering gaze of the man he had become. The man inflamed her in ways she did not understand. It was as if the boy she once knew and the man he was now, were two entirely separate people and she could not reconcile them in her heart.

Emily realized quite suddenly that she needed her mother. Lady Kentleworth was the epitome of the proper lady. She would lecture Emily with a cool civility and practicality that left no room for sentimental feeling. It was everything she hated about her mother, and everything she desperately needed. Emily loved her mother. She was a gentlewoman, and yet being gentle was not in her nature.

No, the viscountess would merely reveal her dismay that Emily was even slightly questioning their agreement. She would be all for Emily to catch a duke for her husband, just not this duke. She would remind Emily of what she already knew: the misery that Alexander's mother had endured walled up in the country while her husband flaunted his mistresses and bastards. She would call her daughter a fool and insist that she return to London. At the moment, Emily felt the fool.

Part 3

Warm Woolen Mittens

15

The duke thought the dinner party went quite well although by necessity many guests left before too late in the evening. Although Alexander had not invited the crowd to stay for the night, he had prepared a few rooms for several elderly guests who remembered his father, and most needed to be convinced of the changes he wished to make to Bramblewood.

None had stayed. Sandstowe was close enough that some guests went there for the night, but most were from nearby estates throughout Northwickshire and returned home.

Even though the sun set early in the winter, all who were traveling home after dinner brought some extra footmen who could walk ahead of the carriage with a lantern to be sure none of the horses took a misstep. In the summer this was not so much of a problem, but this far north, one always had to worry about the condition of the roads.

The duke thought it had been a fruitful evening. He controlled the urge to whoop with joy when Emily had agreed to his calling upon her. Still, it was only the first step.

After his guests left the manor, the duke considered what sort of call would be best. He hoped the weather held. He wanted to take Emily riding as they had done in years past. It would give them a chance to talk. Even though they would, of course, take a groom with them, or even her aunt or uncle, it would afford them a form of privacy.

The duke smiled at the thought. He realized at the card table how very much he wanted to kiss her. He knew he would have little rest tonight with thoughts of Emily on his mind. It would not be the first time. He had dreamed of her for as long as he could remember although his dreams had taken on a decidedly more heated note of late.

He woke the next morning with an aching need for her that did not dissipate with the chill as he took his greyhounds for a romp. The weather was clear, and he once again considered his desire to call upon her. He thought perhaps Edmund could be persuaded to accompany them on their ride.

Edmund would not be so stiff and that would perhaps help Emily to be at ease. He missed the easy camaraderie of their youth. The duke had teased a smile from her at dinner and he dearly wished to do so again. He loved to see her smile.

When the duke returned to the manor after leaving all the dogs, save Lucky, at the kennels he told Franklin to bring him some hot mulled cider. Now that company had left, Lucky followed at his master's heel.

The duke knew it was most improper to keep a hound within the manor. He didn't much care. Alexander trained Lucky himself when he was only a pup. The dog had slept at the foot of his bed ever since he was a child and was a comfort within the cold and empty manor when his mother had passed. The hound was too old for hunting now, but the duke would not part with him.

Lucky went directly to curl up at his favorite place in front of the library fire which reminded the duke he could not immediately go calling. He sighed as he thought of the pile of paperwork in the library which he had yet to go through. He had work of the duchy to do, but soon, he would call on Miss Emily Ingram; as soon as he was able.

"Bring that cider to the library," he told Franklin.

"Very good, Your Grace," the man said with a slight bow. His shoes sounded like a sepulchral march on the cold floor.

As the duke sat at his desk, he realized that all the guests had gone home and the house felt cavernous. Save for the servants, he was once again alone in the enormous manor. He wanted to fill it with Christmas cheer.

One day there would be loud children playing in the nursery. An heir, of course, and several beautiful little girls with auburn hair and freckles to fill the cold halls of Bramblewood with their laughter.

At the thought of their preferred mother he remembered Emily's sweet hand under his. A thought struck him and he put aside his work. He intended to find something. A smile graced his lips. As he stood, the old greyhound also stood, stretching lazily ready to follow at his heel.

He gestured for the old dog to lie back down. "Stay," he ordered Lucky who after the morning romp was ready to for a long nap. Grateful with the order, the dog made three circles, tucked in his tail and lay back down in front of the fire. The duke would start his search with his mother's old rooms.

SEVERAL DAYS HAD PASSED since the duke had last seen Emily. Regretfully he had been far too occupied with the goings on in the duchy to be social. Final preparations for the town's welfare had been completed and he was pleased with the result. For the first year since the death of his father they would not be crawling out of winter or scrambling to prepare for the spring when it came.

He had done the best he could do for his people,

including the crotchety Mr. Marksham. He allowed himself a breath of fresh air on the steps of the church before entering. The threat of a real, lasting snow was upon them, and he could not wait for the world to be blanketed in white.

It was Sunday and the entire town had gathered for the service. It was an age of enlightenment, and the duke knew that there were those in London who questioned the church, but here in Northwickshire, the people expected to see their betters in the parish each Sunday. It had been so since Alexander was small.

The truth was, the chapel at Bramblewood Park was in no shape for use. Even if it were, Alexander thought, with the goings on at Bramblewood in his father's lifetime, he should probably have the place consecrated to God once again. The thought of anything sacred had been absent from Bramblewood for far too long, but change took time.

The bells had rung and all entered the church; some for the service, and some to get out of the cold.

The duke had the front row reserved for his family as it had been for years. His staff occupied the wall at the back several rows behind him. The duke was spotted by Edmund and Mr. Marksham as they came into the church.

The duke put an arm over Edmund's shoulder to direct him to the empty front seat. "Sit with us," He gestured Marksham forward and both men joined him. It would feel less lonely with his friends beside him. "How are your chickens?" the duke asked in a whisper as he sat beside Marksham.

"Laying quite nicely for winter," the man replied with a grin. "Except for that rooster, of course; he will be the death of me."

"Yes," the duke laughed. "He always was a pest. That was why we chose him. My staff is ever so pleased he is gone," he admitted.

"He was the devil to catch," Edmund added and they all chuckled together.

Angry eyes around them demanded silence even though the service had yet to start. Still, the gentlemen took their seats and bowed their heads piously. Alexander took the time to think.

The duke had greeted many of the people on his way into the church and would greet many more on his way out. Again, it was Lord Stratton who urged to him mingle after services.

"People will say things at church that they will not voice in the town meetings or most especially to your face." Cecil had said. "You will hear what you need to hear."

"I thought I was there to pray to God."

"Yes, well, I am sure The Lord will hear what He should hear as well."

The duke smiled at the man's very practical form of religion as he looked around from his front vantage point.

The church had been added to over the years and

boasted two annexes that broke off from the central hall. Together, with the altar ahead, the structure created the illusion of the shape of a cross. He noted the stones along the wall needed repointing. Did everything need to be repaired? He wondered.

The duke was in the main room, but off to his left, he saw the Albright family sitting piously in the annex. William sat with his two young sisters on either side of him. With them, was a figure he recognized at once: Emily.

Emily's head was bowed and she looked every bit the devout lady that she ought to be. She was perfection. He felt a stab of shame that she had turned out so well, while he would always have his faults hanging over him. His and his father's. Guilt suffused him. He should be praying.

She sat as still as a statue with her eyes front. The duke shifted and continued to watch her, just like he had used to do as a boy when he came to services with his mother.

His father had often been sick on a Sunday. Alexander remembered once after services, he had got into fisticuffs with one of the village boys over the verity of that fact. Both William and Edmund had jumped in to help him pummel the liar, who was not a liar.

The duke's eyes found William seated with his aunt and uncle. He shushed his youngest sister, but then he leaned down to hear what she whispered and smiled. The girl had her mother's curls. Poor Kate, Alexander thought. He had an understanding for the girls losing their mother at such a time.

Alexander remembered, his own mother explaining, when they returned to the manor after the fight. She spoke with tears brimming, telling him that he should not have bloodied the boy. "You shall be a duke, a gentleman. Gentlemen do not act so."

"But he said Father was not sick. He was a liar."

"Your father is sick after a fashion," his mother said thoughtfully. "But it is not an illness many understand. They believe your father has chosen his way, but I am not sure he has. I am not sure he can. The drink has captured him surely as a demon, and he can no longer escape."

"A demon?" Alexander had said. "I don't understand."

"It does not matter. What does matter is that gentlemen do not engage in fisticuffs. They negotiate, sometimes they give orders, but they most certainly do not resort to violence."

"Father engaged in fisticuffs," Alexander argued.

His mother had sighed.

As an adult he could appreciate his mother's dilemma. His father gave no clear example of gentlemanly behavior; quite the opposite. Three years ago he threw the Baron Shudley straight through the side window.

The sight had been quite spectacular actually as Father picked up the smaller man and quite literally tossed him out of the house. He also could appreciate that his father and the baron always had a strange relationship: almost rivalry rather than friendship. They had fought more than once, though nothing like their last fight he thought.

Over the years they enjoyed the same revelry and tried to get one over on each other, but of course the duke's funds were greater. No wonder then that the men had such a spectacular falling out. He was filled with guilt for his part in it, and for Henrietta. He bowed his head and tried to pray, but it did not expunge his guilt. He wondered if like his father, he could not escape who he was.

Still, Emily distracted him.

She was distant with him. Sometimes, she acted as if she wanted no part of him. He knew she agreed to his offer to court her with no little reluctance. Why?

He was a duke. How could she not want him? Still, he did not want her to want him because he was a duke. He wanted her to want him because he was Alexander, her friend, and a person who had loved her since they were children. But perhaps she was wiser than his mother and saw him for who he really was. Perhaps she saw the same demon that followed his father also stalked him. Certainly, he was not blameless.

The duke turned his attention to the vicar as the service began, but after a while, he could not sit easy. His eyes strayed back to Emily.

Her hands were folded in her lap, and she looked positively angelic. The duke admired her control and hated it at the same time. He prayed for a hint that the girl he had once known and loved, was still present beneath her austere shield. If he saw but a glimpse, then he knew that, in time, he could draw her back out again. She seemed so rigid. It was almost like she was not the same person she had been.

Edmund insisted that Emily was the same girl who romped with them and followed in their games. That she was still the freckle-faced mer-creature who scolded him and pelted him with pinecones when he was being a dolt, but he could not see it. Please, God let me see it, he thought. Was that a prayer? Surely not.

He turned his attention back to the vicar who had been droning on for a full half hour about something the duke had lost track of in his musings. He tried to get his mind back on the lecture, but it made no sense now that he had missed a part. Rather, his eyes began to wander about the room to see if he was the only one who had been left in the dust. Marksham was listening. Edmund was dozing.

Lady Stratton was asleep, but Cecil was listening intently, nodding somewhat, and leaning in to hear. Alexander wondered if he ever would come up the man's high standard.

Emily remained firm in her prayer. Almost as if she were not even breathing. The duke repeated his paltry prayer with more force. Give me some sign, Lord. Should I pursue her, or let her go? He thought with more conviction. Perhaps The Lord had not heard him properly the first time with all of the other more appropriate prayers.

The duke did not put much faith in prayer. The Lord did not hear him when his mother was sick, or when his father was not. He was not sure he believed in Christmas miracles.

He opened one eye and glanced back at Emily.

Nothing.

He pursed his lips and prepared himself to accept the sign, or lack therefore, when it happened.

Anne, Emily's fondest companion, made a slight movement that could hardly be seen by anyone save one who was paying close attention. Although her hands were still clasped in devotion, her elbow reached out and poked Emily in the ribs. Emily peered in question at her friend, who whispered some unheard words.

That was when he saw it. Emily bit her lip in an attempt to control her laughter, but from the shaking of her shoulders he could see that it would not hold. She hid behind her praying hands, but that too failed. Emily was forced to bow her head so low that none could see her face behind the bench ahead of her. In the silence of the church, one small snort of laughter rang out like a bell. Of course no one reacted, for they could not say from whence it had come. Only now, Anne and her sisters had also bowed their heads low. The entire row was shaking with silent laughter.

He watched them with a smile upon his face. There it was: the sign that he had needed and he thanked The

Lord for it. Then he said an extra prayer for those who did not pay attention at Sunday service.

How long his attention had been focused on the ladies, he could not say. It must have been a decent while because he had not taken any notice that Edmund had awakened from his dozing and was watching him with shrewd eyes.

16

*A*s the service finished, his friend leaned close. "You really are in love with her, aren't you?" Edmund whispered so low that Alexander could have ignored it if he chose. There was no point in pretending that he did not know about whom his friend was speaking.

The duke remembered Edmund asking much the same the summer before Emily went away to finishing school. When he had shaken his head and denied it, his friend had poked him in the ribs, as Anne had done to Emily, and announced with more assurance, "You do. You love my sister." The moment came back to him clear as the church bells ringing out through the town of Northwick as the service completed.

"How long have you suspected?" The duke asked with a slight bob of his head.

"Oh, ages," Edmund admitted. "Since we were eight."

The duke shook his head. "That is not possible. I have only just recently discovered it myself."

"Well, it has been obvious to all others," Edmund argued, as they lingered in the vestibule. "For both of you."

"Both of us? Do you really think she returns my affection?"

"Emily?" Edmund scoffed. "She'll fight it best she can, but I have no doubt. She has been taught to hate all fun and must be reminded of it quite stringently."

"Has she made any mention of me?" The duke leaned closer with hope for an affirmation, and Edmund lowered his tone to keep the words from the gossipmongers.

"Not to my ears," Edmund replied. "She never would. She is too determined that the most practical solution is to marry Robert Hawthorne or some other natter-headed fool from the *Ton*."

"What!" the duke hissed. The vicar's head and those of several parishioners swiveled their way and the duke waved a hand. "Just some unexpected news," he explained and the parishioners went back to their conversations.

"That was my reaction," Edmund agreed.

"She wouldn't marry into the Hawthorne family," the duke said with certainty. "The Albright family is related to the Firthleys." The truth was her marrying into any family but his own was painful. "The man, and I use that word loosely, cannot even take a piss without his grandfather's permission."

Edmund chuckled. "My thoughts exactly. On the other hand Em might think Robert is used to taking orders." Edmund gave a little shrug. "You know, she is bound to give them."

The duke shook his head. He knew Emily was full of bluster. It was one of the things he liked about her. For the most part what she said made a lot of sense. For example, she would delegate and find a way to make the villagers work together. She would not dither and question. She would act.

He needed her by his side. She would be good for the duchy and more than that, she would be good for him. She always had been. The duke moved to exit the church, and put on his hat. He gave a quiet order to his driver. The carriages should be brought around shortly.

Edmund sighed. "I cannot believe it either, but Hawthorne does meet all of the qualities my mother desires."

"Do those qualities involve being a spineless prat who..."

Several parishioners turned their way again. The duke lowered his voice, but could not control the fervor that had struck at the knowledge that Emily would give herself over to such an unsuitable match. She would be bored for the rest of her life; he was sure of it.

"She is determined to have a man who is proper, rcliable, and good," Edmund explained.

The duke sighed. "I can make no claim to be any of those things."

"Of course you may," Edmund argued slapping his friend on the back. "You have gone beyond what anyone expected for Bramblewood and you have only just begun. You take your responsibilities to heart, but you are allowed to have fun now and again. What is the fault in that?"

Alexander wanted to tell his friend that he had more faults than Edmund could possibly know, one in particular that seemed to always be hanging over his head and reappearing at inopportune moments. He kept the secret, as the agreement between his father and the baron had demanded, but the sin was his to bear.

More than anything he knew that he kept the secret because he did not wish word of it to reach Emily's ears. Her good opinion of him would be lost forever. His conscience said that her good opinion should be lost. He was not a good man, no matter what Edmund thought.

"You are allowed to be lively so long as you steer clear of shame," his friend continued, giving his full support to the idea of the duke pursuing his sister. "Emily needs to see that she can live too. You are not your father, Alexander. Never forget that." Edmund shook a finger under his friend's nose.

The duke smiled weakly. What if I am? He wondered silently. Edmund was ever refuting the rumor that had followed Alexander. He was a good friend. Alexander hoped the man's trust in him was not misplaced.

The duke realized he would not only lose Emily if the truth came out; he would lose Edmund as his friend as well. Well, then. It must remain a secret.

"I thank you for your vote of confidence," he said even though confidence was the last thing he felt. He watched Emily moving through the crowd in front of him. His friend's hand on his shoulder gave him courage.

"I would never believe ill of you, and Emily would be daft if she did," Edmund said with a firm nod. "One thing my sister is not, is daft. She is smart as a whip, that one. Now, the only question that remains is what are you going to do? I expected you yesterday."

"I got caught up in estate business and could not get away. It was dark before I realized."

"Emily will be going back to London at the end of the holiday. So I warn you, do not dally."

The duke nodded just as the object of his interest glanced back to see her brother. Emily's eyes connected with Alexander's as if she had felt his gaze upon her.

Her deep amber eyes seared him. The duke felt a smoldering heat fill him and had to remind himself they were in church; only the vestibule, but still.

Before he could offer a smile or nod of acknowledgement, Emily turned away offering a greeting to the vicar. She hid from him once more, concealing herself within the crowd of parishioners as they moved out of the church.

The cold December wind struck him, though not so biting as Emily's dismissal. He hated the distance between them, but he could not speak to her as he had once done. Everything he did seemed to drive her further away. He must find way to reach her and make her understand. He could not bear it if Emily's eyes ever looked upon him with scorn as the servants had after Polly; the way the town had after Henrietta was sent away.

Please, I may not be a good man, but let her know that I love her and let that be enough. The duke made his final plea to heaven. Then he, like the others, proceeded out of the church.

17

On Monday, Emily and Aunt Agnes, along with William's sisters Claire and Caroline were joined in town by the Albright sisters and their mother Lady Aldbrick.

Northwick was a booming town with several rows of shops and gathering places. Lady Aldbrick took her youngest daughter, Susanna to find trimmings for their Christmas gowns and promised to meet the other ladies back at the carriage before too long. Aunt Agnes kissed Emily upon the cheek. She went with Lady Aldbrick, ushering William's young sisters away like a mother hen with her chicks.

The remaining three, Emily, Anne and Eliza giggled and clasped each other's arms as they hurried off to a trinket shop to see what treasures might be found. Trudy's Emporium was a perennial favorite. It always had interesting items. Mostly they were shipped from

London, but Emily humored her friends. Anne and her sister, Eliza wanted to visit the shop.

Nonetheless, Emily found herself fascinated with the sheer volume bobbles and odds and ends that could be gathered in one place. She had to admit the emporium was a wonder. She conspired with Eliza to keep her sister busy and spent much more than she had intended on a pair of glass earrings that looked to have been made just for Anne. She tucked them away after purchase so that her friend might not suspect her gift.

When Emily returned to the sisters after her purchase was completed, Eliza was teasing Anne about a possible suitor, a gentleman Emily did not know.

She prayed that Eliza did not tease about the duke for she might not be able to hide her feelings from her best friend. Thankfully, Anne was distracted by her sister. Eliza, giving up on her game brought Anne's attention to a chain and watch fob.

"Do you think Father will like this?" Eliza asked and Emily was saved from a failed attempt at acting coy.

Emily considered those gifts she still had to purchase. She thought of Henrietta. Emily was not a close friend of the lady since she had been away for so long, but she did not want to be embarrassed if Henrietta bought something for her. She purchased a silk scarf in cornflower blue that would set of her eyes and make her blonde hair shine.

"Also more sweetmeats for William's sisters," Emily added.

The young ladies walked down the street to the candy shop and were happy to get out of the wind and cold. They had to wait behind others buying treats. Then, they lingered a bit warming themselves after making their purchases and deciding where to go next.

The heady smell of peppermint and chocolate brought back memories of Christmases spent at Sandstowe. Emily remembered her own Christmas stocking filled with the sweets and sharing them before the fire with Edmund and with Alexander.

Anne popped a peppermint into her mouth and gave Emily a look of appraisal.

"What is it?" Emily asked.

"I could not say," Anne shrugged slightly. "Something is different. You seem most distracted. Are you in love?"

Emily shook her head. "I had a letter from Robert Hawthorne yesterday," she admitted.

"It is not Hawthorne that has distracted you," Anne said with good humor. She offered Emily one of the peppermint sticks and then popped another in her own mouth.

"Don't eat them all," Eliza scolded.

The truth was Emily thought of the duke more with each passing day, and Robert Hawthorne less. She had pressed aside the notion of deeper feeling, but the letter from Robert Hawthorne the previous morning had confirmed her fears. She read the letter with dread rather than excitement. The London gentleman meant nothing to her; nor did any of the other London gents who could not hope to hold a candle to Alexander in her estimation. There was no comparison.

Emily had not spoken to the duke since the dinner at Bramblewood, but the more that she thought about it, the more that she had come to believe that he had meant his request to call upon her. Was it possible that his intention had been the beginnings of a real courtship?

She heard the bell as the door to the sweetshop opened, but Emily was so lost in her own thoughts that she had taken no notice of the duke's approach until he was standing before her.

Her heart skipped a beat and she felt for sure that the pounding was audible. He watched her for a moment with a soft expression that she could not comprehend.

"Might I assume Mr. Danvers has made a new batch of peppermint sticks?" he asked softly as he eyed the queue of other customers.

"Yes," Anne said. "We bought some for William's sisters. In fact, I do not think I bought enough."

"Not if you keep eating them," Eliza admonished. The two of them moved back to the candy counter.

"As I remember, you liked chocolate better," the duke said to Emily and she was sure she blushed.

"It is wonderful in a cup on a cold night," she agreed.

He looked at her in that way he had, his mouth turned up slightly at the corners. She could almost hear the risqué turn of his thoughts, but he said nothing, only smiled.

Why on earth had she mentioned cold nights? She

felt heat fill her face, only made worse by her perusal of his lips.

"Are you enjoying your visit to the country," he asked at length.

"Very much," she admitted with a contented sigh. "It has been far too long and I have missed it dearly."

"Then, you did not stop visiting because you had grown tired of our monotonous existence?" His smile revealed that he had guessed it to be so and hoped her opinion to be otherwise.

"Not at all," she explained. "Mother heard about the bout of influenza. Kate was ill and mother wanted to be sure that it was not catching, which of course, it was. Mother is most afraid of contagion."

"That is no small fear," he said. "It brought sadness to many this year past."

Emily refused to be melancholy so close to Christmas. "Besides, Mother was too busy parading Edmund and I about the *Ton*."

"You always did love London," he said.

Emily nodded agreeing. "Mother had exclusive passes for the season. She managed to get us into Almacks and was determined to find us both settled according to her standard."

"You have a suitor waiting in London for your return?" he asked. Something in his tone told her that he already knew the answer. Having always been so close to Edmund, she would not be surprised if her brother had spoken of it.

Emily hesitated with her reply. "Mother has two options that she has... encouraged me to consider."

"Have you?"

She shrugged. "I suppose so, but my brother and I have both grown weary with her persistence."

The duke reached out clasping her gloved hand for just a moment while Mr. Danvers went to find more candies for his customers.

Emily's voice wavered. "Every season it is the same... balls, theater, parties, suitors..."

The duke released her. "But you like that," he said.

"The balls, yes, but not the reason for them," She hesitated. This was not a topic to discuss with a gentleman, especially in not so public a venue.

"Go on," he urged.

Years ago he had been privy to all of her thoughts and worries. She had never felt so about anyone else she had met. It felt nice to share again. Everything came rushing out like water from a mountain stream.

"It is only, how can one make a decision about something so important as marriage when they barely know a person?" She lifted a shoulder. "Hundreds of people at a party and they all seem a blur, as if painted with one brush. The next day, there are a hundred more faces, ever changing, yet constant. It is as if I could close my eyes and choose at random and it would not matter."

"It matters," the duke said softly. Then he waited for her to continue, as if afraid that any further words might halt the open conversation.

She was forced to admit that, since her return, she had shared with him less than she had used to do, and now, the moment stood before them, the aroma of chocolate and peppermint bringing back fond memories.

"Mother did not want us to come," she blurted. "Father was at Lords when we left. The truth is it was only with great resignation that Mother and Father even allowed us to leave," Emily admitted in a breath.

"I am glad you have come."

"Edmund and I were given the holiday to rejuvenate our spirits with the promise that, upon our return, I shall delay no longer."

"Then it is decided?" The duke asked when she did not continue.

"No," Emily shook her head and took a breath, "but it will be."

"You mean, Robert Hawthorne," he said in a soft voice. She was not surprised that he had been made aware of the frontrunner of her London suitors, but she was surprised to discover the sadness that pulled across his features.

"He would be mother's first choice," she admitted, "but..."

"He is a sap," the duke interrupted, his voice tight.

"You must not say so," she began, but Alexander stopped and turned her toward him, taking both of her hands into his own and nearly pleading. "He hangs on his grandfather's...well, apron strings, or whatever the male equivalent might be, as if he hopes that his grandfather might pass over his father in the entail, but that shall not be."

"If I marry Hawthorne," Emily began, and the duke interrupted again.

"I should never see you again."

"I said that would be my mother's first choice," Emily repeated. "Not that I would accept it."

The duke waited for her to continue. Emily spoke slowly, almost wonderingly, as if she had only just become aware of the fact.

"I do not love him." She said the final words slowly to be sure that Alexander understood.

His hands tightened on hers.

Perhaps a few weeks ago she might not have said such things to him, but Robert was no longer an option, she knew that now and so must Alexander.

He brightened instantly.

"Perhaps you will find something in the country that has more appeal." He looked down upon Emily with an expression that begged her to open her mind to the possibilities that she had previously refused to consider. "I will not deny that I have long wished for your return."

Ever so gently, he took her packages and placed her opposite hand into the crook of his elbow. His eyes strayed to Anne and Eliza who were hovering a short distance away, having completed their own purchases.

"Allow me to escort you ladies wherever you are bound."

"But you did not get your sweets, Your Grace," Eliza said.

"On the contrary," he said smiling down at Emily.

"Your Grace…" Emily began but could not know how to express what she was feeling.

Any chill that she had felt prior was gone even as they stepped out into the cold street. With the duke beside her, it was as if a flame had lit beneath her skin and the winter air had begun to stifle. Emily wanted to speak of her emotions, and yet, at the same time it was terrifying. She swallowed past the lump in her throat. It was one thing to care for him in her mind and quite another to say it aloud. Perhaps another day would be a better time for it.

"I do hope to see more of you during your stay," the duke continued as they walked back towards the carriage. A slight pressure on her hand was the only difference from what had previously been an ordinary conversation. "There are pleasures in the country, as well as the city," he said, his voice low and deep.

She was unable to answer him. Was he wondering if she would be happier here, in Northwick, or at Bramblewood, with him? The thought suffused her with heat.

"Tomorrow," the duke said in an abrupt whisper before they parted. "Might I call upon you, tomorrow?"

Emily nodded and offered a small smile before he hurried away, nodding to the Albright ladies as they passed. She felt as if she might burst with excitement.

"Well, about time!" Anne covered her mouth with her hand and then said more softly, "I thought it would never happen."

The others were coming into view. Susanna's features were alight with the merriment of the season, but Emily took no notice of her friends as Eliza waved to her mother and sister across the way. They were soon joined by Aunt Agnes, Lady Aldbrick and the other girls, all chattering about the ribbons and lace they purchased for their Christmas dresses.

"Shall we get something warm to drink before we head home?" Aunt Agnes asked, but Emily was warmed through already. The duke had asked to call upon her. He had called her sweet. She felt rather gooey inside, as if she were made of melted chocolate.

18

*T*he morning crept by at a cumbersome pace while Emily and Aunt Agnes tried to teach Cousin Caroline how to make a Christmas sampler. Her needlework was crooked and knotted which precipitated much picking of stitches which was doubly tedious as they were pulled too tight as beginners might do.

"Caroline has always been awful at needlepoint," Claire offered while Emily tried to help the younger girl. "Mother says..." Claire stopped suddenly with the remembrance that their mother was gone. Her breath hitched and her lower lip trembled.

Aunt Agnes embraced the older girl which left Emily to help Caroline. Emily remembered when her mother had taught her to sew. She was very young; much younger than Claire and Caroline.

She couldn't even remember it properly, but she remembered practicing buttons, attaching them quite permanently to a spare piece of cloth. Quite a lot of buttons, she was sure were purchased expressly for her distraction.

The thread was doubled so that she did not misplace the needle with clumsy childish fingers and she had made a heap of tangled thread, but that was the way of young children. They made a mess. That was how they learned.

Emily did not think that long ago button sewing elicited a more tangled mass of thread than Caroline's excuse for needlepoint. Eventually, she decided there was no help for it. She cut loose a particularly tight knot on Claire's sewing, and pulled out what could not be saved. Had she ever been this horrible at the craft Emily wondered?

"I hate sewing," Caroline said with a sigh as she watched Emily trying to save at least part of the pattern.

"You will get better at it with practice," Emily promised.

"No, I won't. I would much rather be riding," Caroline confessed.

Emily had often felt the same. Truthfully, she still often wished she was with her brother out of doors, but she only said, "There is a great accomplishment in finishing a project."

Caroline sighed and tossed back her braids. She obviously did not believe her elder cousin.

It was nearly noon when the duke came to call. A thrill soared through Emily as he entered the room.

"Look who I found," Edmund announced coming into the sitting room with the duke by his side.

Emily stood. "Your Grace," she said as she curtseyed and the younger girls awkwardly followed suit.

"Miss Ingram. Ladies." He bowed to Aunt Agnes and the girls. Caroline giggled, but Claire was very serious.

The duke turned back to Emily. "The true purpose of my call was to see if you might be willing to accompany me for a ride?"

"Ride with you?" she gasped. She cursed the breathiness of her voice. It was not so shocking. She and Alexander had used to ride together quite often. Yet, this felt different. It was intentional and their age made it seem most romantic.

He had said he wanted to call upon her. She had not quite credited it. She supposed they would sit under Aunt Agnes watchful eye, but riding, riding would allow them time to talk.

"Yes," he laughed. "Unless your schedule is full."

"Can I come?" Caroline piped up.

"May I," Aunt Agnes corrected, "and the answer is no."

The girl went into a pout.

"No," Emily stammered in answer to the duke's question of her full schedule. "What I mean is, no, it is not full. I will ride with you."

"I will see the horses saddled," Edmund said while Emily returned to her room to don her winter habit.

Each day grew colder than the last and she did not wish to catch a chill before all of the best activities.

She pinched her cheeks for color and then chastised herself for doing so. Firstly, they would be reddened by the wind soon enough. Secondly, she had no reason to care how she looked in the presence of the duke. It was not as if she meant to encourage his suit, did she? This was Alexander. Alexander all grown up who made her insides turn to liquid heat.

She returned downstairs to find the duke praising young Caroline's choice of color in her sampler. The truth was, there was not much else to praise, but the thought was a sweet one. She paused a moment in the doorway to consider him. He did, at moments like this, seem to be the old Alexander; the friend she had known.

He saw her in the doorway and straightened. "Shall we go?" he asked, offering her his arm.

"I need not tell you to be back before teatime, do I?" Aunt Agnes said.

"We will be back soon, Auntie." Emily promised.

Emily stepped out into the brisk air and thought her fashionable London riding hat did little to protect her from the chill and she knew her cheeks would redden in a moment. Still, it did not matter. She looked down to hide the flustered expression that the duke seemed so skilled at drawing forth whether she willed it or no. Once they were sheltered by the trees the wind would not be so biting.

The stable boy held both leads and was a far cry too

young to hand her up. Edmund had already mounted and was some distance away walking his horse at an ambling pace. She looked around and told the boy to lead her mount to the mounting block. Where was Gerald? She wondered.

"Belay that," the duke said, and the stable boy hesitated uncertain. She was a guest in the house, but the duke was the duke.

She raised an eyebrow. "What are you about?"

But his meaning was clear. There was only the duke to do the job of seating her on her mount. Drat, she thought as a little thrill raced through her.

"Are you ready?" he asked as he stepped close.

"As I shall ever be," she replied with a tensing of her shoulders.

He looked crestfallen at her response. "We do not have to ride, if you do not wish it," he whispered for her ears only.

She blushed. Of course, she wanted to ride with him and moreso, she wanted him to hand her up, but that very desire was where the problem lay.

"Do not be silly," she said, not meeting his eye.

The stable boy hovered, holding the horses, still uncertain.

"Come along you two," Edmund called, and Emily had to smile.

Emily knew she ought not to feel such pangs and fluttering around a gentleman who could very well be a rake and philanderer like his father.

Could such things be passed from father to son? She wondered how many a lady had fallen, or would fall, prey to his charms. If not his charms, then his title. This power that he possessed over her should have her falling in to his arms or send her running back to the manor and to lock the door firmly between them.

Robert Hawthorne would never dare to make her feel so out of control. He was steady, and she felt steady beside him. This... this was something different: a nervous anticipation like a horse that stamped its hoof as it prepared for the run. It made her feel altogether off balance.

The air fairly crackled between them like a storm brewing, and when she brought her eyes to his deep blue gaze, she could not look away. She wanted his hands on her.

Why shouldn't I? She thought with a firm set of her jaw. We are friends; are we not? I should have no reason to decline. So long as the gossips did not paint her in a sour light, one of what must be his many exploits, but no one was here except Uncle Cecil's stable lads and Edmund waiting impatiently on his own mount.

"Are you going to take all day?" Edmund called.

Emily gave the duke a nod. She placed her gloved hand in his out stretched palm and then upon his shoulders as he lifted her. Those shoulders were so impossibly broad. A thrill shot through her as he put his hands upon her waist and lifted her into the saddle.

His hands nearly spanned her waist, she thought

with wonder. He lifted her so easily. Propriety told her to look away, to turn her head in modesty during the contact, but she could not. Rather, their eyes held and her breath caught. She imagined she could feel his hands on her skin through his gloves and her riding attire. It was ridiculous, of course, but when he had seated her in her side saddle and took his hands from her waist, she felt the loss.

The duke handed her the reins, and turned to take his own mount.

When Emily was secure, she turned her mount and herself away from the duke's heated eyes. She did not need him trying to read her, as he used to do. She was afraid at what he might find. She did not want to look too closely herself.

Robert Hawthorne she repeated in her mind, but the words fell flat. There was nothing that flared her interest about the gentleman, especially not when she was seated a mere arm's length away from someone who did possess the ability to rouse her blood.

They rode on in companionable silence. Emily looked about and soaked up the wonderment of the countryside. She would miss this when she returned to London, and all the more if she were to be restricted from this beautiful land in due time. It was, very likely, her last visit, especially if she married Hawthorne. The thought filled her with sudden dread.

"There is a patch of winter berries up ahead," the duke said.

"Only holly berries, not blueberries," she said.

"That is true," he said. "You would have to be here in summer or at least autumn to pick blueberries."

"I no longer pluck them from the bush," she said.

"Could you not be persuaded?" he asked.

"Absolutely not," she teased.

"I shall remember," he said with a curt nod. "Then I shall have to pick them myself and feed them to you one by one, dipped in cream, while you sit at your leisure."

The image he conjured in her mind filled her with heat. He was flirting with her. The smug grin and way he glanced over his shoulder as he nudged his horse ahead to the location told her so.

"I shan't," she replied as she flew past him and Edmund as well. She knew these paths well. She urged her mount into a canter, and headed for the path which ran through the upper road. She knew that juniper and holly grew there.

Perhaps even some rowan if it had not been picked to make jelly earlier in the year, although she was not sure there were any sweet berries left. In any case, it felt wonderful to ride free, the wind in her face.

"You have not forgotten our Bramblewood," the duke called as he caught up with her. As they reached the top of the hill, they brought their horses back to a walk. They rode for a while side by side.

"Of course not," she agreed.

Edmund caught them up, but held back allowing them some privacy as if they were a courting couple.

As they wound down the path into the valley, they spoke of her time at finishing school, and his plans for Bramblewood in the coming spring; all safe topics. Conversation meandered on to some of their daring escapades as children.

She allowed herself a covert glance when he was not looking, and she could not help but think how attractive his form was. He had grown into a fine man, and it was very likely that he knew it. She smiled to herself at the curl of his hair that left a small bit of his boyish appeal in the grown man.

How many a lady would fall for that appeal? She could not forget the feeling of his hands on her waist and the decadent image he had conjured of him feeding her berries and cream.

They had eaten berries and cream many times as children. They had made quite a mess of themselves. The thought of such things should not put a flush to her face, and yet it did.

As they recounted old tales, at one feat of daring, the duke admitted, "I was in awe of you." He looked at her with those passion-dark eyes. "I am in awe of you still," he admitted softly.

She knew they were near to where the berry patch used to be, and she suddenly felt confused and hot. She urged her horse into a canter. "I shall race you," she called over her shoulder. It was but a short run up the hill, and since she surprised the duke, she reached it first. They both left poor Edmund in the dust.

Emily dismounted with a leap before the duke could offer to hand her down. The last thing that her nerves needed in this moment was for him to touch her again. If he touched her, she would fall into his arms. She realized that she had never felt this way.

A number of times, various suitors had tried to maneuver her into walking alone along garden paths or leaving the ballroom for a breath of air. They had never moved her. She had never been tempted, before now. She knew the heat between them would not be denied. If she allowed him a single touch, she would go up in flames.

If she focused solely on the berries then she might not have to look at him. When Alexander reached her, she pretended to be busy searching.

"I think we are too late," the duke said. "Birds have eaten them all leaving us bereft."

Was he bereft as she was? Emily thought. She searched frantically for a safe subject.

In polite conversation, she would ask of one's family, but that was a loaded topic considering his father. She asked after his butler, Mr. Barnes, of whom she had always had a fondness. She had not noticed the man at the dinner party. Another had greeted them.

"I have promoted Barnes to be my steward," he said.

"And the previous steward?" she asked.

"Retired," he said. "He was more my father's man." The implications were clear there. He was my father's man; not mine. Still, she could not quite relax. She chattered on inanely sounding like the ninnies in town that she had despised. She had never had trouble holding a conversation, and yet somehow, she could not keep the dialogue light. They stumbled upon innuendo and each innocent brush set fire between them.

There was a purpose in the duke's every move and her own feelings were like kindling to each smoldering look. This ride was a mistake, she thought. This was dangerous; and where was Edmund? He was not taking his chaperoning duties seriously.

Emily told herself that she must focus on more important things, like Robert. She could not even picture his face. She saw only Alexander.

"I fear there are no berries," she said inanely.

The duke murmured something soothing, but she was too on edge to hear the words. With gentle fingers he reached forward and tucked a stray lock behind her ear. She wanted to lean into his fingers but stood frozen and trembling. Then, as he had used to when she was a girl, he folded a sprig of holly berries into her tresses.

"You found some," she said amazed.

"There," he whispered, just as he had done so long ago. "Queen of the Yule."

A dozen times when he had murmured similar words raced through her memory: Queen of the fairies, Queen of the May...mermaids...Lady of the Lake. She forgot to breathe.

He looked down upon her, his eyes searching her face for some answer that she refused to give, and she felt in the pit of her stomach that if she encouraged him in the least, he would kiss her. She wanted him to kiss her. She was trembled with the desire.

He brushed a gloved finger against her cheek. Then abruptly, he lifted the glove to his mouth and used his teeth to pull the offending fabric from his hand, dropping it on the ground. Again, he touched her cheek. His fingers were hot against her skin. She leaned into them as if they were the only warmth in the world.

"You are shivering," he murmured as he ran his fingers from her cheek to her ears "And your ears are red with cold." He pulled off the other glove and cupped his hands around her ears.

It was an oddly sensual feeling, the world held at bay while he cupped her ears, warming them with his hands. The rush of her own heartbeat was amplified, pounding in her ears and in his hands. She looked up at him and there was so much emotion in his eyes. She did not know how to read it: desire, need and uncertainty.

She realized the fretfulness was somehow dependent upon her. She did not know what to do, but she wanted to wipe away that disquiet.

"You must be cold," she said.

"Not in the least," the words were whispered.

Emily nodded. The rush of heat pooled within her as well. She knew if she closed her eyes he would kiss her. Surely the flames would consume them both if they kissed. She could not.

His hands left her ears then and he pulled her cloak closed between them. His hands remained fisted at the seam and she wondered if he needed something to hold on to lest he do something foolish like pull her into his arms. The thought set her blood to boil and her cheeks ablaze.

She wondered what might happen if he gave a gentle tug and pulled her forward. It was such a simple thing. Such thoughts were traitorous to everything that she had planned for herself and yet, she could not move away from him.

"You are trembling. Are you chilled?" The duke asked.

"Yes," she lied in a breath.

He released her and stepped away, drawing a very obvious steadying breath of his own.

"Then we should return," he said retrieving his gloves.

She nodded and allowed him to lift her once more into the saddle. This time, she turned her head and closed her eyes for she had little enough reserve in willpower to be sure that she could be trusted to meet his heavy gaze.

Their return was silent, although on occasion they cast estimating glances at one another. What must he be thinking, she wondered? Probably that she was soon to return to London, a place where she had no longer had any desire to be.

"Ho!" Called Edmund. "Did you find any berries?"

"One lonely sprig of holly," the duke said.

As they rode, Emily forced herself to consider her

own feelings. Was she receptive to the duke's supposed suit? She did acknowledge that the emotions she felt were much stronger, and more vibrant, than those she had experienced around any other gentleman. Could it be that his appeal had to do with the warm memories of the past? She thought not.

No, if she were being honest, she had come to appreciate the gentleman for what he had become, for what he had overcome, and for the kindhearted companionship that proved that, even after all this time, he still knew her truest self better than any other. The knowledge brought a flutter of excitement to her breast.

She glanced at the duke mounted proudly at her side. He glanced back as if he could feel her scrutiny and her breath caught. For the first time, she realized that love did have the power to hold sway over her choosing. She was already in very real danger of falling in love with the duke. If it so happened that she found herself in love with Alexander, and she very nearly could be, she realized that she would be inclined to accept his suit.

That is of course, if he offered. It would be forward for her to give any true indication of her feelings, but she felt as if her heart would burst. She felt the holly branch still tucked behind her ear, warmth roiling in her core. She should have closed her eyes and leaned into him, she castigated herself. He would have kissed her. She was sure of it, and she wanted his kiss.

————

19

The duke paced his study. He was nervous. He had not thought he would be. He was a straightforward man. Intrigue did not come easily to him, save for this: this must be secret.

The duke knew that Emily would be upset if she knew about Henrietta. Still what was he to do? He paused, remembering the day he invited the banished lady back to Northwickshire.

When Henrietta appeared at his door, he caught her hands. "I thought this would be the best place for us to meet," he said. "Far from gossip."

"Yes," she replied. "Thank you."

He hesitated a moment and then closed the door.

"Sherry?" he said. He remembered she was partial to the drink.

She nodded and he took a brandy for himself. "I

must offer condolences. I am indeed sorry for your father's death."

She laughed with a touch of sadness. "No, you are not," she said. "He was a miserable old man." She took the sherry and sipped it. The duke thought that was true and yet...

"Still he was your father," He said.

"Yes," she drew a shaky breath. "You do understand, Alexander. You have always understood. I thank you for your letter, and for inviting me back. I missed Northwick... and you."

"I was remiss in not doing so sooner," he said.

She shook her head. "It would not have been wise." She laughed bitterly. "It may still not be wise."

"Let me be the judge of that."

She inclined her head and then gave him a cheeky grin. "As you wish, Your Grace."

"Oh, do not," he said. "The title feels strange enough. I am only Alexander, as I have always been." He laughed and the tension eased. "In any case, I doubt, I could have done this while either of our fathers lived, but now..." He let the sentence hang.

"Now, it is just us," Henrietta supplied, "and we may do as we wish." Her voice was a husky whisper filled with emotion. She took a hearty drink of the sherry and drew a shaky breath. "Alexander, I do not know what to say."

"You don't have to say anything, Henrietta." She inclined her head and set her glass aside.

It had been sherry they drank that night.

Henrietta had let him into her room.

It was already past midnight and Henrietta's father's party was in full swing which meant most of his guests were ape drunk, including Alexander's own father. Henrietta was meant to stay out of the way in her room.

Alexander had procured half a bottle of sherry and two glasses. They toasted each other and their friendship. They had visited before when Henrietta's father held a party. There was little chance that anyone would see them. It was late and both of their fathers were already tap-hackled.

Usually, the parties lasted until the early hours of the morning and the servants had their hands full cleaning up after the guests. Alexander only had to slip out before dawn and no one would be the wiser. He had done it on several previous occasions. This seemed no different.

They had played some cards and read for a while. Then he had tickled her because she wouldn't tell him the answer to some riddle, and finally he had asked her, if he might kiss her. A few fumbling tries later they laughed and went back to reading. The drink made them sleepy.

He remembered thinking that the fire was burning down. He should stir it up and put on another log, or he should leave and Henrietta could call a servant to tend the fire; only he doubted that anyone would hear the call bells with the revelry downstairs.

Next thing he knew he was being dragged awake by Henrietta's most irate Father. His own father was red in the face as well, although whether that was from anger or hangover it was hard to tell.

He remembered the day vividly and the high price for the stupidity of falling asleep together in a bed.

No matter that both Henrietta and himself swore with all manner of promises that nothing untoward had happened, their fathers would not see reason.

Henrietta's father had demanded their marriage for the ruination of his daughter, not that he would have cared at any other time, but with the promise of a future duke as her husband, he had put on a good show of outrage.

Alexander's father had seen the trap and rebutted accordingly that his son would not be ensnared by a half-grown hoyden who had been left to do as she pleased. He said all manner of awful things about Henrietta and accused her of everything from harlotry to witchcraft for tricking his gullible son with her well-practiced charms.

Alexander had not been sure if he should be angered for being called gullible, or enraged on Henrietta's behalf. In the end, it had not mattered what either of them said.

The friendship between the baron and the duke had fallen out; coin had been exchanged to settle the matter, and Henrietta had been sent away.

He had caused her banishment. He should have

invited her home after his father died, but he had not. Alexander had followed the letter of the document written up on that fateful day. He continued to pay the yearly sum to Henrietta's father, the price for their foolishness, but it was time to put an end to it.

"So what do you propose?" Henrietta asked.

He pulled a folder from his satchel and showed her the paper. "Does this meet with your approval?"

Her eyes widened. "It most generous," she said. "More than generous in fact."

What might Emily think if she ever discovered the stain upon his past, the duke wondered? She, who was so pure and kind, was sure to suspect that he would be no better to her than his father had been to his wife.

Still, he had to find a way to repair the injury, for Henrietta's sake as well as his own. He owed the lady that much at least. No matter that he had not truly despoiled Henrietta; his thoughtlessness had marred her good name.

He loved Emily, of that he had no doubt, but was he worthy of her? No, not now. Perhaps not ever. At least not until this matter was settled once and for all. He was tired of suffering for something that had never happened. And yet, implication was enough to damn, and Emily was a London girl. Such things where even more anathema in Town than in the county. He would not see Emily besmirched.

She was better off with Robert Hawthorne, he

thought with a surge of jealousy. Hawthorne would not have made such a careless mistake. His family had guarded his good name since birth and would continue to do so as he grew nearer to his inheritance. At his best, Alexander thought, he was a far sight short of what Emily deserved.

Still, having Emily returned to his life had been like a bright light that had cast away the darkness. Alexander could not help but hope. He had forgotten how much they had shared and how right they were for one another. Emily made him better. She made him want to be better. She made all the foolish goings on that passed the time between then and now seem like nothing. If he could only be with her.

He could not bear the thought of her becoming a Hawthorne, and his never seeing her again. He could not, would not, allow it to happen.

This had to be settled before he could even consider Emily.

Henrietta was depending upon him. She had no one else, and he could not disappoint her.

"The originals are with the solicitor, Mr. Mills." The duke explained. "I simply wanted you to have a copy, and if you have changes..."

"No," Henrietta interrupted shaking her head. "Alexander you did not have to do this."

"You will need the originals," The duke continued. "I thought it best to leave the documents with the solicitor until you are ready to collect them."

She nodded her agreement and tucked the letter into her reticule and put it aside.

"Oh, Alexander, thank you," she said softly tears brimming. She leaned into his arms and he held her as of old.

20

*A*nother week passed and the weather turned chill. Christmas tidings were in full swing. Several evenings of cold had forced the cancellation of parties and travel so that when Uncle Cecil announced that Lake Brakenbrush had frozen solid, Emily leapt at her brother's offer for a turnabout the ice.

Skating had long been one of her favorite winter pastimes, and there was nothing quite like a country lake on which to take the pleasure. She remembered with fondness the many afternoons spent gliding across the ice until Uncle Cecil would come shouting that they had made the kitchen hold dinner late and their aunt was cross.

Of course, when they arrived at the manor with Alexander and Anne in tow, Aunt Agnes had never been cross. She had given them hot cocoa with peppermint sticks and warmed them before the fire until they were toasty and ready to eat.

She and Edmund had stopped, on their way, at Aldbrick Abbey to inform the ladies of their intent to take to the ice. Their friends had begun the trek several minutes before and were expecting the Ingrams' to join them forthwith.

Upon their arrival to the frozen shore, it seemed as if the entire town had turned out in celebration of the winter festivities. Those that had once been young in her memories were now grown. Tiny children raced and tumbled into snowdrifts, couples glided arm in arm, and groups of single gentlemen and ladies socialized while taking their turns across the small lake.

The children were unknown to Emily. Save her cousins, there was not a single face that Emily recognized. It was strange how life goes on without you, she thought. Northwickshire was both the same, and changed, since her last visit, and she found that she was glad that it could manage to be both at the same time.

"We are late," Emily laughed as she looked for others that she knew within the crowd. "It seems that the whole town is here!"

A breathless Anne skidded to a stop and clung to Edmund's arm for support.

"Oh, I am sorry, Edmund," she cried. "I was making my way over to talk to you, Emily. I have grasped the skating, but I seem to have forgotten the stopping. Never fear, I shall get my feet under me soon enough."

"I am out of practice as well," Emily admitted. It had been years since she had attempted the pastime and it would surely be comical.

Anne giggled as Edmund pretended to push her over before setting her back to rights a moment later.

Emily could not contain her girlish excitement and looked around to see if the duke had arrived. She hoped that his new position did not mean that he refrained from such simple joys as skating.

He had used to be one of the first on the ice and one of the last to come off the frozen surface. Bramblewood Park bordered over half of the lake, and therefore, had the easiest access for skating as well as determining whether or not the ice would hold.

As far as Emily could see there was no sign of the duke. She frowned, disappointed. Then, she spotted him along the far side of the lake. Alexander. She was instantly aware of the way he moved although he was some distance away. He glided along with accomplished ease. When someone spoke to him from the shore, he turned gracefully and stopped to talk to the group of gentlemen.

Emily felt a rush of heat as she watched him pull off his hat and push back his hair as he had done so many times when they were children. Now, she wanted to run her own fingers through his curls. She wanted to touch him, to feel the jolt that sprung between them at the contact.

Emily realized that she wanted to skate with him.

Skating would give her an excuse to be held in his arms. The thought brought a blush to her cheeks and a flutter to her heart. She applied herself to her skates.

"Are you not yet ready?" Anne chided, as she and Edmund stood waiting for Emily.

Emily laughed and promised a round once she had buckled on her skates. In the meantime, Edmund offered his arm to Anne, and the pair was off before Emily could toss a handful of snow in their direction.

She was about to step out onto the ice with tentative feet. She glanced back towards where Alexander stood. The last thing that she needed was the duke to witness her falling flat on her bottom.

Henrietta was off in the distance, gliding with ease. Those who did not, or could not, skate had gathered on the far hill to watch the fray. Some had packed picnic baskets from which to feed their children and several even had a bottle or two of mulled wine or cider that steamed from their cups and warmed their hands. In a few hours, someone would start a bonfire and the entire gathering would settle in for the day.

"Miss Ingram," Mr. Eldridge appeared by her side and offered his greeting. "May I offer my services?" She accepted with a glance back at the duke, still conversing at the lake's opposite end. She allowed Mr. Eldridge to escort her onto the ice. The turn around the lake was invigorating, but Emily was not up to much discussion.

She had to concentrate on her footing. It had been a long while since she skated. It was a good thing that Mr.

Eldridge did not require her active participation in the conversation. Emily found that the agricultural instruction did not need answer, which suited her fine as she focused most deliberately on where her skates met the ice.

In spite of his passion with all things agricultural, she had decided that Mr. Eldridge was a fine, steady man. He had made a respectable name for himself in the area and seemed to have done so without artifice. Just because his interests were not akin to her own should not make him a bore, she reminded herself. It was a blessing that he had something in which to pour his passion for he was unmarried and certainly in want of a wife.

Emily was just getting her feet under her when the duke skated near. She caught her breath nearly losing her balance. He had seamlessly turned around backwards and glided in front of Mr. Eldridge without interfering with the man's skating. He was quite marvelous. Emily remembered when she was so confident on the ice. She was indeed out of practice.

"Might I have a turnabout the ice with you, Miss Ingram?" He asked. Emily nodded eagerly and Mr. Eldridge allowed the duke to take over partnering her. She stumbled a bit in the exchange. The duke caught her and held her close. She marveled at the strength of his arms which held her upright easily.

"I was wondering when you would have heard enough about the projected yields of the south quadrant," The duke laughed with the confidence of one who had allowed her to languish just long enough before rescue.

"Oh, you let me suffer," Emily said with mock severity. She tucked her hand into the crook of his elbow using him for support as she worked to synch her pace with his long stride.

"Just long enough for you to appreciate my gallantry," he said laughing. She realized he had slowed to accommodate her. Still, she chided him.

"Gallantry? Oh no. You should have rescued me sooner. What sort of hero are you?" She said recalling their games of childhood. He had felt like her hero. How many times had he rescued her from some villain?

She glanced up at him, and realized he was gazing at her. Their eyes met with a near physical snap, heat pooling between them. Her concentration faltered then, but he held her steady. He settled her in closer, his right leg nearly against her left. She could feel the heat of him at her side, but she was steadier on her skates now regardless to the fact that her heart was beating like a drum.

The wind felt wonderful on her face and she remembered the rush of joy that came from skating, or perhaps it was being held in the circle of his arms. His footing was sure and although he was skating faster than she had previously attempted, while the duke held her, Emily had no fear that she might fall.

She hoped he didn't think she was exaggerating her clumsiness to convince him to hold her closer. She would not. On the other hand, it was quite exhilarating to be held so. Perhaps she should have done. The thought brought a smile to her lips.

The duke spoke, his voice a soft rumble in her ear, stirring her hair.

"It was you who skated past without even a *hello*," the duke said, his voice softly teasing.

"I did no such thing." Emily protested breathily. She would have said she had not seen him, but she knew that was not true. She was intensely aware of him. She noticed him almost instantly across the ice, watching him even as she buckled on her skates. She had been wanting to skate with him, but she did not tell him so.

"You were too far away," she pouted. "Would you have had me shout?"

"Yes," he said. "You should have shouted." His voice was low. Tingles of anticipation reverberated through her although she could not place exactly what it was she anticipated.

"I could not."

"I want to hear you shout my name," he said, his voice decidedly deeper. It seemed to touch some secret part of her. She felt as if she were strung tight as a bow.

"That would be most improper," she whispered.

"I suppose it would," he agreed.

She glanced up, thinking she would see a playful expression, boyishly sweet and teasing.

His expression was playful, yes, but there was nothing boyish about it. His eyes could have melted the ice around them, and the heat of it transferred instantly, to Emily. It suffused her body in a wave of desire. She hit a little nick in the ice, or perhaps just lost concentration in that moment and their easy glide was interrupted. It wasn't a stumble exactly, just a bit off balance, but his arms tightened around her.

He pulled her close to keep her safe, and she could feel the hard line of him against her body. He was so strong, so virile. The strength of his arm beneath her hand proved that he was no boy. He chuckled softly, the sound going straight to her core.

"Were you not enjoying your skate with Mr. Eldridge?" the duke asked with an edge of laughter. "Or, perhaps I was misinformed. Are you not fascinated with all things agricultural?" He grinned. "In particular, the balance between livestock and acreage; not to mention the proper work load for a two-year-old ox."

"I am shocked that you are able to recollect that. You do have a marvelous memory," she said as they resumed their skating.

"For what I wish to remember," the duke replied.

He pulled her into a spin. Emily squeaked, much to her chagrin as she held on tightly to the duke's arm. The flirtation was exciting and she felt a thrill at the banter.

She had regained her balance and when he loosed her to spin her; she was no longer overly awkward. In a moment, she was securely back in his arms, held so close she could hear his heartbeat. His skating was confident and he was so deliciously warm. She felt both secure and excited. There was nowhere she would rather be.

She did not remember when she had so much fun. Emily laughed aloud.

"Oh, that is a marvelous sound," he said with a smile. His lips were close to her ear and she could feel his breath warm upon her. "I adore the sound of your laugh."

When she looked up, his eyes sparkled with mirth. She thought that the sound of his voice was quite intoxicating too, but she did not say so.

His tone dropped a little lower. "Let us speak of pleasurable things. I should wish to hear more of your laughter."

She thought, simply listening to him whisper in her ear was entirely pleasurable, and brought to mind salacious feelings, but she could not tell him how moved she was by his very presence so she said nothing. She only sighed, content to be in his arms.

"You must know I shall ever be your knight in shining armor. Well, perhaps a little tarnished," he added.

"I do not mind," she said and his arm tightened around her suddenly. It made her catch her breath. "But I should have appreciated your gallantry all the more had you come to my rescue one quarter hour sooner," she teased.

"And I would appreciate your holiday more if you should choose to extend it," he quipped, but his tone was serious.

"Oh, how long would you have me stay?" she asked trying to keep the conversation light although her heart was beating faster than a hummingbird's wings.

"Oh," he said suddenly spinning them in a wide arc and pulling her in front of him, for a moment and turning them both backwards before he righted her.

She found herself leaning in to him to keep her balance; trusting him.

"Forever and ever," he said in a tone that recalled their conversations of yesteryear, but she heard wistfulness in his voice.

It did feel good to skate with him like this. He was skilled in the pastime, and she assumed that he had spent hours on the ice.

"I would have you stay," the duke said softly and leaned in to her so that he stood like a protective shield above her willowy frame. What exactly was he asking? Emily was unsure how to answer.

21

The duke suddenly reversed direction, pulling her close and spraying ice as he suddenly stopped, making a sharp turn to avoid some children who had cut in front of them. The sudden turn caused him to pull her close, and Emily felt wonderfully secure, but the emotion was lessened, perhaps by the children, or perhaps by the spray of ice itself.

She took a breath, settling herself.

Two young boys came to a skidding stop in an ungainly heap only a hand's breadth away from where the lovers stood. For, Emily was quite certain, lovers they were. The pair broke apart before anything more might be said and the duke helped the children to their feet. Emily was unsure she was yet steady enough to aid anyone. She smiled at the children.

How many times had she and Alexander skidded to a stop, narrowly missing an adult when they were children? She exchanged a glance with the duke and wondered if he was remembering too.

"Thank you, Your Grace," the smaller of the two boys chirped with a bow as Alexander righted him. "You know, my father has been real sick this year. He cannot shake the chills since the influenza. It was awful nice of you to send over those baskets of food. He says you are the best thing that happened to Bramblewood." The boy patted his stomach. "And your cook sure knows what she's doing. I think I shall miss it when Father gets well."

The other boy, who was a head taller poked his little brother, for they were surely brothers. Then the taller boy spoke in a hushed reverent voice, "Good day, Your Grace," he said somewhat nervously.

"Good day to you. Are you brothers, gentlemen?" Alexander asked sizing up the elder boy.

The little one nodded vigorously and spoke again regardless to his elder brother poking him. "Quit poking me," he hissed at his brother, and then turned back to the duke.

Emily had to stifle her laughter.

"John and Jimmy. I mean James Morgan, at your service, Your Grace." The little boy gave an elaborate bow, and Emily had to smile as the taller boy followed suit albeit shyly.

"I think my cook may have need of an additional kitchen boy this winter," Alexander said to the taller boy; John Morgan, Emily assumed. "But you would have to present yourself before the dawn on the morrow. You know the fires always need wood brought in by strong young lads?"

The boy's eyes opened wide.

"You mean that we could be servants in your household?" John said.

"You may," Alexander nodded. "If you are up to the task, Mr. Morgan. I think your brother is still a bit young."

"Thank you, Your Grace. You won't regret it," John said his eyes wide.

Alexander gave a slight shrug. "It will save a man the trouble of having to deliver supper to your father," he said. "Of course, kitchen boys eat in the kitchen."

"What about me?" the younger boy asked.

"Hush," his brother admonished him.

The duke smiled and assured both boys that the baskets would continue to come until his father had improved. "After which," he leaned forward with a conspiratorial whisper to Jimmy. "I am sure we can work something out for a fair price. Do you like to pick apples?"

"I sure do, Your Grace!" the young boy beamed. "I like to eat apples too!"

The duke laughed and it was a joyous sound. Emily wanted to hear more of it.

"Well, come next season, I could use some good climbers for the picking although you mustn't eat too many apples. I would not want you to get a belly ache."

"Oh, I won't," Jimmy said seriously. "My mum says it all goes in my hollow leg."

Emily burst out laughing and then covered her mouth.

The duke grinned at her and then turned back to the boys. "Will you spread the word among the village boys for me?" The boys nodded with enthusiasm. "None younger than you, mind? The cook makes a fine meal for all of the pickers, and usually some spare to take home."

"And apples?" pressed the younger boy.

"Yes," the duke said. "Apples."

Emily fondly remembered climbing the apple trees with Alexander. Some tree branches she could not reach, and the longer limbed boys climbed leaving Emily and Anne on the ground, but the apple trees tended to have low hanging branches that the girls could reach. Many times they sat in the branches and ate the fruit too. She found she missed those times. She was happy then. She wondered if she ever had been truly happy since.

With a whoop young Jimmy raced off to tell their mother, but the older John bowed with as much dignity as his lanky form could manage. "Thank you, Your Grace," he said seriously and then turned to hurry after his younger brother while their mother waved with gratitude from the hill.

"That was a very fine thing to do," Emily said as she tucked her hands into the crook of the duke's elbow and allowed herself to lean against the surplus of heat that radiated from his coat.

"It was nothing, really," he replied with a shrug.

"It was everything to those boys," she added. She could tell that the duke was uncomfortable with such praise and so it did not surprise her when he soon changed the topic.

They resumed their skate side by side. Emily glided ahead for a moment to collect her thoughts and then made an abrupt stop, turning around, to drift backwards before she spoke. Yes, she thought, she definitely had her skates under her now and unlike a dance in London, they could skate together for as long as they liked. The duke's thoughts must have run along the same lines.

"I am glad we were able to skate," he said.

"Why wouldn't we?"

"Year before last it never got quite cold enough to trust that the ice was thick enough to hold the skaters."

"How sad. Everyone must have been disappointed."

"Yes," he agreed as he took her hands in his, and swiveled her around so that he was going backwards instead of her. In a moment he pulled her back into his arms to skate with her.

"I must say, I have missed this," she said with a wistful sigh.

"The skating, Northwickshire, or..." he hesitated, "me?"

"All of it," she grinned. "Although I shall thank you for not getting an inflated opinion about it."

His deep chuckle resonated in her soul. "I have missed it as well," he replied. "Though, I have always had the skating and Northwick, so, mostly, it is you." He brought a gloved hand up to stroke her face and she remembered his warm hands on her face when they had gone riding. "I have missed you. I had almost gotten used to you not being here, but since your return, I have been reminded how much was lacking from my days."

Emily was overcome with emotion at his admission. It was the closest thing to a profession of love that she had ever received and her heart soared to the clouds. She pressed her cheek to his shoulder for the briefest of moments to revel in the pleasure of his words. His scent bore the sharp tang of wood smoke from the bonfire and his own musky aroma. It caused tremors of delight to flow through her. She was trembling for all the joy that wanted to burst forth from every inch of her being. Alexander mistook the tremble for a shiver and assumed a chill.

"Are you cold? We could move closer to the fire."

There was a raging bonfire on the shore at the other side of the lake, and people were gathered around it warming their hands, but she was happy right here in his arms.

She shook her head. "I am not cold."

"Do your fingers still lose feeling when you skate?" he asked.

"Always," she positioned her hands closer to his warmth. "I have always had difficulty with the cold in my hands even though I wear lined gloves."

"Yes," he chuckled. "I do recall." He stopped along the

far side of the lake and reached into his pocket. He revealed a spare pair of woolen mittens, just as he had done so many years before.

Emily gasped and cradled the mittens in her hands. He had remembered. She paused and turned to stare up at the man before her. "How did you..." she murmured.

"As I said, I remember what I wish to remember. They were my mother's," the duke said. "She made them the year before she died."

Suddenly the mittens felt even more special.

Emily looked into his kind eyes as he helped her to place the extra woolen layer over her own fine gloves. She could feel the outline of Alexander's fingers on hers and the warmth of the mittens as he pulled them over her hands.

"I think, you have not changed so much as you profess," he said.

But she had changed. Emily knew that now. She had come here, a girl toying with the idea of marriage. She thought that once she said yes to some gentleman, all would be decided and she would be content, but now she saw that was not so. She saw her whole life stretched before her. She knew marriage was so much more than a few words said in a church. It was love.

She was in love with Alexander. She felt she had always loved him. She loved him for a million small reasons. She loved him for cups of chocolate, and for ice skating and secrets shared on rainy afternoons. She had once thought that London had everything she needed.

Now, she knew that was not true. Everything she desired was right here, reflected in Alexander's eyes.

"I do hope that you will consider staying for a while here in Northwickshire. Here with me," he whispered.

Forever and ever, she thought, as he held out a hand to her. She found her heart was beating in her throat and she could not answer.

"Shall we?" he asked.

She looked up at him and putting her hand in his said, "Yes." He pulled her close and they resumed their round of the lake, their steps perfectly matched.

22

*E*mily still had not decided what she was getting her family for Christmas. Of course, she had already brought gifts from London for Aunt Agnes, Uncle Cecil, and her cousins. The youngest of which had taken to shaking the boxes daily and making wild guesses about what might be inside. Emily had taken Anne's idea and knitted Edmund a new scarf that he could wear skating. She still had her mother and father though to find some little trinket to show her love.

"Why didn't you get something in London?" her brother asked her when she begged him to take her into Northwick. He sighed and complained, but Emily coerced him into accompanying her to town.

She considered sending Robert a letter so that he might not think that she had forgotten him, but decided against it. That would be too forward. She did not think it wise to continue to encourage him until she had figured how to diplomatically inform him of her choice, and she was beginning to hope that choice would be the duke.

"So Father?" she said, hoping to elicit Edmund's help with the Christmas gift.

"Box of cigars," Edmund said without hesitation.

Emily wrinkled her nose.

"He doesn't have any hobbies," Edmund said. "He does nothing but work. What else can you get him? Personally, I thought of a bottle of fine brandy, but he would know that I only bought it so I could drink it myself."

Emily laughed. "That is not the purpose of a gift. The purpose is to make the person realize you are thinking of them and that you really know them and care about them."

"So, that's the problem," Edmund quipped.

"Do not tease," Emily said. "You know you love Father even when he annoys you."

"Do I?"

"What did you end up getting him? If you didn't get him the brandy, which was really for you?"

"Cravat."

Emily shook her head. "Didn't you get him a cravat last year?"

Edmund nodded. "But last year's was blue. He said it was too dark. This year it is white. He can't say that is too dark."

Emily laughed and then coaxed Edmund into showing it to her. She exclaimed that it was quite nice. "I don't suppose you would trade me?"

"Trade you?"

"Why don't you get him the cigars?"

Edmund considered his sister for a moment. "Then I would have to go into town to get them," he said.

"Exactly," Emily said with a smile. "We could go into town together."

"Alright," he said at last with a long suffering sigh. "I spoil you," he said.

"Yes, you do," Emily agreed. "That's because you love me."

"I will have someone hitch up the carriage." He pointed a finger at her. "But no more favors. You should have bought something in London. It is not like you to leave things to the last minute."

"I know, but I was so distracted with the suitor issue in London."

Edmund would have commented, but Emily quickly changed the subject back to Christmas presents.

On the way to town, they discussed Cousin William and his sisters as well as their other friends. They talked about gifts and skating and horseback riding. Edmund brought up the topic of the duke several times, but Emily adroitly side stepped her brother's inquiries.

Edmund patiently accompanied her to several stores looking for something for their Mother, but they remained empty handed. "I did see a sewing basket when I was browsing the other day," Emily said thoughtfully. "I suppose I could purchase that and perhaps put several skeins of embroidery thread inside."

"I think she would like that," Edmund said. "She does say sewing relaxes her."

"Yes, that's true," Emily said. "It is a very relaxing hobby. It's decided then."

By the time the siblings arrived at Harry Cole's Haberdashery a few minutes later, Edmund was decidedly bored with shopping.

They unexpectedly met with Henrietta and her maid. They spoke for a few minutes and Emily mentioned that she and Edmund still had to stop at the cigar shop.

"Why don't you join us for tea?" She invited Henrietta. Emily had started to warm to the girl and thought they could really be friends. She had her doubts the last time they took tea, but Emily thought perhaps she had in her own jealousy misjudged the lady. She wanted to be charitable this Christmas season.

"I would like that," Henrietta said with a genuine smile as they continued to browse the various notions on display in the shop.

"Why don't I buy the cigars?" Edmund said seeing a way to escape shopping with his sister now that Henrietta and her maid were also present. "I will meet you both at the teashop when you are finished. In fact, if you do not mind, I shall be at the pub side of the Arms. Have the footman bring you both over to the Northwick

Arms tearoom and send word when you are ready to
return home."

"That sounds fine," Emily said. "Henrietta and I will
not be long." She promised.

"No, certainly not," Henrietta said.

Emily fully felt herself increasingly at ease with
Henrietta while they selected the basket and Emily
picked out threads for her mother. Henrietta laughed
and found interesting things for them to add.

She talked about many things without any hint of
spiteful gossip or rumor. Emily learned much about her
reaffirmed friend. She discovered that Henrietta had an
eye for color and helped her choose just the right threads
to include.

"Is there anything else you wanted to purchase,"
Emily asked while the haberdasher, Mr. Cole, wrapped
her basket and threads.

"I just need to find a palate of watercolors."

"Here? In the haberdashery?" Emily inquired.

"Yes, they carry a limited amount of watercolors and
brushes. I keep telling Mr. Cole he should stock more,
but I don't think the other ladies go through paints as fast
as I do."

"Have you done many watercolors?" Emily inquired.

"I have," Henrietta said. In fact, Henrietta revealed
that she had sold several paintings in recent years to
well-moneyed buyers. Even the Regent had taken one
miniature for his mother's bedside table.

"You must be quite the skilled artist," Emily said.

Henrietta smiled at her with a slight flush. "You are kind for saying so."

"They sound quite lovely."

"Of course I gave all the proceeds to charity as I should," she added with a wave of her hand. "I would never have need to keep such things for myself. After all, I am not a professional artist."

"A philanthropic hobby, then," Emily observed. "I am afraid that I have no such talent."

"Nonsense," Henrietta said. "Your embroidery bests any I have seen."

"My mother taught me," Emily revealed. "She loves that sort of thing, embroidery and needlepoint."

"I remember. Those needlepoint pillows you made did well at the auction for the orphanage."

"Oh that was years ago," Emily said.

"Nonetheless, it is true."

Emily nodded. She did donate her work as well, but she did not have the passion for it that she saw in Henrietta, and she said as much. For Emily, it was a productive way to pass the time, and besides, a lady must have a talent.

They walked out onto the thoroughfare and Emily looked each way to get her bearings. She saw Griffith with the carriage across the way.

"The Arms is this way," Henrietta directed. "We could walk."

They started to amble along as they waited for

Griffith to bring the carriage around on the busy street filled with all manner of Christmas shoppers, carolers and Christmas cheer.

"Miss Ingram?" a voice came from behind and she turned to make sense of it Mr. Benedict, a playmate from her childhood, and one who had always been far too willing to force his aide upon Emily, approached with a grin and clasped her hands in greeting.

He completely ignored Henrietta. Could Benedict not see that Emily was with her companion, whom he rudely spurned in spite of Emily's multiple attempts to bring Henrietta into the conversation?

"You look to be in need of an escort," he said.

Mr. Benedict had set upon her and would not budge. Emily plastered a smile upon her face, but felt dread that she might not be able to politely rid herself of the man as he walked with them.

"We are only going a short distance," Emily protested. "My brother is waiting at the Arms."

The man pursed his lips. "In the pub?"

Emily could sense the censure in his tone. She began to explain that the footman would go find Edmund when they were ready to return to Sandstowe, but she realized she had no need to explain to the man.

"I am glad to see that you are well," he repeated for at least the third time.

"Why, might I ask, would I not be well, Mr. Benedict?" Emily asked finally with an edge to her voice.

"It is only that I have thought," his eyes strayed to Henrietta whom he had still not addressed, and he continued a little nervously. "It must by trying on your nerves to constantly have to curb your brother and his wayward friends. Surely, he does not expect to have you find him in a pub."

"Of course not. I shall send, Griffith," she said indicating the driver and footman who was struggling through traffic to get to them. Several carriages had pulled aside for other ladies and were blocking the narrow way.

"It is just that you have always been so proper and refined, ever the victim of their unruly ways." Mr. Benedict's eyes again strayed to Henrietta and Emily thought it was both Henrietta and her brother that he felt were not fit company.

Emily ruffled a bit in his saying that Edmund was less than genteel company even though she had chided her brother for the same. "I would not say that I was a victim in the past," she replied with cool civility. "Rather a willing compatriot."

"Oh, I meant no offense," he stammered. "Only that if you would prefer more refined company; why then, I would be your willing companion. Have you seen much of Northwick since your return?"

"More refined company?" Emily repeated.

"Mr. Benedict," Henrietta stepped forward and pursed her lips. "I hardly think you shall gain my friend's regard by insulting her brother." Her words were stern and yet delivered with a smile which was particularly cordial since the man clearly included Henrietta in his insult.

"Or my friends," Emily added turning away and tucking Henrietta's arm around her own. "Good day, sir,"

For a moment Emily thought that Mr. Benedict might follow and in that moment she wished to turn in a shop for ribbons and lace, but Henrietta gave Mr. Benedict her best reproachful stare and he desisted.

The man finally bowed away with a mumbled apology.

"Honestly," Henrietta hissed. "That some men can think to endear themselves by putting others down grates my nerves. I have never cared for Johnathon Benedict and I only pray that someday he gets scalded for all his stirring of the pot."

"He did seem rather self-righteous." Emily considered Henrietta and her words to Benedict and was glad of her help. "That was done as a friend," she said in amazement.

"I am your loyal friend," Henrietta replied with a squeeze of Emily's hand, "and hope you are mine."

"Of course," she reassured Henrietta. "I should tell you, my good opinion was restored long before this moment," Emily said and it was true.

Emily started to turn to wait as Mr. Griffith brought the carriage up, but noted a gentleman's shop with a silk shirt in the window. The silk shirt sported silver cufflinks and she realized that the shop was for metalworking. The store was not here when she had last been in Northwick, but Emily thought the metalsmith was quite talented. The cufflinks were unique.

"May we?" she said to Henrietta, looking at the shop.

"If you wish," she said and with a brief wave to Mr. Griffith so he could see that they stopped at this store, the ladies went into the shop.

All of Emily's other gifts had been decided, and she had thought her shopping was reduced to browsing, but she was sure the cuff links were perfect the moment she laid eyes upon them. The shopkeeper took them from the window for her to see.

"Would you mind very much if I just popped next door to the solicitor?" Henrietta asked.

"No, of course not," Emily said. Mother would be horrified that she was alone even for a moment, but the shop was bustling with other shoppers, both men and women, and it seemed no harm when the carriage with Mr. Griffith would be right outside.

Henrietta and her maid went next door while the shopkeeper retrieved the cufflinks from the window. Emily considered them. When she held them in her hand, she was decided. For the duke, she thought as she recalled how he had always used to remove his cufflinks and roll up his sleeves.

She had not seen him in shirt sleeves for years, much

less bare arms. The thought made her smile. She wondered if he still rolled them. Probably not. He would wear his jacket like a proper gentleman, and he would wear cuff links. Still, she remembered his mother, the duchess, had been in a constant state of agitation over how many cufflinks Alexander misplaced. No doubt some of them belonged to some long dead relative, and the duchess was always searching for replacements.

Henrietta returned, shoving an envelope too large for her reticule into the pouch. She looked up at the lady and smiled. Henrietta seemed to be glowing. She must have had good news at the solicitor, Emily thought, but she did not want to pry. Perhaps it was something about her father's will.

"Those are very nice," Henrietta said indicating the cuff links.

"They are, aren't they?" Emily said admiring the etching.

"For your Father?" Henrietta asked and suddenly it hit Emily how very improper this gift was. She could not give something of such value to a gentleman who was not her intended; even for an intended, such a gift was on the edge of propriety. She did not care. They were perfect. Emily nodded to the shopkeeper.

"Yes," she lied. "For my father." She handed them back to the shopkeeper. "Please wrap them," she said.

"Did you find everything you wanted, miss?" the shopkeeper asked.

"Yes. I believe so," Emily said.

She and Henrietta picked up their packages and walked out of the store. Mr. Benedict was nowhere in sight. Mr. Griffith had pulled the carriage close to the door; blocking other traffic in just the same way as previous carriages had done. It was not far to the Arms, but it was brisk outside, and Emily would rather be out of the wind.

Mr. Griffith handed them both up into the carriage and told the driver to take them to the Northwick Arms.

They rode in companionable silence. Henrietta seemed preoccupied. She was smiling from ear to ear, which made Emily smile too. She thought that perhaps Henrietta must have had good news at the solicitors. It would not be good manners to ask, but Emily could not deny she was curious.

In any case it was the season of good cheer, and Emily found her own mind went back to Alexander as they rode the short distance to the Arms. She could not wait to see his face when he opened the package with the cufflinks. He was not the only one who remembered things, she thought.

She realized that Henrietta has spoken to her.

"I do apologize. I was wool gathering," Emily said in request of Henrietta's forgiveness.

"Not to worry," Henrietta assured her, "I too have had much on my mind these past months. Is it a gentleman?"

The companionable squeeze and conspiratorial giggle that followed had Emily denying such a claim.

Although she liked Henrietta and found her a worthwhile companion, she also knew rumor followed the lady. The last thing that Emily needed was a rumor floating about her and the duke before she had a better grip on her own emotions and of course, until she could be certain that Alexander felt the same way. He had alluded to it, but had not declared himself outright.

"No," Emily said. "It is nothing."

"Oh," Henrietta looked disappointed. "I was hoping for good news," she said.

"There is a rumor that you have good news of your own," Emily said, fishing for details, but primarily attempting to turn the conversation away from herself.

"Yes," Henrietta said, her face breaking into a wide grin.

"So it is good news!" Emily said catching her hands. "Who?" she asked.

"I cannot say as yet. I should not want to jinx my luck." Henrietta said hugging her reticule close with excitement.

"But you have received an offer?" Emily congratulated her friend on a promising future.

"Not in such a formal way, not yet," Henrietta admitted, "but if it comes to pass, I would certainly be glad of the possibility."

"Then, I am happy for you." Emily pulled her friend into a hug. She knew that she had misjudged the woman in the past, but truly hoped the best for Henrietta these days. Her friend had every right to feel the same happiness and Christmas cheer that Emily wished for herself. "Truly, I am," she said.

"I would tell you," Henrietta explained, "but I think it is best if I do not. Not yet. Oh, I am sorry, Emily. I simply cannot. I cannot risk leaving a stone unturned. I must be absolutely sure of it, and its benefits, before I would wish our association made public," Henrietta confided. She put a finger to her lips. "I am sworn to secrecy."

"Well, then, perhaps you should not share if you have been sworn to secrecy." Emily offered her friend a smile so that she might know that no offense had been taken by the withholding of information.

"Oh," Henrietta groaned and waved her hand through the air as if keeping the secret was silly to consider in the first place. "I know that you will not tell. You are a true friend. I suppose I could tell you," she said, but seemed uncertain as to the wisdom of such action.

"No," Emily repeated laying a gloved hand on the lady's own hand. "I should be just as happy for you without you breaking your promise. You need not tell me anything other than that you feel joy."

"I do. I feel such joy, I can barely contain myself," she said. "You are a good friend, Emily," Henrietta said hugging her again as they pulled up in front of the Northwick Arms tea room.

Mr. Griffith helped Henrietta first, and as she began to step down from the carriage, the overly large envelope meant to hold documents and deeds caught on the side of the door and nearly fell out of her reticule.

"Oh," Henrietta said clutching at the satchel. She turned back towards the carriage and hastily stuffed the packet back into her reticule, but Emily saw the seal on it. She recognized it at once. The crest emblazoned on the front was unmistakably that of Bramblewood, more specifically, that of the Duke of Bramblewood.

She bolstered herself for a moment and clenched her fist. A thousand uncharitable thoughts sprang to her mind. She tried to push them away.

She knew that any assumptions that she might make would only breed hurt and confusion, and yet, that hurt had already taken root. She would not look at it. She would not confirm her suspicions.

There must be a reasonable explanation, Emily thought but she could not imagine what it could be.

"It bears the crest of Bramblewood," Emily blurted in accusation. "The duke's. If you have been in some congress…"

"No, it is nothing of the sort," Henrietta hissed. She grabbed Emily by the arm and nearly pushed the lady back into the carriage that they might not be heard by others.

Henrietta shut the door of the carriage in the footman's face leaving him standing on the street. Her voice was low. "You have promised me secrecy and I trust you more than any other. You must not tell anyone of this. You promised."

"Why should I keep the secret?" Emily replied. "How do you have such a thing?"

Emily was torn. She felt as if she were about to be ill. Why would Henrietta possess some legal paper with the crest of Bramblewood? Why would she wish to keep it a secret? Emily's mind raced as it ran through all manner of unhappy scenarios to explain the occurrence. None of them brought her joy.

"Please," Henrietta begged once more.

Emily felt her heart sink to her knees. Her doubts began to rise again against the lady. Every bit of her past animosity for the woman came rushing back. What had Alexander given her?

"You promised to keep my secret?" Henrietta begged and clutched at Emily.

The footman opened the door of the carriage. "Are you quite alright, Miss Ingram."

"Yes," she said.

"Tell Edmund I shall wait for him here. Henrietta and I will not want tea. The lady was just leaving," she said coolly.

Henrietta's frantic expression indicated that some members of the town had already noted a disturbance. "Swear it," she insisted. "Upon your honor and our friendship."

"Upon my honor," Emily said although it crushed her to do so. She was no longer certain she and the lady had a friendship.

Henrietta gestured to her maid and the two of them departed.

Emily sank back in the chair. She was beginning to

suspect that Henrietta was up to her old games. She remembered the rumors of Henrietta and the duke and the talk of a scandal before the lady went to Scotland. Her father had sent her away and now she was back. Emily realized with a sinking feeling that the duke had requested her return, and had made her a gift that required a solicitor's transfer.

A moment later, Edmund stuck his head in the carriage.

"Are you well, sister?" he asked immediately noticing her upset.

"Yes fine," Emily said her eyes closed against the pain.

Edmund climbed up and sat beside her, closing the carriage door against the chill. "I do not think so," he said. "I saw Miss Milford hurrying up the street. Did you two have words?"

"In a manner of speaking," she said. Emily laid a hand over her chest. She felt as if she had run a race.

Edmund sighed. "I cannot say I am sad about that. I know, you thought to be charitable to invite her to tea, but rumor follows that woman. Always has."

Emily caught her breath on a sob. Edmund was not helping.

"I want to go home," she said.

"Very well," he said, "if you are sure." He made no move to tell the driver to be on his way. "It's a good half hour ride after a long day of shopping," he reminded her, pulling out his handkerchief.

She took it from him, wiping her tears before they fell. "I know," she said.

Edmund nodded and opened the door of the carriage. A rush of cold air filled it as he spoke briefly to the footman. In a moment they were on their way.

"Do you want to tell me what happened?" he asked as the carriage moved forward.

Emily shook her head.

"Well, then, take a deep breath, and we will have tea once we return," he said. "It will make you feel better."

Emily nodded.

Edmund patted his sister's shoulder. "You know Mother says tea solves everything, and Mother is never wrong," He said.

Emily had to smile, but was a wan thing.

Inside, Emily was breaking apart. Although she did her best to remain calm on the exterior, inside Emily was in turmoil. The secret fiancé of Henrietta's was none other than Alexander, the Duke of Bramblewood. It must be. Henrietta was to marry the duke, and to make matters worse, she had even begged Emily to keep her confidence. Emily couldn't stop shaking.

Perhaps Edmund was right. A cup of tea would warm her. "I should wish tea sent to my room," she said, "I don't want anyone to see me just now."

"I will see to it," Edmund said, while Emily willed herself not to cry. "As soon as we are at Sandstowe, but Em, what on earth upset you so?"

Emily just shook her head. She could not tell him.

What could the duke have given Henrietta other that a promise of some sort...a promise of marriage or was it a more indecent proposal? Either way, it was something so important that it required a solicitor. So, where did that leave her? Emily felt her heart and her hope, break into a thousand pieces and felt that she might never recover.

Part 4

Let it Snow

23

*E*mily agonized over her knowledge for several days. She was so melancholy that Anne pressed her to rest to ensure that she was not at risk of illness. Emily did feel ill although she was certain that her symptoms were more akin to a sickness of the heart. Aunt Agnes worried over her niece's loss of appetite and offered to call for the apothecary, but Emily refused. An apothecary could not bring a cure for what ailed her.

How the duke might deign to offer for two ladies was beyond her comprehension. No. That was not accurate. He had obviously made some promise to Henrietta. He had never made any such overt commitment to Emily, but he had made overtures toward her. How was it that she had misunderstood?

He had called upon her regularly, made an effort to discover whether or not she had a beau in London. He had made no mistake at his flirtations. Whether he had intended to or not, he had purposely led Emily to believe that he cared for her as more than a friend. How had she let this happen?

The old Alexander she had known would never have been so false. Nor would Emily have expected such behavior from the man that she thought she had come to know in recent weeks. Yet, a small part of her brain reminded her that this was just what she feared. The duke's father had had a reputation for toying with ladies, even in the very presence of his own spouse.

Perhaps, Alexander had grown to see no fault in such behaviors. Perhaps, it was the single surviving flaw passed from father to son. Emily bristled at the thought. One who behaved in such a way had no right to call himself a gentleman. It soured her opinion of the duke.

She had made excuses to remain behind from several parties in the hope that any memory of her affection for the duke might be dulled over time. However, her family often returned from their excursions with tales of the gentleman in question and his expressions of concern for her health. She could not believe he still asked after her when he kept company with Henrietta. It was disgraceful.

Emily curled up in the plush chair in front of the fire in her bedchamber and had done little else all evening, but wonder about the party that she had refused to attend.

"His Grace asked after you again," Aunt Agnes said as she peeled the gloves from her arms and then pulled them off finger by finger. She stepped forward to press the back of her hand to Emily's forehead. "As did Miss Milford," she continued. "They both hovered all evening so that they might hear news of your state."

Emily scoffed and pulled the blanket tighter around her. Of course, Alexander and Henrietta would remain at one another's side, she thought. How they must be laughing at her. How much longer would it be until the call for the banns was made and everyone in Northwickshire would know that they were to marry?

Emily remembered the rumor of Henrietta's loose virtue before her removal to Scotland, and now, she had proven rumor true, or was Alexander truly in love with her? The thought hurt more than was bearable.

"Emily," her aunt knelt at her side. "Are you ready to tell me true? People are beginning to worry in earnest."

Emily sighed. "I simply feel out of sorts. That is all."

"Do you think me simple?" Aunt Agnes offered a pitiful smile. "I am not so inexperienced as to not recognize heartbreak when it is before me. I know the signs."

"You do?" Emily sat up and looked into her aunt's eyes with hope. "You have felt the same?"

"Yes." Aunt Agnes gave a solemn nod. "Although, I must tell you, your uncle still wishes to call the physician, and I cannot put him off much longer."

"I am sorry," Emily said sitting up and pushing her strangling hair from her face. "Who broke your heart, Aunt Agnes?"

"The very same fool of a man I married." She said. "In time, we got it sorted, but that was a long while ago. Tell me what ails you, Emily. I cannot help you mend the hurt if I do not know the cause."

Emily shook her head. "No one can fix what ails me. He is planning to marry another."

"I do not think so. I believe the young duke is true in his intentions," Aunt Agnes said as she squeezed her niece's hand.

"How do you know it is he who has given me this heart ache?" Emily asked.

"Darling," her elder smiled. "The duchess and I used to fantasize that you two might one day accept the love that blossomed between you. Even as children, it was obvious, although neither of you seemed to know it. You have always been drawn to each other; understood one another. We remembered the two of you with your heads together even as babes. That made the bond all the more special."

Emily could not believe it. Whatever was her aunt saying?

"He has been enamored of you for years. I cannot believe he would be untrue now." Aunt Agnes shook her head. "No. I am certain he would not."

"True?" Emily scoffed. "True? True to whom?" A tear rolled down her cheek in spite of her willing it to remain at bay at least until she could be alone. She felt stupid, silly for being so upset, and yet, never before had she felt such a soul-crushing agony.

"True to you, of course," Aunt Agnes replied.

Emily snorted in a harsh and unladylike manner. "Me and however many other women he has fooled into such thoughts."

"I am sure there is no other," Aunt Agnes said gently, and patted the younger lady's arm. Emily didn't think her aunt would be purposely hurtful, but she was belittling Emily's feelings. It was clear that she did not believe her.

"I know for certain of one other save myself," Emily sniffed. "That would make two without question."

"Tell me who and I shall give you my estimation." Aunt Agnes resolved.

Emily pursed her lips. Would Aunt Agnes estimation be more believable than evidence she had seen with her own eyes?

"Henrietta Milford," Emily said flatly. "We have all known for quite some time that she has a secret betrothed. All this time it has been Alexander."

"It cannot be," Aunt Agnes gasped. "All that business with Henrietta was pure rumor." It was clear that Aunt Agnes had no rebuttal other than a simple claim that she had never noted any particular affection between the pair, save friendship.

"And others would only note friendship from my position as well," Emily hiccuped and wiped her eyes upon her sodden handkerchief. "He has played us both false; just like his father before him."

"Oh no. He is nothing like his father," Aunt Agnes continued. "I cannot think it so."

"Then we have both been fooled by his duplicity," Emily declared. "He has given her a promise. I saw his seal upon the paper myself."

Aunt Agnes' mouth dropped open. She sat heavily on the bed.

"You see," Emily cried. "That is why I can no longer face him. I have been made a simpering fool when I would have been better off maintaining my resolutions."

"You must speak to him," Aunt Agnes said to Emily's never ending surprise. "I am sure that there is an explanation. You must not be distraught until you know the truth of it. He owes you that much. At which point, if it is true, you may walk away with your head held high and be better for it."

Emily nodded. She knew that her aunt was right, but she did not think she could do it. How could she stand before him and hear him say that he would marry Henrietta?

There were too many questions, and she needed to speak with Alexander before she jumped to conclusions, but how could she? Just the thought was enough to make her burst into tears. Oh, she should have kept her resolve. Robert Hawthorne never made her feel so!

She sniffed and considered. Could it be a misunderstanding? Could this all have been Henrietta's doing? It was true that Henrietta did not have the best reputation when it came to her pursuance of men. Emily cursed herself for such low thoughts of the lady with whom she had only recently renewed her friendship. Still, she could not help but harbor ill will.

Emily felt duped. Henrietta had chased a title and gotten exactly what she wished. Emily, on the other hand was left bereft for the foolish hope that childish friendship could blossom into love. She should have kept to her plan and accepted Robert Hawthorne. In fact, she should write to the man this very night.

That evening, she lay in bed and agonized over her predicament. She would have to meet Alexander with confidence. She could not fall into a flurry as she very much wanted to do. No. She was stronger than that.

She would not bow to her own emotions. Emily closed her eyes and willed away the thoughts of her love. Try as she might, they continued to roll through her mind. She told herself that she felt only compassion, nothing more, for the hurts that he had endured: the loss of his mother and the wayward upbringing under his father's care.

He was a child of her past; a companion. That was all. She was in search of a gentleman that she could call husband certainly not a boy who used to tuck sticks into her braids while she lay in a field. Why did such thoughts produce heat? She asked herself.

The thought of him touching her hair, tucking it behind her ear, brought back images of the holly he had placed there just days ago. Desire twisted within her. How badly she wished he had kissed her that day, or any other had the opportunity arose. At least then she might know what it felt like to be in his arms. Now, she would never know, and worse yet, she would always wonder for what might have been.

She turned her pillow over, trying to find the cool spot and sleep, but rest would not come. Soon enough she would need to face the man that she loved, who would not, could not, love her in return. At the very least she could conserve her pride and her dignity. That is, she reminded herself, if she could resist him.

Emily prayed for a simple answer; that Henrietta had lied or that she had mistaken the Knoxington emblem for that of Bramblewood. They were not altogether that different. Please, she begged of any who would listen, let there be some explanation.

ALEXANDER HAD neither seen nor heard from Emily in over a week. She refused all visitors and had missed several gatherings that her family had attended. It brought fear to his heart that she was not well. So many had not fared well after the influenza bout and were still harboring remnants of the illness.

He cursed and slammed the almanac shut upon his desk. Something was wrong. Last they had last spoken at the lake he had been certain that her feelings were similar to his own. What occurred in the days after to change matters, he could not discover. All Edmund had been able to tell him was that Emily had taken to bed after an excursion to town where they had met with Henrietta.

It made no sense. Henrietta was well. Alexander had seen her in town several times in recent days and her spirits were high. They had worked out a solution to their difficulty and the matter was settled, but that was nothing new, or indeed anything to which Emily ought to have been made privy. Edmund had been certain that his sister was not ill, but could not say what may have caused her upset.

"Perhaps she had a row," Edmund suggested once when they had met in the pub for an afternoon meal. He raised a suggestive eyebrow at Alexander.

"Not with me," the duke replied.

Not Henrietta either. Unless, Henrietta was lying to him. He could not imagine it so. He had always considered the lady a close confidant and friend. Perhaps that was the issue.

The duke slammed his hand into the table, causing several other patrons in the pub to jump. If some busybody was re-spinning rumors then he would rain down upon them a wrath unlike any other. Even then, it would not be enough. Not if he were unable to win back the hand of his love. Not if Emily accepted Robert Hawthorne; a man with no complications, who could give of himself without concern. If the duke disliked the

Hawthornes before, he hated them now, if only for the knowledge that Emily deserved nothing less than the perfect life Robert would provide.

Blast it, he loved her so. He would not allow the sins of his past to cost him Emily's affections. With Emily at his side Alexander knew that Bramblewood would be a success. Beyond that, he would be happy. He would never bring her shame as his father had done. He would not have her fear that there was any other in his life but her; only his Emily.

He took a deep breath and ran his hands through his hair.

He tried to reassure himself that Emily would remain resolute, but it did not take long for him to recall that she had never truly given anything, but a vague reply. Not that he had ever outright asked for her hand he amended.

Still, the thought lingered. Might she refuse him?

He was a duke. The title meant nothing to Emily. He considered sending a letter to her father, but he wanted Emily to want him, and not agree to marry him because her father insisted. Would the viscount insist or would Emily's mother advise caution due to his own father's reputation? The thoughts made Alexander's head ache. The possibility that Emily would refuse him was high and the risk was an ever present concern, still there was no help for it. Emily must be fully certain of his intent.

The next time that he saw her, he determined, he would leave no doubt as to his feeling. He would lay his heart before her. He would let her know that he loved her and leave the cards to fall as they may; as she willed. The thought terrified him.

He prayed that she would accept him. His happiness depended on her word.

24

---

*C*hristmastide was meant to be a time of joy and celebration and Emily could no longer avoid the outings. She could no longer feign illness. There were only so many headaches of which one could complain before someone threatens to call the physician. Since Emily knew her melancholy could not be cured by medical means, she would have to at least pretend to enjoy the gaiety of the season.

It was one of her favorite times of the year. The greenery was hung and the tables were covered with apples and holly berries decorated the doorways. As she set out the gifts for the children's enjoyment she thought that she might never look at Christmas holly the same after this year.

In only a few weeks' time, her cousins would open their gifts and exclaim over the wonderful things that she had brought them from Town. The small box of cufflinks she had purchased for Alexander felt like a heavy stone amongst their number.

When she had rediscovered the package she wished to cast the offending item away. She could not give them to the duke, but neither could bring herself to return the gift. She placed the box in the back of her dresser drawer. Perhaps she would give them to Robert Hawthorne one day. No, she thought. She could not do that either. She would give them to Father, as she had said. Yes, that was it. She felt like her heart had hardened into a lump of coal within her chest.

The Christmas Ball was to be hosted at Hedgewick, the residence of a local marquess. Everyone who was anyone in the district had been invited and Emily could not miss another party, particularly one that promised to be so full of holiday spirit.

The snow had turned to slush with the carriage wheels and the trampling of horses, but inside the festivities were in full swing as Emily entered the ball escorted by her brother.

Hedgewick looked like a magical land that had bloomed within the spacious manor. Candles twinkled from every surface and there was little by way of décor that had not been draped or sprinkled with every possible type of holiday greens. Bursts of color from the flowers and holly kept the rooms from becoming overwhelmed by a single color.

Emily had chosen an elegant gown of forest green in the hope that she might not stand out amongst the crowd. "Yes," she told herself. "Blend in with the greenery." With so many people in attendance, she had high hopes of avoiding the two in particular who had been most on her mind.

Her plan was thwarted; however, as the duke himself was waiting to greet his friends near the entrance hall. He expressed his concern for her health and pleasure that she was now feeling well enough to attend the ball. He offered to escort her into the ballroom. There was little that Emily could do but accept, the ice that encased her heart cracking painfully.

The duke searched her face and Emily was reminded how observant he was. She knew he was looking for any remaining sign of illness. He secured her a seat so that she might not expend what little energy she had recouped.

"I assure you, there is no need," Emily repeated with a tight smile, but Aunt Agnes countermanded that suggestion.

"It would do me well to know that you had stayed by my darling niece's side, Your Grace," Aunt Agnes said with a look of convincing concern. "She has been so weak that I fear she cannot be left even for a moment."

Emily narrowed her eyes at her aunt who only smiled blandly at her.

"I shall take the task with pleasure," Alexander said with a nod of stern commitment.

Emily supposed her aunt's reasons for throwing them together were twofold. Firstly, she had charged Emily to speak with the man and in her aunt's experience such matters had been resolved to a positive end, although Emily did not expect such a result. Secondly, it seemed to be a sort of penalty that Aunt Agnes was exacting for Emily's falsifying illness.

She gritted her teeth and realized that she was meant to be punished for her dramatic behavior. That chastisement, in full, was an entire evening under Alexander's care. She could not decide how she felt about that fact. On the one hand, she was terrified to know in truth that he was to marry Henrietta, and on the other hand, just being near him made her heart beat with the cadence of a drum.

Aunt Agnes waved a jovial farewell as she disappeared into the crowd, but not before she threw a wink in Emily's direction. She seemed quite pleased with herself, Emily thought.

An unladylike word rose to mind, but Emily kept it to herself. She looked up at Alexander, and then over to Edmund. Both were watching her with rapt attention. She sighed and made for the refreshments. If she could lose her guards she might just be able to find a relaxing corner in which to pass the evening.

"I have missed you," the duke said.

"Truly?"

"Yes. Your family said you have been ill. Was influenza the difficulty?" he asked.

She gave him a look as if to say, I am not going to

discuss my illness with you, but she still felt soiled with the untruth between them.

"My apologies," he said quickly. "I do hope you are well." He took her cup and began to fill it with wassail punch from the bowl.

"Well enough," she replied without looking at him. Instead, her eyes scanned the crowd for Edmund who had already slipped off to leave the pair alone. Traitor, she thought. She could have used his ever present wit.

Emily refused to reveal the hurt that the duke had brought to her for fear that he might request an explanation. Instead, she did her utmost to appear as if his calls upon her as well as the afternoon at the frozen lake had never happened at all. She would behave as she had upon her first arrival in the county; warm and friendly, but not encouraging of any interaction beyond a pleasant acquaintance.

She certainly would not mention that she was aware of the lovers' secret. No, Henrietta had been correct in her assumption that Emily would hold her tongue. She knew how to keep a secret. The confidence that she had shared with her aunt would be kept, and Emily had no fear that any rumor would spread from Aunt Agnes' lips.

The ballroom soon filled with dozens of guests vying for a turnabout the dance floor. In spite of the thorn in her side that was otherwise known as the Duke of Bramblewood, Emily found herself enjoying his company. She tried to hold herself apart, but it was no use.

The atmosphere was over all jolly and there seemed to be no reason to allow one gentleman to dampen her mood, even if that gentleman stuck to her side like a burr. The holiday season was in full swing and there was no better way to celebrate Christmastide than in the country. Alexander kept a close attendance upon her and each time he touched her, her heart did a little flip-flop no matter how she told the organ to be still.

"So how do our country balls compare to London?" The duke asked with an ever-present smile.

"I cannot pretend to have experienced anything quite like it," she replied.

It was true that the celebrations and decorations of the holidays were shared with more freedom in the country than a town residence allowed. There was something magical about it that made Emily wish that she could live in the moment forever. She was ever conscious of the topics they must not approach, namely his intended or the possibility of hers. The skirted around the topics adroitly like accomplished skaters weaving in and out of danger.

"Ah yes, you were not yet out upon your last visit," the duke recalled taking the conversation to an easier time.

"No," she confirmed. "Nor for several years afterward. Mother has strict rules as to what is appropriate in that regard."

"And you always follow the appropriate rules?" He teased.

The whispered comment suddenly incensed her.

"Yes," Emily snapped. "Someone must."

The duke looked stunned; perhaps it was hurt.

She turned her back to him just in time to avoid the extension of his hand. She caught the movement from the corner of her eye. She pretended to have not noticed the duke's offered arm. It was simpler that way, and although her heart raced with the thought of dancing with him, she knew that it would break the fragile resolve that she had mustered. Even now, being so near him, she feared it would crumble.

"Miss Ingram," his deep voice spoke from behind her, so close that she could feel his breath stir the loose tendrils of hair that fell from those that were piled on top of her head. She closed her eyes in sweet agony, glad that he could not see the difficulty that it took to collect herself.

"Would you do me the honor of joining me for a dance?" The duke asked.

Emily's breathing was fast and shallow. She had to get control of herself. She blinked rapidly and looked up. When she turned, she made certain that the tears welled in her eyes had abated even though the pressure that they might reappear at any moment still remained.

"I do not think it prudent," she said with much difficulty.

"Why-ever not?" The duke questioned.

"I am not entirely well enough," she lied with a small shrug.

The duke took a single step forward under the guise

of looking out over the crowd, but the truth of it was that it gave him the opportunity to speak directly into Emily's ear. "I think we are both aware that you were never ill," he said.

"How dare you!" She hissed, but she gave away the truth of the matter by looking up at him with a sharp gasp. How had he guessed? A moment later she set her jaw with firm resolve, clenching her teeth.

Edmund, of course, she realized. Her brother would have no way of knowing that it was from the duke that she was hiding, and therefore, had meant no harm by his words. She ought to have spoken with Edmund and warned him to hold his tongue so that this might have been avoided, but it was too late for that now.

"I am afraid that I do not know of what you speak," Emily replied with surety.

"You know exactly," the duke murmured his lips so close to her ear that she felt the brush of them against her skin like a kiss. Her breath caught in that instant, but she knew that the contact had been fleeting enough that there was no chance at being overseen. The room was far too crowded. As such, Emily had must do her best to hide the visceral reaction that had taken hold and left her trembling.

"You can tell me, you know?" Alexander coaxed. "We've always been able to share with one another. If nothing else, I can listen. Please tell me what has upset you so?"

"There is nothing," she snapped. "Everything is just the same."

Emily could see from his expression that he did not believe her, but what did it matter? He had said that they had always been able to share with one another, but he had failed to tell Emily about Henrietta. He had led her to believe he cared for her alone. If he could keep secrets, then so could she.

"Alright," the duke sighed and stepped away. Once again, his hand lay out between them. "If all is well, as you say, then you should have no reason to decline my offer."

The equivocation shook her. She knew that they were speaking of the dance, but there was a resolve in his eyes that made her wonder if he had chosen his words with a different meaning intended. Either way, she had been cornered. She could either stick to her insistence that nothing was wrong and dance with the duke, or refuse and be forced to explanation.

Her fingers shook and she willed them steady as she laid her cool gloved hands against the warmth of his skin. His fingers folded around hers and she thought of his enfolding her hands in his own as he pulled on the woolen mittens.

She looked into his blue eyes and realized they were dark as night. Be still, she told her rebellious heart. It was beating fast as a galloping horse, and yet, going nowhere. She knew that the battle within her could not be won.

Alexander tucked Emily's hand into the crook of his elbow and led her toward the floor. Her first country dance would be with the duke. At least it was not a waltz. The very thought sent a shiver of excitement through her.

She reminded herself that she was meant to be cross with him, but her heart would not obey. She wanted to dance with him. She always had and knew that she had no power to decline this chance to be in his arms no matter what he had done.

His expression softened now that she had capitulated, and try as she might, she could not help but return his smile. Was it possible she could be mistaken? Slowly, she released her breath, hopeful that he could not feel her trembling beside him. If there was one thing that she knew about the duke, it was that he was observant. She doubted he had missed any of her tells. He only smiled at her.

Emily noticed that from the edge of the dance floor Henrietta's eyes followed the pair as they made their way to their positions and the moment was destroyed. Emily felt her cheeks burn under the lady's observation. Would her friend interpret this as a betrayal of Emily's confidence?

Not that there was anything inappropriate about two friends partnering down the line. After all the duke could not dance more than two sets with his surreptitious love without inciting gossip, especially if he was intending to keep their association secret for much longer. Emily placed her hand in the duke's and tried to convince herself that the flutter in her stomach was merely the result of her enjoyment of the party and holiday cheer.

ALEXANDER KNEW that something was deeply wrong from the moment Emily entered the hall. Her entire demeanor had changed. They had only just begun to feel natural around each other again, and now that was lost. Emily had shut him out, hiding behind a mask of propriety.

She kept him at an arm's length as best she could, but he could feel that she wanted to be with him as badly as he longed to be with her. They were drawn to one another, like moths to a flame, and perhaps that attraction was just as dangerous. It hurt him to think that after everything going so well, she now resisted their attraction. Why?

Had she accepted Robert Hawthorne? The very thought made him sick with worry. What if her mother forced her hand? He knew the viscountess had no love of him. It could be that Emily had no choice.

The Lady Kentleworth was a force to be reckoned with and was not above arranging her children's marriages herself. Still, he thought, as he drew Emily closer by instinct, as if holding her in this moment would keep her close to him always. Could not Emily resist such demands for the sake of the friendship they had once shared?

He wanted to take her in his arms and never let her go. He wanted to declare his love for her right now in this very moment, but the middle of an open dance floor was neither the time nor the place. He wanted to grasp her by the shoulders and demand to know why she was being so stubborn, demand to hear that she loved him in return.

That approach would not go over well either, he thought as he monitored her struggle to quell her enjoyment. Besides, he admonished himself, Emily was not the dramatic type and would certainly be cross if he embarrassed her by making her the center of a spectacle.

The country dance lasted nearly a half hour and the duke was glad for it. After a time, Emily stopped glancing around to see who was watching and even softened the firm set of her jaw so that he stopped worrying for the sake of her teeth. A time or two, she even leaned into him and he could smell the faint floral scent of her hair.

They had never danced together, not really. Children playing on the lawn and hopping about was not the same thing. This was something different, and the ebb and flow of the music, the coming and going of their dancing, was as natural as if they had practiced it a thousand times.

Couples turned and parted, wove amongst the other dancers, and made their way between the rows with a flare of excitement and skill. By the time the music stopped Emily was breathless and laughing. The duke's heart soared, and he felt as if all were right in the world just for the pleasure of that feminine sound.

"You approve?" The duke asked. The question was directed at Emily's enjoyment of the ball, but he wondered if she understood the deeper meaning of his words. He knew that her mother wished her to return to London and remain close, but could she stay? Would she stay, for him? He searched her eyes for confirmation, and when they widened, he knew that his meaning had not been missed.

"The Marquess hosts a magnificent party." Emily's reply was the safe response, and the duke was wise enough to recognize it as such.

It seemed they were still dancing, only now in conversation. He could not understand why she was now holding herself aloof. Was it not only a short while ago that she had returned his flirtations? He recalled skating when she had settled against him in such a way as lovers do. How he longed for a return of that openness, but she had shut him out.

Had he pressed two hard, been too obvious in his pursuance of her? He had meant to make himself clear, but Emily had rigid expectations of what was proper, and perhaps she had thought him too persistent. What else could he do with Edmund reminding him that Robert Hawthorne was in the offing?

He could not give up now, not when his future, his happiness, lay on the line. He needed to know how she felt and needed her to know, beyond a doubt, of his devotion. They had moved to the edge of the floor so that the other dancers might begin, and he followed her to a seat in a remote corner. Now was as good a time as any, to confess his love, he thought.

"If Christmas balls are not reason enough to consider extending your stay in the country," his gaze pressed her to give him any sign of her affection, "then, perhaps, there might be some other reason that you might be persuaded to consider?"

Her eyes narrowed and her gaze hardened as if he had upset her with his words. He felt at once that she was slipping away from him, and he did not know how to stop the decline. Why was she so hardened against him?

"I think not," she replied in a cold tone that was unlike anything that he had ever heard from her gentle voice. "There is nothing that could convince me to continue on as things have been."

The words felt like a stab to his heart, to his gut. Nothing, she had said. What she felt was nothing. He was bereft.

25

What on earth was he asking, Emily wondered? For her to stay in Northwickshire? She agonized over his words and the only conclusion that she could come to was that he was a rake. He must have found his father's tactics acceptable and thought that he too could enjoy the comforts of several women at once.

What did he expect of her? That she might be willing to live her life under the guise of their friendship, as his mistress? The very thought brought a blush to her cheeks. Or had she misunderstood entirely? Was it Henrietta who was to be his mistress? That thought brought her a wave of disgust. He intended to marry one woman and toy with the other. Did it matter which he wanted as a mistress and which as a wife?

He was an awful man, just like his father.

How could she ever have thought that he could love

her? Even as the thought went through her mind, a spike of pain followed it with swift vengeance upon her heart. Emily had suspected, had wondered, and even hoped that she was in love with Alexander, but in that moment she knew it to be true. She was in love with him.

It did not matter that he would marry another. It did not matter if he was false. Her heart belonged to him. She felt the tightness in her chest and the tears filling her eyes. She could not breathe. She could not stand here in front of him and allow him to say such wonderful and heartbreaking things. Love or no, she would not stoop so low as to be any man's mistress, nor the wife of a man who would keep one.

"Emily," he whispered and reached for her, but she jerked her arm away like someone who had been scalded with boiling water.

The use of her given name felt like an affront. Without another word, she turned upon her heel, and rather than listen to whatever it was that he might try to say, she ran. She did not stop until she had reached the isolation of the breakfast room which would be abandoned until the card players gathered later in the evening. If she could have been sure where the ladies retiring room was, she would have escaped there, but in her upset she was lost in the unfamiliar manor.

Emily wrapped her arms around herself as if to hold herself together. She was gasping for breath, and it was all that she could do to prevent the tears from falling. The turn of the latch upon the door told her that he had followed her, but she refused to turn, afraid that he might see the truth, the devastation, in her face.

"Emily," his voice was low and calm, "I am sorry if I have caused you distress. I never meant..." She heard him approach and stop several feet away. "I would never have spoken if I had not thought that, somehow, you might feel the same."

"I do not," she whispered, but the hitch in her voice gave her away.

"Turn then and tell me outright that there is no hope for me. Tell me that you do not love me, and I promise that I shall never bother you with my affections again."

He waited.

It took Emily several minutes to gather herself, but even then, she could not bring herself to face the man that she loved. For that was the truth. It would always be the truth. She loved him desperately. Even though he was promised to another, she loved him still. The knowledge crushed her soul, and she felt as if the world had crumbled beneath her feet. There was no solid ground.

"Emily, look at me."

She could not.

"Tell me what I have done to turn you against me, and I shall correct it," he begged.

She almost believed the hurt in his voice. Almost believed that he cared. Yet he was false. He had to be. He had learned from the best. Learned how to convince more than one lady that his intentions were true, even when he only had his own interests at heart. He was a cad. How could she possibly be taken in by him? The deception of it tore through her like physical pain.

"Emily, please."

"I know about Henrietta," she blurted.

Emily finally worked up the courage to face him. His shoulders sank like one who had been dealt a great blow. The truth was there, written on his face; the shame that he had been caught.

"What?" he muttered. The word was a question, but there was no confusion in the duke's eyes. He knew exactly to what she referred, and he did not deny it. Her own words felt like a sword through her heart.

"You do not deny it?" Emily whispered. She was not quite sure how she was speaking; how she was standing when she was dying inside.

The duke shook his head sadly looking at the floor like a chastised child. He did not meet her eyes, but muttered, "How? How did you learn of it?" He raised pain filled eyes to her.

"That is all you have to say for yourself? How did I find out?" The hurt turned suddenly to anger. It welled up in a great wave that drowned the pain. Emily was livid now. "Henrietta told me herself," she replied with as much pride as she could muster. "Is it untrue then?" Even now, she hoped he would deny it.

"No," he grunted. "If you have heard it from Henrietta directly then she would have told you true. After all, she was there," he whispered.

Emily felt crushed by the thought alone. How she managed not to burst into tears she did not know, but her lips kept forming words as if she needed the torture of them. "How could you have kept such a secret?" she breathed.

"Because I was afraid that I would lose you." The duke reached out as if to touch her arm.

Emily recoiled. "How dare you!"

He ran his hand through his hair instead, looking thoroughly bereft. The rumpled waves were mussed and the gentleman appeared utterly out of sorts.

"You should be ashamed of yourself," she hissed. "You owe Henrietta better, and myself as well."

"I know."

Emily could not quite bring herself to stop. She wanted to chide him, perhaps to hurt him as he had done to her. Her tone was hard. "You are no better than your father. No man worth his name would abandon a lady after having acted so."

The duke's recoiled at her harsh rebuke, but his head snapped back as he took her meaning. "You would have me marry her?" he said through gritted teeth.

"Yes!" Emily cried. Tears were now streaming freely down her face. "No more hiding. No more secrets. You owe the lady your honor and respect. You know it is right." She crossed her arms before her both to help keep herself steady and to create a barrier between them. "The time for childish excuses is past," she said at last. "This is your folly and I want nothing to do with it or with you."

"I love you," he said plaintively, like a child begging for a sweetmeat, as if love made any difference at all now. There were plenty of couples who were in love and could not be married, she thought. There were just as many who had been required to fulfill the promise of marriage even when there was no love involved.

"It does not matter," she replied with a shake of her head.

His pained expression was anguish itself.

"It matters." His voice was raw with the depth of his emotion. "If you love me?"

Emily could not bring herself to answer. He repeated the question and she cried all the harder for her inability to deny it. Silent tears coursed down her face. She ignored them. They did not matter. She brushed them away angrily, and yet she clung to the anger so that he would not see that she simply wanted to disappear into a cloud of smoke so that he would not witness her mortification. She stepped forward taking control even as her heart was breaking to pieces before him.

"Emily, please, say that you love me."

She should ignore him. She should leave. She could not make her feet move. She hesitated in the doorway and leaned upon the frame. After several minutes had passed and she still had not moved, he stepped forward.

"You are standing under mistletoe," he pointed out with a soft voice.

Her head shot upward and searched for the plant as if she could will the thing to shrivel and die by her very gaze. The action had caused her to reveal herself and she was sure that the duke was granted with a clear view of her heartbroken expression.

"Em," he began again, so softly. The use of her nickname almost undid her. She shook her head, but did not move or speak. He stood close enough that they were both canopied by the offending bough. He reached out just shy of touching her.

"I won't if you would rather not," his voice was a whisper, but it reverberated around her. "I would do whatever you wish."

Her mind screamed for her to tell him to go away, but her heart pleaded that she loved him. She could not deny him. Not this once or else she would forever wonder. Only a strangled sob slipped from her lips and she knew that her heart lay exposed.

She reached for him, and he took her into his arms in one swift motion. She did not fight him. He was so unutterably gentle, and she wanted this. She wanted him. He clung to her desperately and she returned his embrace. Her ear pressed to his rabidly beating heart.

He reached down to her face and thumbed away a tear as she looked up at him. For one frozen moment she thought that he would kiss her. His mouth hovered, but an inch away, and she could feel his breath upon her lips. His breath trembled, like her own.

He cupped her face in his hands most tenderly as if she would break. He thumbed one tear from her cheek and then the other with unutterable gentleness, a question in his touch.

Her eyes drifted closed in preparation. Just one kiss, she thought and then I shall have to let him go, but for just this moment, she would cling to him and pretend that he returned her love. She would pretend it was real.

His lips were on hers, gentle at first, and then more insistent. Her hands went up around his neck, fisting in his hair, those wonderful curls that she would never touch again. She opened to him and the entire tenure of the kiss changed as he crushed her to him. With his arms wrapped so tightly around her, she felt blanketed in the scent of him, as if he would never let go; as if this moment could go on forever.

She felt as if she was dying and living her entire life in this one single moment. There was nothing but this moment. There was nothing but him. She drank him down as if she would die if she did not get enough of him, and he of her.

A gasp from the opposite doorway revealed an intruder, and the couple sprang apart to find Henrietta's wide-eyed gaze upon them.

Every flutter of hope that Emily had just felt was crushed in an instant. She pushed herself away. Her fingers went to her lips. She turned and she fled the room.

"Em!" The duke moved to follow her, but Henrietta waylaid him.

Emily found an empty room soon enough. She flung

the door closed and leaned her back against it sliding down to the floor. "What have I done?" Emily groaned to the empty hall.

She could not say how long she sat there before Edmund found her.

"Emily," He grasped her quaking arms. "You look as though you have seen a ghost. Are you alright?"

"I'm not feeling well at all," she told her brother. "Please, take me home."

"I shall call for the carriage," he sprang into action. "Uncle can call for the doctor."

"No," Emily pleaded. "No. I want to go home."

"I will take you home," Edmund promised.

"No, to London," she said. "I want to go home to London."

Edmund stared at her for a long while, but did not press his sister for an explanation. His eyes flicked to something over her shoulder, and Emily prayed that it was not a sign of the duke's approach. A moment later, Edmund threw his coat over her shoulders and ushered her out into the night.

26

*A*lexander paced his study and ran his hand through his already disheveled locks. He looked at what he had written. It was rubbish. He crumpled the letter and tossed it in the fire and began again.

The entire staff knew of the young duke's distemper.

He had stood like a dumb-struck fool looking after Emily. He had let her go. Why had he let her leave?

He was numb, and Emily was right. She had always known what was right and proper. He never did. It was Emily who always steered him and Edmund in the right direction. But this?

The duke took a deep settling breath. He would lose Emily forever. He watched her retreating back. Hadn't he lost her already? Her slim shoulders were set in a rigid line. She did not look back.

Years had passed and Emily wasn't here, and

Henrietta had been. He wasn't in love with Henrietta, but she was his friend and he needed a wife. He needed someone beside him. Why not Henrietta?

Henrietta had warned him to chase after Emily would invite even further scandal. Henrietta understood such things and Alexander could not bear for censure to fall upon Emily. The duke watched as Edmund bundled her out to the waiting carriage. His friend gave him a searching look, but he did not know what he could say.

Emily's words whirled in the duke's mind. Emily really told him that he was shirking his responsibilities. She had called him a child, and less than a man. The rebuke stung bitterly, but she was right.

Alexander had taken on many of the problems of the town, but taking responsibility for his own actions; that had been pushed aside again and again until it seemed so far away that it might not have happened at all.

His father had said it would be so, but Father was wrong. His father was wrong about so many things. Alexander had worried for years that he had inherited his father's demons, but he had never heard it laid so plain. The injury had faded, but it was not gone and not forgotten.

Certainly, Henrietta had not forgotten the wrong he had done her. How could she? Emily had put the matter right in front of him where he could ignore it no longer. You should have married Henrietta, she said. You should have married her.

Alexander knew that was right. He knew, and still he hesitated.

Henrietta suffered more for the incident than he had done. She was banished from her home. She was ridiculed for being a loose woman. She had not found a husband of her own because of the shame he had brought to her name. He had been dropped from some of the local guest lists and been forced to endure their sidelong glances, but no one dared to really give him the cut. He was a duke's son, and now he was the duke, himself. There was no censure, and the guilt nagged at him.

His father had insisted that the wench was well paid; she would go away, and he would do well to forget her. So Alexander had done, and for a while, his father was right.

The problem and Henrietta were out of sight.

But Alexander had missed her.

She was one of the few people his age that was not forbidden visits to Bramblewood. Even Edmund's aunt and uncle preferred that he stay at Sandstowe and Edmund's own father wanted him more and more in London.

Other friendships had dried up after his mother died because people wanted nothing to do with his father and his wicked ways. Just as Emily now wanted nothing to do with him.

Alexander closed his eyes against the painful

thought. He had no right to her. She had refused him. No. She had not even allowed him to ask.

Only Henrietta was left.

Because her father and his father had been much the same.

She at least understood.

He swallowed down a glass of brandy and allowed the burn of the spirit to numb him.

EVEN THE WEATHER was against Emily and the roads were not suitable for her desired departure. Uncle Cecil would not give her the carriage no matter how much she begged. Instead, Emily had made no attempt to feign illness, but blatantly refused to go out. She would wait until the roads were clear and make her return to London as soon as could be managed.

Emily lay on the window bench of her aunt's parlor and stared down at the blanket of snow that continued to accumulate on the lawn. Three days darkened by winter storms and gloomy winds reflected her mood.

In London, snow only fell in several polite English snowflakes and was conveniently melted by midday as was proper. Now, that she wanted to leave, the snow piled up for several days. It was most unaccommodating.

Edmund had still not pressed her for details. The entire household had tiptoed around the issue, but she knew that it would not be long before they began to demand answers.

Two letters had arrived from Bramblewood and both had been flung into the fire unopened. Emily could not bear to view his writing, or hear whatever excuses the duke might present.

She knew that she had spoken out of turn. She regretted her words, but she could not take them back. She could not bear to see him. Just the thought made the tears collect in her chest. She had refused his visit, saying she was indisposed.

"Em, you are being ridiculous. He knows you are here," Edmund said, but she would not come down and even Edmund, in solidarity for his sister, kept his distance from his friend for a time at least.

Another letter arrived from Bramblewood, which Emily pitched into the fire, and one from her Mother. She was surprised that the letter made it to Northwick, but perhaps the road south was passable. It gave her hope.

"Emily," her aunt had looked up from her book and asked across the room. "Cecil told me that you received a letter from your mother this morning. I wondered what she had to say?"

"Nothing much," Emily yawned. "She asked if I had made a decision between the gentlemen that I had been meant to consider."

"And what will be your reply?" Aunt Agnes asked with concern.

"Whichever she most prefers," Emily replied without care. She did not see that it would matter one way or the other. She knew she had to marry eventually. If she was not marrying for love, it did not matter much who she married. There was some comfort in knowing that if she married Robert Hawthorne she would never have to come to Northwickshire again. She would never have to lay eyes upon Alexander. The sense of loss almost overwhelmed her.

"Em, do not speak so callously," Edmund said. "You cannot make such a flippant decision."

"Edmund, hush," Emily said. "It is my choice, not yours."

"I know," he said, "and I want you to make it. You know this is wrong."

"I shall not have this conversation with you," she concluded. Emily turned to march up the stairs to her room.

Within moments, Edmund followed. He rapped sharply on the door to her chambers.

"Go away," Emily said without opening the door. "I will not be made to feel a fool." She had flung herself across the fainting couch in her sitting room.

"You are a fool." Edmund pressed on, entering anyway. He stalked into the sitting room. "So you want to return to London and marry some dullard like Hawthorne and live a dull life, raising dull babies awaiting his dullard grandfather's praise?"

Emily wished to slap her brother for his cruel words;

instead she clenched her fists in anger. "Robert Hawthorne is a good choice."

"Hawthorne? Really? He is your decision?" Edmund threw his head back and stared at the ceiling as if he could not comprehend her words.

"He meets all the necessary criteria."

"Of course he does," Edmund scoffed as paced away. He turned back to her with all seriousness. "You shall never love him, Em, and you know it. Worse, *he* will never love you."

"You do not know that."

"Then you love Hawthorne?"

"No, but..."

"Don't you want that?" Edmund demanded catching her shoulders and forcing her to look at him. "Do you not long for love?"

"This isn't a fairy tale, Edmund," Emily replied with confidence as if she meant it. "Love only gets you so far. Look at mother and father. Theirs was not a love match, but they are content. They do well enough. Love can grow from such matches."

"Are you daft?" Edmund hissed. "Robert is too proper to love you properly. He shan't do so without permission from his grandfather." Edmund's voice took on a singsong cadence. "Might I take my bride, Grandfather? Might I kiss my bride, Grandfather? Might I take a piss, Grandfather?"

"You need not be vulgar." Emily huffed.

"Oh, *that* was not vulgar," Edmund said and Emily

realized that Edmund had another even more uncouth thought for what act Robert might ask permission. Emily blushed profusely as Edmund continued unabated. "Look at what you are doing with your life, Em. You are throwing it away on that nodcock."

"What would you know of it?" Emily said waspishly.

"I know that I love you, and I refuse to stand by and let you make the biggest mistake of your life."

Edmund grunted before he stomped out slamming the door behind him. Emily had pursed her lips and shot a piercing look at Edmund's back. He appeared very determined, for whatever he was about.

Several hours later once her anger had abated, Emily could not help but to ponder her brother's words. Robert was somewhat of a nodcock, but he meant well, and he would not hurt her. There would be no scandal or violence. He may not love her, but he would be good to her. She would never worry about debt or drink or scandal.

As Emily slipped beneath her covers that night, she reminded herself that her father had plans for a fortuitous match. Not that any decently placed nobleman wouldn't do, but Father would rather a political man; conservative, of course, one who would join him at parliament during the days of debate and lobbying. Her father would approve of a political ally since his own son seemed so recalcitrant in that regard. Her mother intended for her to remain in London.

What did she want? The image of the Duke of

Bramblewood came unbidden to her thoughts. She had no right to ruminate upon him. Emily closed her eyes and willed away the rebellious feelings that threatened to take hold. She took a deep breath, but the image of the handsome duke seemed to lurk beyond her eyelids.

Alexander, she whispered, not the duke, the man. She thought of his kiss. He had set her heart aflame and she was filled with heat. Her body burned with the memory of his touch. She wanted Alexander, but her yearning was more than desire. She thought of days filled with adventure, lazy afternoons spent together and the years of longing in between.

Emily stifled a sob. She pushed away the old thoughts and wishes: dreams of love and a suitor to sweep her off her feet. Fairy stories were not real. They were things for children, and those days were gone.

She had spent years preparing herself for this phase of her life. It was, quite literally, all that a finished lady worked toward. Now, with one visit to the country and a reminder of the freedom she had once enjoyed, all of her resolve was crumbling. She refused to allow the pull of fancy to bring her to grief. Tomorrow, she would rise with renewed strength and with it stay the course. If she did not want to choose between Hawthorne and Barton, she would find another. The resolution brought her no comfort as she drifted into a fitful sleep.

27

The Milford butler welcomed the duke grudgingly and let him cool his heels in the bare drawing room. Alexander supposed that if Henrietta's father was still lord here his welcome may have been much less cordial, but the man was gone for good now; just like his own father.

He had mulled over this decision for several days. He had sent letters. He had gone to Sandstowe himself to speak to Emily, and she had refused to see him.

He knew her. He knew when she made up her mind; she didn't change it. He closed his eyes.

Edmund had tried to speak with her, but even he had not been able to convince her to see him.

In his heart, the duke knew this was the right thing to do. He knew it years ago. His Father had cheated and told him he could flaunt propriety, but he couldn't, not if he wanted Emily's respect. He knew he could never have her love; at least he would have her respect.

He glanced around the Milford drawing room. Last time he had been here, there were paintings by the masters on the walls and silver candelabra on the tables. Now, the walls had been stripped bare. The sconces were lit, but there was the scent of tallow in the air. There were no candelabra. There was not even a chair or table in sight.

He had known that Henrietta's financial situation was dire, but perhaps he had not known quite how dire. Apparently, her father had sold the furniture before his death, and now the debts would pass to her young cousin. In some ways, Henrietta was free of her father now, but he doubted she would see it so. In their own ways, they both loved their fathers, flawed though they were.

Henrietta came into the room with a maid at her heels. There was a time when she would have received him alone.

"May we speak privately?" he asked eyeing the maid.

Henrietta nodded and walked with him through the corridor to the dining room where there was a table and chairs, but still no paintings. The maid followed.

"Do not worry," Henrietta confided. "Gwen is near deaf."

He shook his head thinking no doubt that was why Henrietta brought this particular maid with her. "I could not turn her out," Henrietta continued. Then she touched the girl on the arm. "Gwen, do go and bring some tea," she said, and then pantomimed drinking from a cup. Gwen nodded and disappeared into the kitchen.

"Have you let go many of your servants?" he asked.

Henrietta sighed. "Most," she said. "I have little need of them. For years I thought if I did not marry well, I should need to take a position as a governess. Can you imagine me teaching girls to be young ladies?" She laughed at the thought, a harsh bray, but Alexander knew it was no laughing matter.

The mention of marriage brought up the topic. He should ask her, but he didn't. "When does your cousin take up residence?" he asked instead. He knew Shudley Hall was the entailed property and passed to her nearest male kin.

She shrugged. "He's nine. It may be a while," she said. "In the meantime, we are closing the house. My aunt offered to let me stay with her as long as I like, but I assume she meant until I marry."

The duke nodded. There was no more putting it off. "I wanted to ask you a question," he said and then he was suddenly shy.

She nodded and waited.

"I just wanted to say...I thought I should apologize. When you were banished from your home...I never meant."

Henrietta gave him a little shove. "Alexander, do not start that again," she said. "I liked Scotland."

"Truly?"

"Yes, and besides, I earned the punishment as well as you."

"Yours was more stringent."

She lifted a shoulder as if it did not matter now, and yet, she had told Emily. It did matter to her.

"I was remiss." The duke continued. "After my father died I could have corrected the course of funds. Of course, I would have had to speak with your father."

"A formidable problem," Henrietta said wryly. The maid brought the tea and retreated to a far corner. Henrietta poured.

"I was a coward. I just left the matter alone," he said as he put a single spoon of sugar into his tea. He noted that there was a half bowl of sugar but no cream, only milk in the pitcher. Alexander sipped the weak brew dutifully.

"Father would not have let me come home," Henrietta sighed. "The original agreement between our fathers was that payment would only be made until I found a husband." She gestured at the barren manor house. "He squandered most everything else. Father was in no hurry for me to marry. It would have lightened his purse."

"I did not know the funds were going to pay his debts. They were supposed to be for you. For your dowry."

"Yes, and you righted the problem when you discovered it," she said. Her hands were wrapped around her teacup. "I thank you for it. You replaced what was lost and more besides, when you were under no obligation to do so."

"The funds were always meant to be yours. You need not be destitute. With the dowry restored, you may marry as you wish. It may not make up for the pain I caused you, but it is the least I can do."

"And I am most grateful, but you said as much last we spoke." She set her teacup upon the saucer. "What is this really about Alexander?"

Now was the time, he thought.

He put his own cup down decisively and stood. "Henrietta, you have always been a good friend." He sank down on one knee in front of her. He knew this at least was the proper way to make a proposal. "We have known each other for years..."

"What are you doing?" Henrietta interrupted sharply.

"Asking you to marry me," he said from his knees. "As I should have done long ago."

"Oh Alexander," she said shaking her head. She stood, paced away and shut her eyes.

Was she going to refuse him too? He didn't think he could stand it.

"Is there someone else?" he croaked out getting hastily to his feet. He bumped the table rattling the teacup off its saucer, but he caught it before it dropped to the floor to shatter. "If there is someone else..."

"No," she said sharply, staring out the dining room window at the new fallen snow. "I had thought perhaps... but no." She turned to face him. "What of Emily?"

The duke grimaced. The question causing a near physical stab of pain to lance through his heart. "She will not receive me." He answered simply.

"I am sorry." She said sincerely, and Alexander felt the lady understood the pain of rejection and scorn. He gathered himself and his purpose and renewed his suit.

"Henrietta, I know you don't love me nor I you, but we get on well." He came forward and took her hands in his. The image of Emily rose in his mind; Emily with her chilled hands. He cleared his throat and began again.

"We have seen each other through some tough times. We know each other's secrets so there should be no surprises between us. I think we would get on better than most."

"And I wouldn't have to be a governess," she said.

"No, I do not want you to feel pressured. The money is yours, Henrietta. Regardless to what you decide. The dowry is still yours. The point was to give you a choice in whom you married."

She laughed bitterly. "I never had a choice, Alexander. I don't think either of us did; our fathers being what they were. I fully expected to remain a spinster."

"Do you want to be?" he asked softly, thinking that perhaps that would be preferable to marrying him.

"No," she said. "But you don't have to marry me because of what happened four years ago."

"I know, but it is the right thing to do. I should have

made the offer four years ago. Father didn't want me to, but…"

"I know. I remember. His words were loud enough for Gwen to hear."

"He said some hateful things, Henrietta. I apologize."

"You didn't say them, Alexander. You are not responsible for his sins. If you were, I would not even consider your proposal."

Her words were kind, but did little to settle his mind. It took him a moment to take her meaning. "So you are considering, then?"

"Yes."

"Yes, you are considering?"

"Yes, I will marry you," she said.

"Well then," he said. "That is good." It felt wrong somehow to kiss her when it was their kisses that brought them both so much grief, but Henrietta leaned in and offered her cheek. There was no passion, but neither was there revulsion.

Their marriage would not be a trial, he thought. Henrietta was a good woman, but his heart protested most ardently that she was not Emily.

He felt as though he had swallowed a block of ice.

28

*T*he duke was not looking forward to Sunday services, but he took his seat on the front bench. He glanced across the aisle to Henrietta. She did not always come to services, but today, she was here. He gave her a brief smile of support, which she weakly returned. Alexander felt empty and a fraud.

Edmund joined him. It was a small comfort. The duke's eyes automatically scanned the room for Emily. He realized she was not with the family. Perhaps it was for the best that she was absent, this Sunday of all Sundays, but worry dogged him. Would he never be able to forget the woman?

He leaned across to Edmund. "Is you sister ill?" he asked.

"Heartsick." Edmund whispered. "You should know more than most."

Alexander grimaced but was saved from an answer

by the start of the service. He fidgeted like a small child. By the end of today, all of Northwickshire would know. The service dragged on interminably.

When the banns were announced at the end of the service, Edmund gripped his arm like a vise.

"...marriage between Alexander Burgess, the Duke of Bramblewood, and Miss Henrietta Milford. If any know cause or just impediment why these two persons should not be joined together in Holy Matrimony, ye are to declare it."

A low murmur passed through the assembled congregation. The duke's kept his eye forward not daring to look at the surprised faces behind him. Edmund's fingers dug painfully in to the flesh of his upper arm. He barely felt it. The vicar muttered some prayer asking God to bless their union. Alexander heard not one word.

Edmund did not release his grip until they were outside of the church where he pushed the duke around the side of the building. Henrietta was nowhere in sight. Perhaps she was waylaid by well-wishers.

Several people attempted to congratulate the duke as well, or perhaps they just wanted some bit of gossip, but Edmund's glare repelled most of them and they retreated.

"Are you out of your mind?" he hissed.

"Not to my knowledge," the duke said evenly.

"You love my sister."

"I do not see that who I love or do not love is any of your concern." Even as the duke said the words he knew they were untrue. Edmund was his friend, perhaps his only friend, and for the man to find out that he was marrying Henrietta via a reading of the banns at church was a blow.

Edmund spat a vulgarity under his breath. "Of course it is my concern. I don't want to see you muck up your life or my sister's."

"I am doing the honorable thing." Alexander said.

"Honorable? How is it honorable to marry Henrietta over a bit of gossip from four years ago?"

Now that Edmund released him, the duke straightened his wrinkled waistcoat and pulled his woolen great coat closed. He drew himself up to his full height and faced Edmund directly. He told his friend what he should have told him years ago. "Because, it is not just a bit of gossip."

That stilled Edmund.

It was the first time the duke had acknowledged the talk or gave it any credence. He was painfully silent on the subject. Whenever the topic came up, Edmund had always dismissed the notion. "Empty-headed blather," he had said. "It will blow by as long as you don't make any by blows," and Alexander let the matter pass without a word.

Edmund had stood by Alexander, defending him when no one else had. Saying that, people only thought ill of him because of his father and they did not know him as Edmund did. Alexander would never dishonor a lady so.

And yet, he had. The untruth weighed heavily upon him.

"Are you telling me that the rumors are truth?" Edmund spat. Alexander could hear the anger in his friend's tone, not only for what Alexander had done or not done, but because he had perpetrated a lie. It was a lie of omission, but he had lied to his friend.

Unable to quite form the words, the duke nodded sharply. "True enough."

Perhaps, he had not embraced debauchery to the extent of his father, but the result was the same. Henrietta was just as ruined because most people thought he had done. Anyone who might have wanted to marry her thought the same. Henrietta said as much when she admitted no one had offered her marriage.

Henrietta was most beautiful. She should have had her pick of the *Ton*. Instead she was anathema. He was the reason. Emily had reminded him of what was right. He was at last doing the honorable thing. It did not matter that Emily's brother did not agree.

Edmund spat another oath.

Alexander did not remind him that they had been within church only moments before.

"But that's all over now," Edmund said, as he attempted to rein in his surprise. "She's not with child..." His face went white. "Was she? In Scotland?" His voice was barely audible, a breath on the cold wind.

"No," the duke said firmly. "She was not, and is not

with child. I would not stoop so low as to burden a woman with a bastard."

Edmund breathed a visible sigh of relief.

"Then you are under no obligation marry her."

"No."

"Then, Dear God, why?" Edmund was raising his voice again and several parishioners looked their way. The duke certainly did not look like the happy bridegroom he was meant to be, cornered as he was with Edmund.

He hushed his friend, but Edmund would not be silenced. "You are daft, man." Edmund hissed. "You are in with love my sister, and she loves you. Why are you not marrying her?"

"She has refused me," the duke said simply.

All of the air went out of Edmund's sails. "Then, you are both idiots," Edmund concluded and with long strides paced away from the duke.

Alexander was uncertain how this had left his friendship with the man. He greatly wished to retain Edmund as his friend, but he knew their relationship would be strained from now on. The truth was when Alexander looked at Edmund, he saw Emily. He could not keep from thinking of her or longing to ask after her. Although it pained him greatly perhaps it was best to avoid Edmund as well, at least for a time. There was too much shared history between them.

29

$\mathcal{E}$mily had tried to remain in bed on Sunday. She had no interest in seeing anyone and of course, if she was absent from church, it was difficult to socialize within the town. She had told everyone she was ill, and she felt as if she truly were. She simply could not manage to drag herself out of bed.

Unfortunately, her sulking was interrupted by the arrival of her parents for the Christmas holiday. Christmas was still a little over a sennight away and she had hoped her parents might not come until Christmas Eve, but here they were, nearly a week early. She heard her Father's booming voice downstairs and covered her head with a pillow.

Her maid appeared to inform her of the fact that her parents had arrived.

"I am aware, thank you," she told Carrie.

Finally, Emily bowed to the inevitable and slid her feet out of bed while Carrie chose a morning dress for her to wear to a late breakfast. She knew that as soon as the others arrived back from church, Aunt Agnes would have food set out for the new arrivals.

If Emily did not go downstairs now, her mother would come up and Emily thought it would be much easier for her to escape back upstairs than it would be to get her mother out of her room.

Emily heard her father as she reached the bottom of the stair.

"The trip was interminable," Lord Kentleworth complained, "and your sister is not even here to greet us, Sarah."

"I'm sure Agnes will be down directly."

Emily's parents, Lord and Lady Kentleworth were seated at the dining room table as servants brought in their belongings and their entourage were fed in the kitchen.

"They are still at church," Emily said as she hovered in the doorway. "You are early." She nodded gratefully to the footman who brought tea and biscuits to the dining room. She was hoping that Aunt Agnes and Uncle Cecil would arrive soon. "We will have breakfast whenever it is ready," she said to the footman.

"No, actually we are late." Her father replied gruffly. "We meant to arrive yesterday, but this dreadful weather held us in Wollington for the night." He softened a bit as he stood to greet his daughter. "Have you enjoyed your holiday thus far?"

Before she could answer, her mother inquired. "If all are still at church, why are you left behind? Do you feel alright, Emily?"

"Yes, Mother. It is nothing. At least it is nothing physical. I am...heartsick. I cannot bear to see him."

"Who? That reprobate duke? I don't care if he is the Prince Regent Himself, if he has laid a hand on you, Emily I shall call him out," Father said eyes narrowed.

"No, Father. Nothing of the sort. He is marrying another," she said as her father seated her.

"Good," Father said. "Bad apples I tell you. It's a pity Agnes' best friend took in with his father. I told your mother that, years ago. Even if the man was a duke, he was a swine."

Emily did not bother to correct her father although, a denial rose within her. Alexander was not like his father, she thought vehemently. But she had called him so. A bitter guilt filled her.

How could she have been so hateful? It did not matter. He was promised to Henrietta, if she were to hate him perhaps that fact would not hurt so terribly.

"Sit," her mother urged. "Drink your tea. It shall ease you." Her mother nodded to the steaming pot.

The viscountess thought tea made everything better.

Emily sat, poured and stirred an ungodly amount of sugar into her cup and took a sip. Perhaps it did.

"Things are not as they were," she said holding back tears. "I thought that I would visit as had done as a child. I thought all would be the same in Northwickshire."

"Nothing is ever the same," Her father said curtly. "You have to learn to live in the present, Emily."

"Oliver," Mother said gently and Father desisted.

"I know that you have fond memories of Northwickshire and your aunt and uncle," Mother said, "Northwickshire is fine for a holiday, but London is your home, my dear."

Perhaps Mother was right.

"It is," Emily said with a false brightness. She took another sip of tea. It was warming her. "Tell me of London. What news?"

"There are Christmas parties every night of the week, but without you and your brother to enjoy them, there was no point in our attending." The viscountess said. She lifted a shoulder in a delicate shrug.

"I'm sorry," Emily said. She knew both her parents loved the bustle of London and right now, she wished for it too. She might lose herself in the crowded ballrooms. The happy festivities would make her forget.

Mother spoke of invitations to Almacks and which parties Emily might prefer for the New Year.

Emily wanted to crawl back into her bed.

"I am really still tired," she prevaricated as Edmund burst through the door.

"Em, you are an idiot," he said without preamble.

"Edmund!" Mother said shocked.

"Do you not greet your parents?" Lord Kentleworth said with censure.

"Greetings, Mother. Father." Edmund gave each a brief nod and clasped Emily's hand around the wrist as he had once done when they were but children. "Come," he said. "I have to speak to you." He hurried her from the dining room to the library.

No doubt Father would have reprimanded Edmund for his deplorable manners, but Aunt Agnes and Uncle Cecil took that moment to enter. Emily heard the familial greetings met behind her.

Edmund shut the library door with a soft snick, caught his sister's shoulders and turned her to face him.

"They announced the banns at church today. Banns! Did you know of this?"

Emily felt the color drain from her face. "You mean they have made it official then?"

"I mean, that in three weeks, Alexander is marrying Henrietta!"

Emily tried to still her heart. It really was happening then. Edmund was pacing in front of the bookcase. Emily sank down into an armchair. Her knees felt weak.

Edmund turned to her. "What on earth did you say to him, Em?"

"Me?"

"Yes, you. You must know he hangs upon your every word. Always has. If you told him to throw himself in the

ISABELLA THORNE

lake, I suspect he would have done so forthwith. Just days ago he could speak of little else but how to win your favor and then suddenly, the vicar is announcing his engagement to Henrietta?" Edmund's voice rose at the question and Emily shushed him. Father would hear.

Edmund waved her off as he paced. "This is daft. Alexander loves you, but is marrying Henrietta. You love Alexander, but are marrying Hawthorne. Eldridge loves Henrietta and is ..."

"Stop!" Emily interrupted. She could not focus. She shook her head. "I've not yet agreed to marry Hawthorne"

"Thank heavens for small blessings." Edmund threw his hands in the air in exasperation. "I don't know why you both are so pigheaded. I know you argued, but what could you have said that changed Alexander's mind so drastically?"

Emily raised her chin. How dare her brother blame her? She had the high ground. "What have I done? The duke is the one who is false. He led me to believe he cared for me, but he and Henrietta...well they..." She couldn't quite bring herself say it.

Edmund clucked his tongue and shook his head. "No," he stated simply.

The wind went quite out of her sails. "But I thought..."

"And you are wrong," Edmund stated flatly. "Alexander said that he and Henrietta only..."

Emily held a hand aloft to stop her brother's frank

words. She altogether did not want details of Alexander and Henrietta.

"It was not the way you are imagining." Edmund protested. "I know she was sent to Scotland four years ago, and there were all those awful rumors, but contrary to public belief, there was no bastard. Alexander said there was not even chance of a child, and I believe him. He hated that his father had by blows on every corner. You know that."

"Wait," Emily said confused. She took a breath and considered. Edmund said four years ago. "We are not speaking of the same event. The duke made promise to Henrietta recently. He has been playing with my heart."

"No Em. He proposed three days ago after your argument. *After* you refused him."

Emily's mind was in a whirl. Alexander admitted to behaving dishonorably, but Emily thought he had given Henrietta his promise. How could she have been mistaken? What was the document she had seen his seal upon? It no longer mattered.

"He did not ask me," Emily said softly her heart aching. She could barely breathe through the pain in her chest.

"He said he did."

"I suppose I didn't allow him to do so." Emily confessed. "I berated him for his treatment of Henrietta."

"And now he's marrying Henrietta." Edmund shook his head in disbelief. "You are in love with each other, Em. You should be together. Do you know how rare that love is? When you find the one, you hang on; you do not let him go, or push him away."

Reality crashed down upon her. Alexander was marrying Henrietta. Once done, he would be lost to her forever. Edmund was right. She had pushed him away. She had not listened. She had been wrong.

"Oh, what have I done," she cried, tears welling and a tightness filling her chest. Suddenly, it all let loose. She fell to her knees, sprawled upon the library rug.

Edmund knelt beside her and held her while she sobbed.

"Oh Edmund," she cried into his shirt. "I have been a fool. What can I do? There's no way to fix this," she hiccuped. "In stories, there is always some fairy to wave a wand and make everything right, but there is no magic to mend this."

"You are right in one respect, Em," Edmund said softly. "Children believe in fairy godmothers and Father Christmas to bring treats unbidden. They have caring parents and aunts and uncles; adults who sometimes manage to put the world right."

"Alexander had no such parent," Emily said miserably. "He had no one to put his world right."

"He had his mother," Edmund comforted, "and he had you, Em."

"I don't know what to do, Edmund!" Emily cried.

"As I understand it, the banns are read three times. The purpose of this is to see if there is any objection to the marriage."

She opened her mouth to speak and then paused. Edmund was right. Children whined for adults to fix their problems. Adults took the task in hand themselves.

"Then, I shall object." She sniffed, dashing away her tears.

It would be the height of unladylike behavior, she thought, and found she did not care. She tried to muster her courage. She could do it. If Alexander could forgive her. If it would stop the wedding, she cared not one whit what was proper. But what cause did she have? She had no legal objection. Only love. She prayed it was enough.

"I will need your help," she said to her brother, proud that her voice did not waver.

"You shall have it," Edmund said immediately, although he paused considering. "Oh, Em," he warned. "If you speak out and this does not work."

She nodded. She would be ruined. "It has to work," she said resolved. She would trust Alexander. She would marry the duke or no one at all.

"I could object," Edmund said thoughtfully.

She raised an eyebrow at her brother. "Do you want to marry Henrietta?"

"Lud, no."

"Well, then," Emily said. "It cannot be you."

Suddenly, Edmund's eyes lit with excitement. "I have an idea," he said already moving towards the door. "I have to double check with Anne and then, I have to see a man."

"Anne? Who? What man?" Emily said, but Edmund didn't explain.

He only paused at the door. "You will see, Em. Together we will put the world right again."

"Or turn it upside down," she whispered as he rushed out.

30

$\mathcal{T}$he duke had invited Henrietta to share the front bench in church. After all, neither of them had much family now and after his argument with Edmund, the man was sitting in solidarity with Emily.

Emily.

She was not in the seat with her aunt and uncle. Her parents had arrived, but Emily and Edmund were absent. He sighed.

It was the second Sunday to read the banns. He had considered what he should do when he got Emily's apology, hand delivered by Edmund. He read it and re-read it. He knew regardless of the apology, Emily meant what she said at the ball. He was being dishonorable. Could he now betray Henrietta again, when she had no one?

Yes, he loved Emily, but he was not sure she loved him. She had stayed away for years. Sure, there was finishing school, but afterwards she had gone to London with her parents. She had not come back to Northwickshire. She had not written. She liked the balls and frivolity. She enjoyed London. Edmund had told him so; Edmund who had managed to visit when Emily did not.

Henrietta was the safe choice. They were friends. He could keep his heart intact, at least the pieces of it that Emily had left to him.

He glanced around wondering at Henrietta's late arrival. Perhaps the proper thing would have been to go by her house and bring her to church in his own carriage. He had not thought of it. Perhaps she had decided not to come. He knew that many of the ladies were unkind to her.

In any case, he sat alone in his family pew. Soon, he would not be alone. Henrietta would sit beside him. He could not help but wish it were Emily.

Just then, there was a stir at the back of the church. Mr. Eldridge had come in along with a great crowd of what could only be his relations. The resemblance was shocking. The duke, in an effort not to stare turned back to the front.

Just then, Henrietta slipped into her seat beside him, Gwen following.

"I must speak with you," she said urgently, but the vicar had already begun the service.

He laid a hand on her gloved one. "After church," he said decisively.

336

EMILY AND EDMUND had a great amount of preparation to do before services and they arrived late.

"Are you sure, Emily?" Edmund asked as they entered the church. "I could do it for you."

"I am sure," she said although she was quite nervous.

The service had already started, and so Emily and Edmund did not join their parents at their normal pew. They found seats as quietly as possible near the back.

Edmund squeezed her hand. "I really didn't want to be sitting by Father anyway," Edmund whispered, making Emily's heart drop to her knees. Their father would be furious.

If she did this and Alexander refused her, she would not marry anyone. No one would have her. Even though Northwick was a remote town, news this scandalous would travel to London.

All through the service, she fiddled nervously with her handkerchief and when at last the sermon ended and the banns were read, her mouth was dry. Nonetheless she stood.

"I object," she said. Her voice was soft, but it gained volume as she spoke. "I object to the marriage because I know them both and this is a terrible mistake. It shall make them both miserable."

The entire congregation turned to look at her.

"I object because marriage is about love and commitment. The duke and Miss Milford, they do not love each other. How can they become one as prescribed by the Bible if there is no love between them?"

Emily paused catching her breath as the whispers in the church grew louder. She took her courage in her hands. "Alexander, I love you. Please do not do this," she proclaimed baldly.

Her words echoed within the crowded church, before the congregation erupted in shocked disbelief.

"Sit down," the vicar said patiently. "Miss Ingram, the reading of the banns is not license for a scorned woman to take her spite out on the man who deserted her."

Emily opened her mouth to protest, but never got the chance.

"Emily is not a scorned woman," Henrietta exclaimed standing.

"I did not desert Emily," the duke announced simultaneously.

ALEXANDER RUFFLED as he realized that the vicar thought he could do such a thing. Of course, he did. They all thought ill of him, but the hurt lingered for only a moment.

Emily had said she loved him. Nothing else mattered. His mind rang with the words, hearing them again and glorying in them. Emily had said she loved him. His heart had taken wing, it felt like a trapped thing within his chest.

But the woman who stood beside him was not Emily.

The duke and Henrietta paused staring at each other both standing in defense of Emily as Mr. Eldridge marched right up the center aisle accompanied by his cousins at his back. He did not address the vicar. He turned instead to Henrietta.

"Miss Milford," he said. "I know you wanted to marry well and although I am well off I have no title to my name, certainly nothing to rival a duke, but as the lady says marriage should be a bond of love, not money. I did not speak for there was word you desired a title, and I believe you should have whatever it is you desire, Miss Milford." Eldridge looked at Emily. "But some of your friends believe this marriage will not make you happy." The man took a deep breath. "I know it shall pain me greatly."

The congregation was certainly atwitter now. Some were standing and pushing forward, blocking the duke's view of Emily who still stood in the back of the church.

Eldridge continued. "I love you Henrietta Milford and if you love me, if you can stand the cold of Scotland, I promise I will devote myself to you."

"Yes," Henrietta exclaimed. "I mean..." She looked back at the duke with a question, and he smiled. He knew that look in her eyes, hopeless in love.

"The dowry is yours," he reminded her. "Whatever you decide, Henrietta."

"Now, just a minute," the vicar said.

Henrietta Milford threw herself into Mr. Eldridge's

arms and kissed him full on the mouth while the entire congregation looked on gasping and shouting. Many were on their feet now, blocking the aisle.

The duke considered pushing his way to Emily or shouting at those gathered to make way, but she would not condone such behavior. She had said she loved him. Had she meant what she said?

"This is not at all proper," the vicar called over the din. He had clearly lost control of his flock and looked to the duke for help. None was forthcoming.

"But I am not in love with the duke," Henrietta said to the vicar and then turned to Alexander. "I am sorry, Alexander. Once I may have thought I was in love with you. I even thought I could marry you, but now, that I am really in love, I know the difference. I think you do as well," she finished softly, looking back at Emily. "I cannot settle for less, even for a title."

The congregation was in an uproar. Mr. Eldridge did not seem distressed at all since he picked up a giggling Henrietta and carried her from the church. He did not care who he jostled out of the way.

The duke sat down in his front pew. Alone.

He said a silent prayer.

Lord I suppose, You heard what You needed to hear. I asked for a miracle. I asked for a sign that Emily could loosen her stiff ways and love me, flawed though I am. I asked that I might be worthy of her.

I did not expect her to proclaim her love, though I am

sometimes a bit daft. I may not have seen the sign if it had been more subtle.

I thank You for creating this Christmas miracle for me. Thank You for Emily.

SHE HAD to get to Alexander. "Let me through," Emily said.

Edmund stood aside and let Emily go to him. She had to fight her way through the exiting crowd to get to the duke, but she managed. Several people gave her sidelong glances.

She supposed no one would ever think she was the proper lady again, but she didn't care. She didn't care if anyone thought she was a lady. She only wanted to be Alexander's.

She slid onto the bench beside him. He looked so lost, so far from her.

"Your Grace," she said. She saw him visibly flinch.

"Alexander." She took his hand in hers. "Your hands are cold," she said. She could feel the chill even though her gloves. She cupped both of his hands in hers and pulled them close to her face.

"I do not have any mittens," she said softly.

"You are warmth enough," he said and they sat still and silent, her hand in his, while the parishioners filed out. He smiled at her. "You know all that was most improper."

"Sometimes there are reasons to dispense with propriety. Friendship and love are more important."

"You are more important." The duke replied, cupping her face in his hand. "Did you mean what you said?" he asked at last.

"That I love you? Yes. I think I have always loved you, from the time I was very young. I only did not realize it." Emily admitted.

"I feel the same," Alexander said, his eyes shining in his passion. "Emily, I can make you no promises of an upright life. I have never known of such things, but I do love you desperately. I find the thought of life without you unbearable. Agree to marry me?"

Emily felt tears pricking at her eyes, but there was a lightness in her heart. "Yes, Alexander. I will marry you. I too cannot live without you."

His hand trembled against her cheek. He gripped her other hand tightly, their lips but a breath apart. "I most ardently wish to kiss you," he whispered, "but if I do I am certain the vicar will have apoplexy."

The thought of his kiss sent a thrill through her.

"Shall we go then?" She replied. The two of them rose and still holding hands and went out of the now nearly deserted church.

Edmund was waiting for them leaning against the duke's carriage.

"What are you still doing here?" The duke asked.

"Oh, I know you two need a chaperone today," he teased. "Anyway, I did not want to ride with Father. Can you believe he thinks I had something to do with this?" He waved a hand towards the church. "I told him it was all you, Em."

"Thank you," Emily said dryly.

"Did you have something to do with it?" the duke asked Edmund.

"Does Marksham have chickens?" he answered and they laughed together as the duke handed Emily into the carriage. "Friends have to stick together," Edmund said and they both agreed.

"Now, I would give you advice on how to speak to my father," Edmund continued, "but I open my mouth and he derides me. I do nothing to please him, so you are best on your own, my friend." He clapped the duke on the back. "If he gives you too much trouble, I shall drive you both to Gretna Green."

"I hardly think that will be necessary," Emily said.

"I must have your father's permission to marry you," the duke said to Emily.

"And he shall give it," she replied eyes flashing.

"Do you always get your way?" the duke asked.

"Always."

"Unfortunately," Edmund added.

"It is because for the most part, she is right," the duke said.

Emily smiled at him and shook her head. "Not this time," she said. "I should have listened to you instead of just assuming I knew best. Alexander, I am so terribly sorry. I said such horrible things to you. I never meant them. You are nothing like your father. Please, forgive me?"

"Always, Emily. I too acted rashly. If I ever display such lack of judgment again throw a pine cone at my head or something."

"Or something," she said softly. Now that they were in the carriage, she turned her face up for his kiss, and Edmund prudently looked away.

The duke gathered her close and she felt the warmth of him in a hard line along the length of her body. She snuggled against him, breathing him in. He was hers. They were to be married. She returned his embrace, clutching him close. Heat suffused through her; so that she thought she might never be cold again.

She ran her gloved fingers up through the curls at the base of his neck, curls that she had longed to touch since they sat together in a snow bank, since they soaked their feet together in the summer lake, since they rode together to find holly berries.

Dozens of moments shared came to her mind, and she wanted dozens more. Thousands. She wanted to tug her gloves off and touch him skin to skin. Instead, she melted against him. The scent of him stirred her blood and her lips parted welcoming him. A mewing sound escaped her unbidden.

Edmund coughed abruptly. "I am meant to be chaperoning," he said with false censure.

They broke apart, a little flushed even in the cold. The duke kept his arm firmly about her waist. His smile and his embrace told Emily more than words of his unbridled happiness at their union.

"Sandstowe or Bramblewood?" Edmund asked.

"Sandstowe," the duke said. "I must ask Lord Kentleworth permission to marry his daughter immediately." Emily tucked herself against Alexander's side. She knew that somehow she had done the impossible and her world was right again, now and forever.

31

---

*I*t was Christmas Day at Sandstowe and Emily had passed out the gifts to her young cousins, who were currently enjoying chocolate and peppermint sticks by the fire. She could not imagine how it must feel to have lost their mother. No gift could replace her, but Emily was certain to be supportive of them as Aunt Agnes had been of her and the other youth of Northwickshire.

Even though she and her mother did not always see eye to eye, she knew that her mother loved her dearly. William and Edmund were enjoying a round of cards and her parents seemed content to visit with Aunt Agnes and Uncle Cecil.

Emily pulled Alexander aside to give him his Christmas gift. He opened the box with the cufflinks in it and smiled warmly. "You remembered," he said.

"I know you used to lose them," Emily said.

They smiled softly at one another.

"I admit I have been extra careful not to lose my cufflinks," he said. "Now, I must be doubly careful."

"I know jewelry is a very improper gift," Emily said, "but I saw them and could not resist."

"You have been most improper lately," he teased. "I must be a bad influence on you."

"Certainly not," she said. She blushed as he took her in his arms. "We were not even engaged when I bought them, but they seemed perfect. They have an etching on them."

He held them up to the light to see the engraving. "They are exquisite."

"It's a candle flame," Emily said. "I thought it was appropriate since you always warm my hands."

"And you are my light," he said as he traded his own cuff links out for the ones Emily had bought him.

A moment later he pulled something from his pocket. "Give me your hands," he said and she laid them both in his. She trusted this man more than any other. "I hope you will wear this as my token," he said revealing a glittering ring. "I should have given you my promise years ago: a promise to be faithful, a promise to be yours. My heart has always belonged to you, Emily."

Emily nodded eagerly holding out her hand. She found that words escaped her at this moment.

He slipped the ruby ring upon her finger and she gasped at its stunning beauty. "Forever and ever," he said being simultaneously the boy who was her friend and the man she loved.

"It belonged to my maternal grandmother," the duke said, "and my grandfather's mother before her. She and my grandfather had many wonderful years together as I hope we shall have."

Her heart was filled with joy. Nothing could make her happier than every day spent at his side.

"I love you, Emily," he said.

"I love you, Alexander," she replied, her eyes shining with tears

They shared a gentle kiss and rejoined the others in their Christmas celebration.

Sometime later after several glasses of wassail punch, Alexander caught Emily under the mistletoe and cupped her face in his hands as he placed a tender kiss upon her lips. "Twelve more days," he whispered.

"Are you sure you do not want to wait until the chapel at Bramblewood is restored?" Emily teased with a twinkle of mirth in her eye.

"Absolutely not," the duke said. "The chapel will take months to repair." He paused thoughtfully. "Perhaps it shall be done in time for the christening of our first child," he said making Emily blush.

They had planned to marry on the Twelfth day of Christmas, although there was some debate as to whether or not the day the duke broke his engagement with Henrietta counted as the first Sunday of reading the banns for himself and Emily. The duke argued that the whole congregation knew of the matter and that constituted a reading of the banns. The vicar was unwilling to argue with the duke.

No one was surprised when the banns were read on the second week. No one opposed. In fact, the church was filled with well-wishers.

"How close we came to ruining this," Emily whispered against Alexander's chest as he held her. They stood swaying under the mistletoe. Christmas carols were being sung in the sitting room.

The duke chuckled. "Your brother would have never allowed it," he assured her. "It seems Edmund knows our minds better than the both of us."

"Gads! Don't tell him that. He will be insufferable."

The duke kissed her again, running his finger along her collarbone, and then following his finger with his lips. It was all very scandalous, as his lips traced the exposed skin just above her décolletage and then turned her head so he could kiss her behind her ear. Emily shot a glance towards the other room. He caught her chin and turned her attention back to him. He planted another kiss on her lips, and then whispered against them.

"I understand your mother wished you married before the Season's end, but this country wedding cannot be what she wished for her only daughter."

Emily sighed. "She is happy that I am happy. Moreover, I am marrying a duke. Mother does love a title. She insists we have an announcement ball in London in the spring."

"What of you?" he asked pulling her close with a grin. She gave a little squeak as he asked, "How does the appellation Duchess of Bramblewood feel?"

"Being a duchess does not matter one whit to me. *Your* wife is the only title that matters." She smiled up at him as he kissed her nose and then her cheeks. "Still, I will not complain."

"You may when you see the amount of effort involved."

"Never," she said between kisses.

"Could you live permanently at Bramblewood, in the country?" he asked. "I hope to only go to London during Lords. Would that be enough to satisfy you?"

"Hmmm?" she said unable to concentrate on his words as he continued to kiss her. He kissed the back of her neck.

He chuckled.

"More than enough," she assured him. "I do believe Father sees a project in you."

"Whatever do you mean?" He lifted his head from her skin to look at her.

She deepened her voice to mock his. "I don't know much about politics, Sir," she parroted his words to her father swatting at him playfully.

"Well, I don't."

"That was a tacit invitation to Father to take you in hand."

"I do not mind it," he said. "I have a lot to learn. I don't even remember my father going to Lords. I am sure many people have forgotten that there even is a Duchy of Bramblewood."

"Well, I believe that Mother and Father would do well to remove from London on occasion, particularly at Christmastime. Father works too hard. He needs a holiday."

"They do not know the country as we do," Alexander said. He went back to nuzzling her neck and sending shivers of delight up her spine.

"Yes, and I wish them to learn to love it, as I do" She caught her breath as he kissed her ear lobe. His breath tickled her as he murmured something.

"Are you counting?" She asked.

"Yes," he said as he kissed her again.

"What are you counting?"

"Freckles," he said. "Now, do be still, or if shall have to start over."

"I shan't mind," she said breathlessly.

He nibbled on her ear.

"Then it is settled," he breathed, his breath tickling her. "Christmas shall always be in the country."

"Yes, as long as you do not presume to know what I am thinking," she said.

"I shan't," he agreed, kissing several ticklish spots on her neck.

"And neither of us would wish to ask my brother," she said.

"Agreed." He said with a laugh.

She lifted her face for another kiss and molded her form to his.

Edmund peeked into the corridor. "What were you going to ask your brother?" He asked.

Emily waved an annoyed hand at him "Go away." She turned back to her betrothed.

"And here I thought I was bringing good tidings," Edmund said waving a letter between the lovers. Emily frowned as she looked at the seal. It was from Henrietta. "How long have you had this?" Emily asked her voice full of suspicion.

"So cynical, dear sister, it has only just arrived." Edmund said as Emily tore open the seal.

"What does it say?" The duke asked.

"It is an announcement of Henrietta's wedding," Emily said looking up with a smile. "She eloped to Gretna Green and married Mr. Eldridge last week."

"So soon?" the duke said.

"True, a lady who breaks an engagement is supposed to wait a year to be wed," Emily said, "but this is Henrietta."

"The man is most fortunate." The duke commented.

"Are you jealous of Eldridge?" Emily looked up at him sharply.

"Most envious, yes." Alexander admitted. "Mr. Eldridge can hold his bride all night long and may kiss her whenever and wherever he wishes."

"You could be in Scotland by tomorrow," Edmund invited.

"I think we shall do things the proper way," Emily said.

"As you wish, my love," the duke said. He ignored Edmund entirely and kissed her quite soundly.

"I am still here," Edmund said sulkily.

The duke paused giving Emily a moment to breathe. He pointed upwards. "And mistletoe is here," he said. "It is quite proper to kiss under mistletoe."

Alexander bent to her again with all the promise of his love and she melted in his arms.

EPILOGUE

$\mathcal{A}$lexander Burgess, the Duke of Bramblewood and Miss Emily Ingram were wed on the Twelfth Day of Christmas. Edmund and Anne stood as witnesses. Emily's parents did not go back to London until spring. Lady Kentleworth commented on the quaintness of the country wedding, and Lord Kentleworth pulled the duke aside to school him in politics. Alexander said he did not mind. He had a lot to learn about London and Lords.

Emily had made a stunning winter bride. She was given a snowy white fur stole from the duke's mother's collection that kept her warm and made her look fine enough for royalty. Aunt Agnes found a bolt of blue velvet at a dress shop in Northwick for her gown and her mother brought a cascade of diamonds to adorn her hair and neck. Alexander gave her his grandmother's ring as a token, but she was most pleased when they were alone after the ceremony he placed a bit of holly in her hair and called her his winter fairy queen.

"I thought I was your mermaid," she teased.

He shrugged. "Sometimes fairy creatures are interchangeable."

"I am no creature!" Emily decried playfully, but the duke insisted that she was *his* fairy creature and captured her lips with his own halting any further protest.

The duke had eyes only for his new duchess and refused to release her from his side for the entire event. The knowledge that Alexander might kiss his wife whenever he wished was enough to leave a constant smile upon his face. He did so as often as possible and without hesitation, to the point where the assembled crowd cheered and whistled causing Emily to reveal her deepest blush.

The duke did not even mind the travel to London since Emily was with him. Their wedding announcement ball was the highlight of the London season. Alexander reminded his bride when she was overwhelmed with her mother's zealous preparations, it was nearly impossible for a member of the peerage to have a small country wedding.

Mr. and Mrs. Eldridge arrived in London for the ball and toasted the bride and groom and Mr. Eldridge waxed poetic about his own sweet Henrietta. It seemed, if possible, he was even more passionate about his new wife than he was about his agricultural pursuits.

"What an unexpected couple they make," Emily

whispered against her husband's shoulder as she pressed her cheek against him. "And yet, they suit one another."

"All that matters to me is that we suit one another," he replied as he pressed her wine glass into her hand. "A toast to my bride!" he shouted and cheers rung out all around.

Emily had never been happier. She had come to realize that one did not have to be stuffy or rigid in order to be good. The countryside had a way of reminding one of such things, she thought with a giggle. If she wished to push her ducal husband into a snow drift and engage him in a furious snowball fight as she had done only a few days before their union, she may and laugh as much as she liked while he counted freckles.

Professions were made all around and the happy couple settled into welcome congratulations. Emily was loathe to admit to her brother that he had known the right of it all along, although she assured him that he would now feel the acute focus of their mother's marital campaigns.

With hearty laughter and a bright future, the duke and his bride ushered in the New Year arm-in-arm. For many years afterward, it was said throughout the Northwickshire countryside that there was never a pair more fated than the Duke and Duchess of Bramblewood.

CONTINUE READING FOR A SNEAK PEEK OF...

The Viscount's Wayward Son
by Isabella Thorne

Book 1 of
The Ladies of the North Collection

1

The grand ball was truly a sight to behold. The polished walnut balustrade of the entrance hall was decorated with carvings of cherubs adorned in leafy attire, strategically placed. Marble pillars towered over the ballroom and mantels filled with what must be priceless statues lined the walls. Miss Anne Albright speculated at the time and care and, of course, the coin that hosting such an event must cost.

Her father was a viscount and a respectable gentleman, though she still felt like a country bumpkin as she gazed up at yet another manor which put her own home in a class beneath it. With every event Anne attended in London, she felt more and more an imposter amongst the grand persons in attendance. She feared at any moment someone may notice that she didn't belong, and she would turn into a pumpkin. The notion was entirely ridiculous.

As the eldest daughter of the Viscount Aldbrick, Anne was not accustomed to such finery, but neither was she common. She had traveled to London with the newly made Duchess of Bramblewood, Emily Burgess, and was currently staying with her. Anne had visited with Emily several times in the past. The pair of young ladies were great friends; at least they had been before Emily's marriage to the duke.

Anne swallowed and attempted to banish these maudlin thoughts. She and Emily had been friends since they were barely old enough to toddle. The pair of young ladies had attended finishing school together, so Anne knew that she shouldn't feel awkward, but she still did. Emily's mother was her chaperone this season, and she liked Emily's mother well enough, but Lady Kentleworth was not *her* mother.

Anne had been most excited when Emily had invited her to Town for a visit and for the opening of Bramblewood's London home. Anne and Emily had gone on several whirlwind shopping trips for the house, while Alexander, Emily's new husband, the young duke, fulfilled his parliamentary duties.

Alexander's father had not been much for Town, and even less for Parliament, especially after the death of Alexander's mother. The large house in Mayfair had been left empty, or let out to other nobles for years. Now, Alexander and his young bride were in residence for the season. Anne was privileged to join them, along with her younger sister Eliza and several servants from Bramblewood.

Lady Kentleworth agreed to chaperone the Albright sisters, spending most of her time with them at her daughter's new London house rather than her own Mayfair residence where Lord Kentleworth resided. The duke's grand edifice was an empty hall in desperate need of a woman's touch. Anne felt comfortable making suggestions to Emily about the decorations. Together the women had spent weeks preparing the house.

Alexander's father, the late duke had a terrible reputation and Alexander was only now starting to redeem his family's name. As the new duchess, Emily wanted to make a good impression at the first major event she hosted. She was nervous, but Anne had calmed her like the good friend she was, and the ball went off without a hitch. It was a great success and the *Ton* had nothing but good things to say about the new Duchess of Bramblewood.

Anne remembered the Bramblewood ballroom filled with important people dressed in royal finery and attempted to recapture the feeling of that first wondrous evening, but the pleasant sensation slipped away. That night, she had been with her best friend. Emily had wanted Anne by her side, and she rarely left it except to dance a few dances with the young duke, and Emily's brother, Edmund Ingram. The thought of Edmund brought a smile to Anne's lips.

Now, she scanned Lord Northrup's ballroom

searching for him. Edmund was as much a friend to the duke as Anne was to Emily. When they were younger the four of them had been nearly inseparable.

That first evening, Edmund and his father, the Viscount Kentleworth, had been solicitous, bringing all manner of gentry to Emily and Anne for introductions. Even though important people surrounded her, Anne felt steady with her friends at her side.

Then, Edmund asked her to dance. She was a bit surprised. He was not the best of dancers, but he was so earnest it was impossible to refuse him. They had danced one of the simpler sets, and at the end of it, he had whirled her out onto the vast balcony, overlooking the garden. Although small, the city garden gave a feeling of the country to the opulent London house.

It was a place for lovers, but Edmund only held her gloved hand for a moment, before exclaiming about the heat in the ballroom with the crush of people. He turned and looked out at the view.

"Yes," Anne agreed, somewhat embarrassed by the romantic turn of her thoughts. It was hot in the ballroom and the outside air was quite welcome. There was the ghost of a breeze. "Your sister is a grand success," she said.

He nodded. "Yes, Em is made for this," he said, "and I am glad for it, but if I have to kowtow to one more of Father's cronies, I may cast up my accounts."

"You wouldn't," Anne said, with a giggle.

"No. I wouldn't. I shall be a dutiful son and a good

brother and stand fast." He looked at Anne for a moment, his bright green eyes sparkling, and her heart did a strange flip flop.

"Thank you for the dance," Edmund said at last. "I thought it would look odd if the brother of the new duchess failed to dance at all, and I knew you wouldn't mind my ineptitude."

Anne grinned at him remembering when they were younger and the many hours they spent practicing dancing. Edmund had trod on her toes repeatedly, and on one occasion stepped on the hem of her dress, tearing it unmercifully. Tonight was a marked improvement.

"Actually, you did rather well." Anne said with a smile that was only for Edmund.

Edmund laughed. "You are a sport, putting up with my treading on your toes and not even calling me out for it. Shall we find some refreshment?" He took her arm to lead her back into the ballroom. Anne wondered when her wayward friend had become a gentleman.

The two of them had spent most of the evening talking and it was almost like old times. After the guests had gone home, the four friends celebrated their success in the drawing room with wine while the servants cleared away the remainder of the food. Alexander had commandeered a plate of meat and cheese and they ate ravenously.

"I couldn't eat a bite at dinner," Emily admitted. "I was too nervous."

Anne nodded, thinking she had felt the same. Now,

with all pretense stripped away, they were just four friends sharing a good time, until Alexander leaned in to whisper something in Emily's ear. She blushed, turning her face up to his. They did not kiss, but the heat was palpable. Anne felt suddenly uncomfortable.

"It is late; we should retire," Anne suggested, and Emily agreed, her eyes shining with love for her new husband.

Edmund snatched a last bite of roast pork and Alexander called a footman to clear away the rest. Emily and Alexander retired for the night, but Edmund and Anne stood awkwardly on the landing. The silence seemed to grow and stretch between them.

CONTINUE READING....
The Viscount's Wayward Son
by Isabella Thorne

WANT EVEN MORE REGENCY ROMANCE...

Follow Isabella Thorne on BookBub
https://www.bookbub.com/profile/isabella-thorne

Sign up for my VIP Reader List!
at
https://isabellathorne.com/

Receive weekly updates from Isabella and an
EXCLUSIVE FREE STORY

Like Isabella Thorne on Facebook
https://www.facebook.com/isabellathorneauthor/

Made in the USA
Monee, IL
23 November 2020

49240006R00218